The Book of Second Chances

The Secret Books of Gabendoor
Book One

J. Michael Blumer

Quails Run Publishing
Stillwater, Minnesota

The Book of Second Chances:
The Secret Books of Gabendoor, Book one.

ISBN 978-0-9900095-0-4

9 8 7 6 5 4 3

First Edition September 2006

Second Edition December 2012

Third Edition December 2013

www.quailsrunpublishing.com

For Jane
Without you, I'd have nothing.

Acknowledgements

What an adventure. Not in any book, but with all my friends. I can't imagine writing this or any story without their help.

First to my younger friends. I thank you Alannah, you were my first fan. You gave me hope by picking Hillary as your favorite book character for a school assignment. Melissa, your kindness overwhelmed me. How wonderful you were to read my draft to the neighbor kids and record their reactions. I owe them each a book. Three cheers to the Book Factory young adult book club in Queensland Australia who gave me my first reviews.

For my older friends, all aspiring writers, you have my gratitude. Melissa Richards, Raven Matthews, BR Hollis, Mads Birkvig, Maureen Murrish, Shoshanna KKeats Jaskoll, Larry West, J. W. Wren, Clover Autry, Marulyn Rude and many more, I learned from you. You made this book what it is. I look forward to seeing all of you published. And to, Tammy, who is published, I may have given up if you hadn't kept after me.

What a great team at Blue Forge Press. Thanks to Jennifer DeMarco for giving me this chance. A special thanks to Buster and Sarah for their help in putting this all together.

Last in order, but not in heart, is my family. Thanks to my wife, Jane. You gave me the chance to chase and catch this dream.

The Book of Second Chances

The Secret Books of Gabendoor
Book One

J. Michael Blumer

1: Journey Wind

Themoon was full, yet the forest stayed Halloween black. The fox stopped, her ears erect. Ending her hunting early, she tiptoed silently through the forest. At the edge of a small clearing, she paused to sniff the air before hurrying across, to reach her den under the ruins of the old cottage.

A circular spot in the carpet of dry pine needles rustled then stilled. They twitched again. The gray fox caught the movement and quickly took shelter under the firewood stacked against the stone chimney at the back of the building. The needles lifted and spun, picking up loose blades of grass and dry bits of earth to accompany them. The dust devil grew as unsettled night air brushed across the meadow circled by age old pines. The whirlwind called to the ferns. The feathery plants straightened from their bent slumber to dance and jerk as the glowing wind-spiral rose, broadened and began to howl. High branches on the trees joined in the frolic, swaying and bending as the swirling gray funnel brushed against them.

Swaying gracefully at first, the funnel lurched and began to gyrate wildly from the three growing forms that plumped and distorted its center. Tired of its load and finished with the task it was summoned for, the journey-wind belched and was gone.

"Get off me."

"That's my foot."

"Ouch! I burnt my thumb. What's on fire?"

"You lit my beard with your pipe, you quarter-wit," Haggerwolf yelled, flailing his hands at the tip of his whiskers.

Larkstone pulled his hickory wand from inside his vest. "Hold him, Fernbark!"

Fernbark locked his stubby arms around Haggerwolf from behind. Larkstone swung. The wand clipped off the tip of the scrawny wizard's beard as cleanly as a troll's razor. The gray hair floated to the ground and sizzled as the last of it burned to curlicue ash.

The fox peeked out after catching the scent of the three odd men; butter and cinnamon. She wiped her tongue across her snout. The smell was familiar.

"That's my vest!" Larkstone yelled at Fernbark. "What are you doing with it?"

"How should I know? Hey! Those are my pants. Get 'em off, you overstuffed bag of lizard lard. You'll split the leather."

"Me! I'm not the one that eats four pounds of boar bacon for lunch."

"Quiet. Both of you!" Haggerwolf said, still plucking the end of his beard. "We're supposed to be doing this in secret. And you're wearing my boots, Larkstone. The journey-wind mixed us all up. It always does that in a trip this far. Let's change, but fast."

The three wizards stripped, tossing everything but their red long underwear into a pile on the ground near the ramshackle door to the cottage. Then they grabbed for what was theirs.

Haggerwolf, the taller one, pulled out pants, shirt, and a long robe. They were all dark blue, almost black and had the outlines of forest animals embroidered in the fabric. Fernbark and Larkstone, both shorter and stout, sorted through the pile. Fernbark's clothes were different shades of green with outlines of plants and Larkstone's clothes light blue with fish and seashell patterns.

"Your buttons made my fingers green," Fernbark said. "Never buy a vest with copper buttons."

"You sold it to me," Haggerwolf said and rubbed his sleeve against one of the buttons. "I'll take that little matter up with you when we're back home. Now give me the book. Let's get on with this."

"You had it when Larkstone conjured up the journey-wind," Fernbark answered as he slipped his arms through his suspenders, letting the blue bands snap against his shoulders.

"One of you grabbed it from me when that blasted wind took off with us."

"There it is." Larkstone pointed back to the edge of the pines near where the whirlwind had expelled them. "Must have blown out of my hands."

The book smelled of skin, but not from an animal the fox recognized. She sneezed to push the scent from her nostrils. Bordering the cover of the thick book, heavy studs glowed faintly in competition with the moonlight. Both the light and smell chafed her instincts. Keeping low, she crept from her den, dashed around the corner of the woodpile, and disappeared into the woods.

"What was that?" Larkstone asked, his voice sharp and fast. He hugged the book close to his chest and spun around.

"Just some critter," Fernbark answered. "Probably one of those cats these hills are named after."

"It's not the cat-hills," Haggerwolf said, rolling his eyes and shaking his head. "It's Catskills and we're in the mountains. That critter was just a porkypie, I think. My aunt used to feed 'em bits of sugar rolls."

"Who else knows about this place?" Fernbark asked and looked in the direction the fox had run. "Maybe we should—"

"It's safe," Haggerwolf said, cutting him off. "My aunt knew what we were trying to do. Just before Fistlock killed her, she told me about her little secret hideaway world. This will be a safe place to stash that leather-bound scourge."

"But we're not the only ones who know this world exists," Larkstone said, still clutching the book tight as he walked back toward the cottage.

Haggerwolf gave the teetering door to the old building a kick. "Ah, but we *are* the only ones that know how to get to it."

Rusted hinges lost their grip and rough-hewn boards gave way. When each board slapped to the floor, a new puff of dust joined with the rest. Haggerwolf braced his hands on the door frame and leaned inside.

The interior was dark except for a strip of floor in front of him and a spot in the far corner of the room where part of the roof had fallen in. In those two spots, the moon eased its dim light inside the small stone and log cottage.

"I'll make some light," Fernbark said and ducked under Haggerwolf's arm. He took a good-sized pinch of dried moss from his vest pocket and rolled it into a ball between his palms. "Give me some water." He reached back without turning around, expecting someone to hand him a water skin.

"I didn't bring any," Haggerwolf said. "How about you, Larkstone?" he asked, looking over his shoulder.

"We're not on a blasted picnic, and my spells don't use water. Why would I bring any? You're the leader. You're supposed to think of those things," Larkstone said and slid past the taller wizard. "Allow me." Larkstone grabbed Fernbark's hand and spit.

Fernbark jerked his hand away. His eyes widened, his face reddened and his mouth opened.

"Don't say it," Larkstone snapped, before Fernbark could utter a complaint. "It worked, didn't it?"

Fernbark grumbled something about garden slugs under his breath as he picked up the glowing pea-sized ball of moss from the floor. He scowled at Larkstone before taking a pinch of orange powder from another pocket. When he sprinkled it on the moss, the room lit up in the bright yellow-green glow of the magic light.

Haggerwolf pushed between them and moved to the stone hearth. "All right, you two. Let's just take care of the book and then get out of here. Help me clear this spot. Fernbark, find something to sweep with so we can see the mortar lines. Larkstone, we'll need a makeshift pedestal."

There wasn't much inside the cottage, except for a few shelves that retained a precarious grip on the log walls and a pile of rubble from the fallen section of roof. Larkstone sifted through the jumble of broken boards and shingles, while Fernbark went back outside.

Haggerwolf knelt in front of the fireplace and began clearing pine needles and debris off the hearthstone. Fernbark returned with a bundle of dried grass and began sweeping the last of the fine dust and dirt away from the spot Haggerwolf had cleared. When they had a three-foot oval area swept clean, the two wizards moved back and waited. Larkstone used several chunks of broken timber and a few moss covered wooden shingles to fashion a short pedestal to hold the book.

"Now are you going to tell us your plan?" Fernbark asked as he set the book in place. "You said it was better if we didn't know until the last moment. I figure we're pretty close to that time now."

"We're going to seal the book and hide it with a layer

of spells. Any spell that can be done can be undone, so we'll each cast our own spells.

"Good plan," Larkstone said and began rolling up his sleeves. "If we're creative enough, even if one person knew all the spells, it would take three ogre-lives to figure out how to work them."

"I do admit, it's one of my more brilliant plans," Haggerwolf said. He reached to tuck the end of his beard behind his wide belt, but grabbed air where the missing end would have hung. He cleared his throat, scratched his side and then tucked the sheared end inside the opening of his shirt, between two buttons. "Let's get started. We'll bury it inside the hearthstone. But first..." He drew a slender dagger from behind his belt and knelt by the book. Holding the hilt in one hand, he placed three fingers of his other hand over runes etched into the blade. The dagger began to glow.

The thick book had a strap and ornate latch to hold it closed. Haggerwolf placed the tip of his blade at the base of a brass acorn that formed the lock for the clasp. He gave his wrist a quick twist. The acorn popped loose and Larkstone snatched it from the air.

"Hm... Magic. It figures. It turned back into a real acorn," Larkstone said. He put the nut on the hearthstone and smashed it with his boot. "So much for the lock, but one of us will have to deal with the acorn in their spell. It'll need replacing to unlock the strap. No one can cut that leather. It's from a glorgwart."

"Then I say it's spell time," Fernbark said. "Let's circle around. Who wants to go first?"

"Book in a stone stays out of sight," Haggerwolf said and waved his wand.

"Not bad," Larkstone said and nodded as he pulled out his own wand. "Seek with a rainbow in the night." He and Haggerwolf looked at Fernbark.

"Tears from a girl with an overbite."

"What in the troll-ear was that?" Haggerwolf asked as he stared at Fernbark.

"Well," Fernbark said and began to blush. "You two rhymed and that's all I could come up with. We're supposed to be spontaneous, aren't we?" He tried to force a scowl on his face.

Haggerwolf rolled his eyes and cast another spell beginning the next round. "Nut with a cap where the pine cones fall."

"Names of love in a mother's shawl."

"Laughs from a boy who ain't too tall."

Haggerwolf and Larkstone both looked up.

"It'll make it harder to figure out. Won't it!" Fernbark yelled at them, his face burning bright red. "Let's place it."

The three men pointed their wands and the hearthstone began to shimmer. A rectangle in the center of the quarried stone turned clear before it vanished. While Larkstone and Fernbark kept their wands steady, Haggerwolf used his to move the book. The bound pages floated from the makeshift pedestal and hovered over the void in the hearthstone. As he lowered his wand, the book settled into place. When all three wizards withdrew their wands, the void filled with clear stone, sealing in the book.

"Now just a single spell by me," Haggerwolf said. "It's an alarm for the three of us if someone tries to tamper here." He pointed his wand at the book. "Shambles re-scrambles." A puff of wind fluffed the end of his beard and circled the other two wizards, flipping their shirttails as it passed.

"What's the alarm?" Larkstone asked as he tucked his shirt back in.

"You'll recognize it if it happens," Haggerwolf said and put his wand away. "Let's finish it. Same order as before.

I'll start. Lightning reveals."

"A tear unseals."

"Blood heals," Fernbark said, his face beaming this time.

Fernbark's look of pride and the surprise on the other two faces were lost in the sudden swirl of dust. The magic light dimmed and the clutter of boards and shingles in the corner rattled until the wind stopped. The three wizards coughed and waved their arms.

"I guess that means it all worked," Haggerwolf said as the dust settled. "If Fistlock, himself, found this place, he'd never figure out all of that."

"And my little creative touch rules out random chance," Fernbark said, looking at his friends expecting to see them nod in agreement. They were looking at the hearthstone.

The stone, the fireplace, the beams and shingles from the pedestal, were all back in their original positions.

Haggerwolf nodded approvingly at their work. "There's absolutely no chance that anyone from this world or any other could ever find and open that book."

"Well, my friends," Larkstone said as he used his hands to brush dust from his shoulders. "One of you call up another journey-wind and let's get home to Gabendoor before Fistlock comes looking for us.

2: Children of the Summer Wind

"Give me a push. My wheels are stuck," Windslow yelled over his shoulder at his older sister.

"I thought you said your new chair could go anywhere? Maybe you need to recharge the battery. I want to go back to the campsite anyway," Hillary said. She grabbed the handles at the back of her brother's wheelchair. Before she gave it a shove, she used an edge on the back frame to scrape dirt off the side of her hiking boot.

Clear of the temporary obstruction, Windslow sped ahead. Hillary watched his brown hair bob up and down as the wheels of his all-terrain wheelchair bounced over the rough ground. She smiled to herself as she imagined his head as a giant pinecone and his freckles as seeds. Her friends thought she and Windslow looked alike. Their hair color and complexion gave them a similar look, so much that people often thought they were natural brother and sister instead of step. She wished he'd let her fix his hair. Cut short, it stuck out at odd angles. She tried to put gel in it once and he freaked.

"These stupid sticks are hard to roll over. My battery is fine," Windslow yelled as his chair rolled over dry needles and small dead branches from the trees. He looked up into the tall pines and stopped. Digging into his side pack, he searched for his bag of acorns. "Watch this."

He loaded an acorn into the leather pad of his slingshot. Holding the wood handle out straight, he pulled hard, stretching the rubber cords back to his chin. When he released the pad, the acorn flew high into the pine trees, clipping free a few needles as it whizzed through the branches. The crow hopped along the branch, cawed once, and flew away.

"You're so mean," Hillary said. "When I filled up your acorn bag, you promised me that you wouldn't shoot at any animals. This is a state park and you're breaking the rules. Stop it or I'll dump the whole bag in the trash."

"If you do, I'll tell mom that you have makeup. You're not supposed to use it until next year when you're twelve. It's stupid to wear it on a camping trip anyway."

"It is not stupid," Hillary said. She closed her tiny lipstick case and mirror and shoved it into the back pocket of her jeans. "Mom wouldn't care."

"Then why do you wipe it off before we go back to the tents?" Windslow said and moved the joystick control for his chair to pivot around and face his stepsister. "You've got lipstick on now."

Hilary stuck her tongue out at him and ran ahead, deeper into the woods. After ducking behind the broad trunk of a pine tree, she pulled a small package of tissues from her shirt pocket and wiped her lips. "Ouch," she said and snapped open her lipstick case. She puckered, trying to curl up her lip. "Stupid braces. Who cares, or even knows what an overbite is anyway." She had to twist and turn the lipstick case to look at her lip in the skinny mirror. Before she put it away, she saw a small reddish chip of bark. It nearly matched the color of her hair and clung to her curls near her shoulder. As she pulled it out, she winced, flicked it away, and sighed.

She liked camping. Bill, her stepfather, knew a lot about the woods and was fun—most of the time. At least he made her mother happy. Windslow was fun too—at first. Hillary liked having a stepbrother. Windslow had been like Bill. Windslow laughed a lot and could think of fun things to do until the accident. Now instead of thinking up adventures, he just got her into trouble. She felt like his personal servant.

But even worse, she felt guilty about the accident. It was her stuffed bear that he was trying to rescue. He liked to show off and had made her watch while he climbed up on the roof of their house. He slipped and fell when he held the bear up like a trophy over his head.

Hillary picked up a handful of dry pine needles and threw them. The gentle breeze blew them back at her. She scowled as she brushed them off her flannel shirt. She knew she should check on Windslow, but also knew he'd yell for her if he needed anything. And almost anything he wanted, he got, including most of the attention. She couldn't imagine what not being able to walk must be like. But she missed the days when she and her mom would do things together. Now everything they did seemed to be for Windslow.

"Hillary? Hillary!"

Hillary jumped to her feet and ran back to the clearing. "Where are you?" she yelled.

"Look for my wheel tracks. I found something back in the trees. It's the ruins of an old cabin."

His wheels hadn't left a clear trail, but Hillary could see the direction he had gone and ran into the woods. "I can't follow your tracks!" she yelled. "Say something."

"You sound louder. Keep coming. I'm in another clearing. I've got a new adventure for us. It starts at midnight."

"Sure!" she yelled as she walked fast through the trees. "An adventure for you, but I'll just get grounded. It's not fair that you never get punished."

"This chair is the ultimate grounding. How'd you like to trade?"

He was right, Hillary thought as she batted away a branch and then saw his tracks just to her left. She was lucky and shouldn't complain. She ducked under a limb and saw him up ahead.

"Isn't this cool?" he said. Windslow had the side of his chair up against the remains of an old stone chimney. He held a dead branch and jabbed it at the old hearth. "We haven't had a good adventure since I got sentenced to this chair. Tonight, we're going to have one."

"Why at night?" Hillary asked as she walked around the chimney. She poked at the stones with the toe of her hiking boot. "This is just an old cabin."

"We need to come here at midnight so we can call up ghosts. That's the only time they come out, you know."

"How would you know?"

"TV. Remember? I watch a lot of it now. People who lived in old places like this didn't use banks, either. Lots of them hid their valuables under the big rocks they made their fireplaces out of."

"Just because you're changing it to a treasure adventure doesn't mean I'll do it. Mom and Bill won't let us come here after dark. You know that. And I don't think they'd want us here now either."

"You know they won't do anything to me. They won't even know. And it's a ghost *and* treasure adventure. We need to call up a ghost to find out where the treasure is. Come on, Hillary. It'll be fun. Just like the adventures we had before I got hurt trying to do something nice for you." Windslow dropped the stick and drove his chair around the chimney to where his stepsister stood. "Please, Hillary?"

"All right," she agreed. She knew it was useless to argue when he had his mind set. And after all, he was right. He used to do nice things for her all the time and she had encouraged him to show off that afternoon. She wanted to impress her friends and had them come watch when he climbed up on the roof. She bragged to her friends that she could get him to do anything for her. Maybe the tables had turned because she acted silly that day. She didn't want to let those dark thoughts drag her back down again. Hillary forced a smile and gave him a playful punch in the shoulder. "But if I get grounded, I'm going to let the air out of your wheels."

"You're the best, sis. We better get back to the campsite. I need to recharge my battery for tonight. Grab an armful of those sticks over there. We'll use them to mark the trail. Put one over there," Windslow said, pointing as he drove his chair back toward the trees. "And another one there."

Hillary grabbed some of the dried sticks. Each time he pointed, she either sighed or shook her head and then shoved a stick into the ground. Twice she threw one at him, but missed.

❧

"Windslow," Hillary said softly as she ducked inside his tent and knelt beside her brother.

"It's about time you got here," he said. "Help me outside."

"How am I supposed to do that? I can't lift you. And how are you going to get into your chair?"

"Easy. Just grab the blanket, wrap it around my feet and pull. Help me roll over onto my stomach first. Then I can push with my hands."

"This is stupid," Hillary said.

"Just do it. We need to get there before midnight."

With his sister's help, Windslow rolled over onto his stomach. He looked back over his shoulder and watched Hillary wrap the end of the blanket around his boots. "Pull," he said and began pushing with his hands.

Hillary strained and pulled. She was surprised that the blanket slid easily on the grass. It was like dragging a big pile of dry leaves on a canvas. Just like they did before his accident, when they raked the yard. But he was heavier than a pile of leaves and she knew he'd be the only one having fun this time.

The bigger challenge was getting him into his chair. Together they struggled, whispered a few sarcastic words back and forth, and finally managed to get him in the seat. When they heard Bill cough, they looked at the tent-trailer where their parents slept. The night stayed silent, except for the spring peepers calling down by the pond.

"Push me until we're away from the tent," Windslow whispered.

"Great adventure," Hillary whispered back a bit louder than he had. "I think it's just going to be a lot of work for me. And look over there. That's lightning off in the distance. There might be a storm coming. Maybe we—"

"Maybe you should push. This is our last chance. We go home tomorrow."

Hillary was about to give his chair a shove that he wouldn't forget. As she pushed, he moved the chair's joystick forward and sped ahead. She nearly fell before she caught her balance.

"Would you warn me before you do that?" she snapped, then ran ahead to catch up with him. Windslow suddenly stopped and she ran into the back of his chair.

"Watch out," he said to her and began searching his pack. "You could get hurt. One of us in a chair is enough. Maybe if I wasn't stuck in this thing, I could be a better brother and watch out for you."

Hillary wanted to both smack him and hug him. It was nice when he was like he used to be. 'In the time before the chair,' as Windslow would say. "Wait," she said and ran back to her tent. When she returned she carried a shawl, knitted from pale yellow yarn. "Here," she said and handed the shawl to her brother. "It's the one mom knitted for me with our names in it. Just in case you get cold."

"If she finds out you brought this camping she'll have a hyper-spaz. But thanks. Here." He handed his sister a long flashlight with a shiny red-metal case. "I fixed mine up with Velcro. Watch." He smiled at her after he pressed his flashlight against the side of the chair's armrest and the light stayed in place. "Come on," he said and pushed his joystick forward. "We're late for our meeting with the ghosts who are going to make us rich. What are you going to buy with your share?"

"A new servant for you so I can go on a vacation," she mumbled.

ജ്ഞ

Black of night and midnight blue from the approaching storm chased colors away from the forest. The longer meadow grass bowed to puffs of wind the storm chased ahead of it through the valleys in the foothills. Night creatures sniffed the air and scurried back into den or thicket, giving the night up to those more courageous or foolhardy. They granted this night to the two children of the wind who moved steadily toward the ruins. Hovering high in readiness the clouds flashed with far off lightning and hid the ruins below from the stars, moon, and all else above.

"Windslow, it is going to storm. I saw lightning again. Maybe we should go back," Hillary said and unconsciously clutched her lucky crystal pendant, hanging from a thin chain around her neck.

"We're almost there. Look," he said as the beam from his flashlight swept across the stones of the chimney up ahead. "Besides, it's almost midnight."

When they reached the ruins, Windslow tried to move his chair close to the chimney. As he struggled with his chair, the wind puffed stray gusts, cooler than the others. Hillary felt their chill, took the shawl from her brother's lap, and wrapped it around his shoulders.

"That's as close as you're going to get," she told her brother. "Let's just get started. I don't like this adventure. We're going to get rained on. And if you catch cold, mother is going to—"

"Hillary. Look there. At that stone. I saw something when the lightning flashed. Help me out of my chair."

"Windslow. What are you doing?"

Hillary moved to her brother, who rocked his chair, trying to get out of it by himself. "All right. Here. Put your arms around me."

She strained while Windslow helped with his arms. Moving him barely ten inches at a time, she boosted him closer to the chimney until he could lean against the pile of round stones.

"There," Windslow said and pointed. "Brush off the hearthstone, that big flat one. That's where I saw it."

"Saw, what?"

"I don't know. Something. When the lightning flashed. It was like the stone turned into a big block of ice. I could almost see through it. I wish it would lightning again."

"If you're doing this to scare me," Hillary yelled at her brother, "then you have! Let's go back. I don't want any more lightning and your chair might attract it. Did you ever think of that?"

"Good. I want to find out what I saw. There. See that?"

Lightning flashed again, still far off. In the seconds between the flash and the distant thunder, the large two-foot square hearthstone turned nearly clear, like cloudy glass.

Brother and sister huddled together, each trying to get a better view of the stone. A stronger gust of cold air swirled past them. The wind rushed into trees and rattled a dead branch against a hollow trunk. Windslow sat up straight and looked into the forest as the branch kept rapping.

Hillary gave a short scream when she heard the sound. "What was that?"

"I don't know. Maybe just the wind. It was nothing," Windslow said. "Get my backpack."

Hillary stayed on her hands and knees and scrambled to her brother's chair. She unsnapped the bag and dragged it back to the chimney.

"What are you doing?" Hillary asked when her brother pulled out his slingshot and pouch of acorns.

"Just in case," he answered and put an acorn into the leather slingshot pad.

Wind buffeted the trees, announcing the closeness of the storm. The dead branch broke loose and crashed to the ground. Windslow pulled back on the acorn, stretching the rubber bands tight. Both Hillary and Windslow screamed when one of the cords snapped. The acorn flew back, ricocheted off the chimney and struck Hillary in the cheek.

"Ow!" Hillary held both hands to the side of her face and began crying. "You shot me," she said between sobs. "Look. You cut me!" She grabbed her brother's flashlight and held her hand under the beam. Her palm had a smear of blood on it.

"It's not that bad. I'm really sorry, Hillary. I—" Windslow's mouth stayed open, but his words stopped. He stared down at the hearthstone.

Hillary looked at his expression and she couldn't tell if she saw fear or excitement. She knew he wasn't pretending. "Windslow?"

"Look. No wait. Sit up a little," he said and used one hand to push her back.

Hillary sniffed and swept her hand across her cheek, both to wipe away the blood from the tiny cut on her face and her tears.

"Give me the flashlight." Not waiting he grabbed it from her. "Lean forward again. Just a bit. Let your lucky crystal dangle into the light."

"Windslow, what—"

"Do it, Hillary. Do it! It makes something happen." He looked up at her, his eyes bright. "This is working. There's something here. Really."

She leaned forward until her crystal pendant hung over the hearthstone. Windslow moved the beam from the flashlight around until the tiny rainbow of light from the glass prism washed across the stone. Lightning flashed. The hearthstone turned milky white, then slowly turned clear as glass. While Windslow and Hillary stared at the clear stone, a single tear ran down the edge of Hillary's nose and splashed near the rainbow. The clear stone shimmered. The change startled her and she sat up straight. Her quick movement shook a drop of blood from her cheek. It landed next to her tear.

Lightning flickered close this time. Thunder boomed and shook the ground. The hearthstone was gone.

"Don't touch it," Hillary said. She grabbed her brother, trying to force him back from the space where the hearthstone had been. "It could be—"

"Let me go!" Windslow yelled and wrenched his shoulder away from her hold. He fell forward and tried to thrust his hand into the hole. Hillary pinned him down.

The wind kicked up stray blades of grass and twigs. Lightning crackled in drawn out choruses that ended in loud, ground shaking booms. Hillary had to let go of her brother to grab the fallen flashlight.

"Hillary, it's a book. Didn't you see it? Help me reach it and then we can get out of here. All of this is starting to scare me too."

She swept the light down into the hole as Windslow tried to get a look. His hand brushed his pouch of acorns and a single nut fell into the hole. They watched the acorn roll across the studded leather cover. When it touched the clasp that held the book closed, the acorn stopped. With a loud "click" it turned to brass and the leather strap fell away.

They both sat up and hugged each other when they heard the clear yet whispering voice carried on the wind that swirled around them.

Book in a stone stays out of sight.
Seek with a rainbow in the night.
Tears from a girl with an overbite.

Nut with a cap where the pinecones fall.
Names of love in a mother's shawl.
Laughs from a boy who ain't too tall.

Lightning reveals.
A tear unseals.
Blood heals.

Windslow grabbed the book.

3: Fistlock

In the midst of his sleep, the muscles in Fistlock's jaw tightened under his skin like knotted ropes and worked his mouth, grinding his teeth. He began to sweat; beads across the furrows of his brow, moistness across his narrow shoulders and dampness down his back that soaked into his bedclothes. He twisted and snaked, rumpling his blankets until they slid from his spindly body to land in a heap on the floor. The trundle-wraith's shadowy fingers reached from under Fistlock's bed to snatch the blankets away, using its own trickery to entice creaking sounds from floorboards and muffled thumps from the walls and doors.

Fistlock sat up so quickly he frightened the gloom-spinner, a gentile shadow beast who gave a muffled scream from its hiding place in the depths of Fistlock's closet. Two startled shadow-glumps lost their holds on the ceiling at the corners of the room. They plopped to the floor and scurried away, changing to hide in the natural shadows shaped by moonlight draped across a high back chair. The trundle-wraith jerked its fingers back so fast that puffs of mingled lint, hair and dust swirled in the wake from its movement.

"The book," Fistlock said at first in a whisper. Then a second time he screamed, "The Book!" so loud the words echoed through his castle, stilling all the night sounds; groans and creeping-cracks, scrapes and skittles. Unnatural shadows shrank away, glowing forms turned transparent and unseen. The crawlers vanished for the night.

"What book would that be, Master?" the trundle-wraith asked from under the bed, its voice insubstantial, more like wind than speech.

"The book of Second Chances," Fistlock said as he slid from bed and kicked at a shadow-glump. "It's open!"

ဢဢ

Haggerwolf settled back in his hammock strung between two hardy branches that curved gracefully up from under the porch of his tree-bode, as he called it. A tree house really, cradled high up in the stout and age-wrinkled limbs of the flute-bean tree. An afternoon breeze played quietly with the oblong leaves and long brown seedpods that gave the tree its name.

Small but sufficient, the house had only two rooms. He cooked, ate and slept in the large and spacious front room, except on pleasant days like today. An arched doorway tucked near the stove gave access to the second room, his laboratory. He spent most of his time on the porch, snoozing as he did now. Evening was for lab work, although he had seen little point to it lately. Fistlock controlled everything but the Forge-Twiddlers. All the races had united to defeat Fistlock many years ago, but lost in the end. And there would be no second chance at that.

"Not without the secrets of that book," Haggerwolf said to himself, sighed, and draped one leg over the edge of the hammock to give himself a small push and swing. "At least the book is hidden away from Fistlock."

Fistlock had been the first wizard to discoverer the book, secreted away by wizards in the *time before.* The old texts described many books stashed in hidey-holes hidden by magic that no one understood. Of them all, the book of Second Chances was the most powerful and the key to finding the others. Ownership changed several times, but no one had ever been able to figure out how the book worked. Just having the book brought danger enough, both for the holder and those who desired it.

"Oh well." Haggerwolf sighed and struck a match to light his pipe.

The wind surged in a narrow blast, nearly lifting him from his hammock as the rope bed jumped and bounced from the air's shove.

"I...

"can't...

"breathe."

His words squeezed out faint and forced, but there was no one else to hear them. His face reddened, making his long beard seem even whiter against the crimson. Close to passing out, he glanced down at his chest, then struggled to pull his short knife from the tangle of cloth that had been his pants. It wasn't there, but his hand brushed across the pommel of a short sword. He pulled the blade from its scabbard and used the sharp edge to cut loose the top two buttons.

"Phew..." he said with his first breath as he cut off the rest of the vest buttons. With his next breath he yelled. "Larkstone, you idiot!" Haggerwolf knew his friend couldn't hear him, but the yell made him feel better. When he looked at himself again, he saw more than Larkstone's vest. Haggerwolf was squeezed into Fernbark's pants and cover robe, which explained the sword.

That's all he had time to notice. The smell of burning fibers grabbed his attention. His mind raced to the last time his clothes had scrambled. Without thinking, he chopped off the bottom three inches of his beard and watched it float lazily down, one hundred feet to the ground. It was then that he discovered his mistake. With disgust, he spit on the charred hammock rope to extinguish the hot spot where his pipe had emptied.

He decided to summon a journey-wind to take him to Larkstone's lakeside cottage. Before he could find his wand, an odd, yet vaguely familiar journey-wind swooped down over the top of his tree-bode and snatched him away.

ཀ

Fistlock's long stride carried him quickly down the hallway from his bedroom to his laboratory. Torches jutting out from skull-shaped wall sconces lit the way. Their fires bent not from flame-fluffers, but from the wind of Fistlock's passing. The fluffers knew better than to puff out or tamper with a flame when their master overflowed with the mood they sensed. They shrunk away from him like his other dark shadow beasties.

When Fistlock neared his laboratory a shutterfling threw the door open for him. The copper clad boards banged with a dull thud against the mortared stones of the hallway and the shutterfling retreated back to its hiding place inside one of the hinges.

Panderflip was waiting.

Fistlock didn't bother to acknowledge his stout assistant who waited silently, shoulders slouched and head down, standing behind one of the many tables. Fistlock paced back and forth. His shadow followed; darting across the table, flowing over the glass beakers, clay mixing bowls, and spilled powders.

"I felt it," Fistlock said and continued pacing, still not looking at Panderflip. "I put a spell on it before that blasted Leaper stole it. I sensed it when he unlatched it, but he closed it again before I could find him. This time it's still unlatched, but very far away—faint.

"Use the Book of Worlds," Panderflip said, more as a question than a suggestion.

"Of course! Fetch it." A smile crossed Fistlock's lips for the first time since the spell's nagging had dragged him from his sleep. While his chamberlain hurried to the bookshelves covering the entire end of the laboratory, Fistlock dragged a heavy chair to the center worktable, sat down and waved his hand. Two tall thick candles scraped their way across the table, stopping far enough in front of him to provide room for the large book.

Panderflip gently placed the Book of Worlds in the pool of yellow light spread before his master.

With the sleeves of his black evening robe pushed back, Fistlock raised his wand above the book. Like a conductor ready to signal the orchestra, he tried to hold his hand steady, but the tip of his crooked somber-wood wand quivered. He drew in a deep breath to ready himself and recited the words the magic of the book required.

"Book of Worlds at my command,

Open to a distant land.

Show a place and mark it well,

That called to me from hidden spell."

Unseen flame-fluffers controlled by the book's magic bent first one candle flame and then the other. Their stronger cousin, the williwaw, puffed the flames out completely and ruffled Fistlock's sleeves with its icy rush of whispered air.

With his spindly, hairless arm still poised above the book, Fistlock twitched his wand and the candle flames relit. Quickly he tucked the somber-wood inside his robe and placed his hands flat on the table, one on either side of the book.

With no great hurry, the leather book cover opened revealing a blank age-yellowed page underneath. The cover stopped, sounding a small tap as it came to rest on the table. The yellow page flipped to join it. More blank pages lifted and turned, quickly now, filling the air with the musty scent of ancient parchment. Midway through the book, the pages stilled and Fistlock waited, watching. Letters appeared in bits and pieces here and there across the page, slowly crowding together in neat, hand scripted lines. With no more space for them to fill, the page turned and underneath lay a map of stars connected by thin shapes and sharp angles marked with numbers and signs. Beneath it lay another map with continents and lines for navigation. Fistlock smiled as more maps and text hurried past his gaze, too fast for him to read. And then the pages stopped.

"There," he said and leaned over the book to bring his eyes closer to the small text beside a blood-red dot.

"Ear -th?" Panderflip asked, leaning over Fistlock's shoulder. "Like fourth, fifth, ear-th?"

When he sat up straight, Fistlock nearly banged the back of his head into Panderflip's already crooked nose. "No, you shadow-brick. It's Earth. Like the ground, like dirt. We'll have to take a journey-wind. Summon one up in the courtyard while I get dressed. And do it right. If we get there and my clothes are mixed with yours, you'll end up dead along with whoever has my book.

ജ്ര

The journey-wind rotated slowly behind them in the five-foot circle of flattened meadow grass where it waited. Fernbark, Larkstone and Haggerwolf didn't bother to rearrange their mixed up clothes. They ran to the crumbling stone chimney and hearthstone that marked where they had hidden the book thirty years ago.

"It's gone," Fernbark said. "If Fistlock has it again..."

"It wasn't him." Haggerwolf sniffed the air by the hearthstone. He wet his finger, wiped it across the stone and touched the dusty tip to his tongue. "The elements of nature haven't been fouled and there's no scent of magic."

"It was something powerful," Fernbark said.

"No magic?" Larkstone asked. "Are you sure?" Ignoring Haggerwolf's nod, Larkstone stooped, sniffed and tasted the ground himself. "Hagger's right," he said as he stood. "But there's something more important. No evil."

"But it was powerful," Fernbark repeated and darted his eyes along the tree line until he had turned full circle. Slower this time, he searched again, taking time to look deeper into the trees as he twisted.

"I wish we had a Book of Worlds," Larkstone said. "Haggerwolf, did your aunt say anything about wizards, or earth spirits, or—"

"Something powerful," Fernbark said, interrupting.

Haggerwolf scowled at him. "Calm down." Looking back at Larkstone, he answered. "She never said anything. It must have been something with great intelligence. A fearless being."

"Fistlock has one," Fernbark said in a whisper and cleared his throat.

Haggerwolf rolled his eyes and shook his head. He opened his mouth to say something to Larkstone, but stopped and turned back to Fernbark. "What did you say?"

"I didn't say 'powerful'." Fernbark held up his hands as if surrendering.

"You said Fistlock has one. One what?"

"A Book of Worlds."

Haggerwolf and Larkstone stared at each other for an instant. "Fistlock. He'll be right behind us," Haggerwolf said.

They both grabbed one of Fernbark's sleeves and began running toward the journey-wind. Fernbark stumbled at first as his friends pulled him along. His mind wasn't concentrating on working his feet. It was too busy trying to figure out what he had said that panicked his companions. When he did, he broke away and reached the bent circle of grass before they did. As the other two jumped in behind him, Fernbark's eyes widened. He bolted back toward the cabin. The journey-wind began to spin.

In a blink, its smoke-grey streaks of magic swirled upward, covering its two travelers. The top of the reeling funnel broadened and tugged at the high branches of the pines. Bottom and top swaying out of sync, the journey wind wobbled after Fernbark.

"What in... are... idiot..." were the only words Fernbark understood. The sound of the journey wind sucked back the other words Haggerwolf had yelled.

The wind tried to suck him in too, but Fernbark braced himself against the pull and struggled forward to the chimney stones. He had to wrap both arms around them and clasp his fingers together to keep from being ripped away.

A second journey wind lowered from the clouds. Its sooty colored form ripped up clods of grass at the far side of the clearing.

"Dream snatch, opened clasp!" Fernbark screamed as well as he could. The collars of his cloak slapped painfully against his face. The smell of mold and decayed wood grew stronger as the other journey wind snaked like a predator across the meadow.

His own journey wind buffeted him, lifting his feet from the ground and sucked away one of his boots.

"Magic match, to the last!" He could barely hear his own words through the black screeching of the ominous funnel. The winds competed, one to feed on him, the other to carry him away, yet Fernbark held fast, his fingers unclasped now and bloody from digging into the stones. One more line and the winds could have him.

"From its lair to my..." He squeezed his eyes shut to save them from the bits of stinging sand and sticks that scratched at his face, as he searched for a rhyming word.

"To my..."

The funnels bumped and coiled around each other, pulling his hands away from the stones.

"Pink chair!" his voice boomed from where his body had been. Fernbark was gone.

4: Trundle-Wraith

Fistlock quickly surveyed his clothing, even opening his black silky travel cloak to look underneath. Wide-eyed, Panderflip watched. When Fistlock was satisfied the journey didn't include rearranged clothes, he studied the surroundings. "Horrid place," he said as he looked at the trees. "A world to stay away from. Too many insects and fuzzy creatures from the look of it."

"This is where the book was, Master." Panderflip held a forked stick shaped like the letter Y. The single branch stretched down from the V of the twigs. It pointed at the hole left by the missing hearthstone.

"Magic. Fresh magic. But not when the book was here," Fistlock said as he walked a small circle. "And what is that smell?"

"I believe it's butter and cinnamon, your Shadowness. That means—"

"Forge-Twiddlers," Fistlock said, finishing the sentence for his chamberlain. "Forge-Twiddlers," he said a second time, emphasizing the sound of each word. He swept his wand around the clearing. The meadow grass withered, turning from fresh green to coarse brown as each blade toppled flat to the ground. Small flames flared and died, leaving a trail of soot blackened footprints marking where the wizards had stepped. "The book's still on this world and the Forge-Twiddlers aren't."

"Maybe I could track it with my delving rod," Panderflip said as he walked across the clearing, checking each footprint with his stick.

Fistlock ignored him and used the chimney stones as a seat. He tucked his wand under his arm and took a thin, round, pewter container from a pocket inside his cloak. Silently he read the words of magic etched into the lid before he opened it. Inside were many short needles. Very carefully he picked one up, barely able to grasp it between his thumb and finger. Closing one eye, he focused on a tiny hole in the tip of his wand where he inserted the blunt end of the stinger. "You didn't think to bring a trundle-wraith along, did you?" he called to Panderflip. "No, I didn't think so," he said, not waiting for an answer. "Come here, Panderflip. I have a mission for you."

ᘓᘐ

A long line of cars and trailers inched ahead and stopped. The last weekend before school was always a busy time and it seemed everyone planned to leave the park at the same time. The Summerfield family used to travel in a cramped two-door car until Windslow had his accident. That's when they got the van with a wheel-chair lift. The van was big enough to haul the camper trailer, too. Windslow had argued with his father about that. Both his father and Trish, his step-mom, decided on the trailer because they didn't want Windslow to sleep on the ground. He insisted, and soon found they gave in easily whenever he said doing something he wanted would make him feel more normal.

He didn't like using his paralysis that way. He only used it when he was sure they were just trying to baby him. He didn't like using it with Hillary. She was fun, and even though she was a month older, he had enjoyed acting like her big brother. It had been a great way to get her girlfriends to come around. Or maybe it had just been stupid. He'd put her teddy bear up on the roof on purpose; just so he could show off to her friends. He was the one responsible and now she had to stay with him like a personal servant. That's what made him so grumpy lately—thinking about it. He was so glad they had the adventure last night. It was almost like the time before the chair.

"Psst..."

Windslow tried to turn his head far enough to look at his sister, but could only see her out of one eye.

"Psst..."

"Hey, mom. Sounds like one of the tires is leaking."

"What?" Trish asked from up front.

Hillary kicked the back of his seat.

"Nothing. Hillary is just making strange sounds to get my attention. I think she deflated."

"Oh, shut up," she said from behind him.

Trish adjusted the rearview mirror to look at them. Windslow waved. Trish gave a small chuckle and twisted the mirror back. Bill gave it another twist, put the van in gear and drove forward another ten feet.

"This thing is blank," Hillary whispered, her breath close to the back of his neck.

Windslow twisted his head again and spoke softly. "I know, and what about the pages? Do you think they got all stuck together from being buried?"

"I don't know. This book is weird. The whole thing still scares me. Maybe we should turn it in at the Ranger Station when we check out."

"No," Windslow said, twisting his head so hard that it

hurt his neck. "Not until we have time to look at it more. It was magic, Hillary. I know it. You know it."

"But you're not supposed to remove archeological artifacts or plants or anything from a park. It said so in the brochure."

"You think this book belonged to a dinosaur or something? Name one time you've ever heard or read about, where the things that happened to us happened to someone else."

"It doesn't matter."

"All right. Compromise. We take it to school tomorrow. I'll show it to Mr. Nick. He's the coolest science teacher I ever had. He might be able to tell us something."

"Ms. Christensen, too. You'll have her this year. She's really smart and easy to talk with."

"I know her. She helped me when my mom died. Okay, double-dust-dish deal." He reached behind his head.

Hillary hooked her little finger with his and squeezed. "Double-dust-dish."

Windslow let out a quiet sigh, knowing the book would stay secret from his parents. He knew they wouldn't understand. Hillary hated dusting and doing the dishes. So did he. It was one of the things his dad wouldn't let him out of. If Hillary broke her promise, she'd have to wash and dust for two weeks. Maybe not two weeks. Just a day, he told himself. He knew that any longer would add to the press of guilt already crushing him.

"Hide that thing someplace," he whispered to Hillary.

"I will. As soon as we stop and mom and dad are in the Ranger Shack."

ꟷ

Panderflip was staring at the ground, searching with his divining rod, and not paying attention while he walked back to Fistlock. With a quick flick of his wrist, Fistlock touched his wand to Panderflip's neck.

"Something bit me," Panderflip said and slapped the back of his neck. He jerked up straight, his shoulders no longer slouched, his back arched. The divining stick clattered to the stones, released from limp fingers that were already swelling. He teetered and collapsed.

"Well, that was careless of me," Fistlock said and grabbed Panderflip's legs. "I should have stuck him over by the trees and saved myself some work."

Sweat beaded on Fistlock's forehead and glistened on his thick black eyebrows from the effort of dragging his stout ex-chamberlain to the closest tree. Before casting his spell, Fistlock braced his hands on his knees and rested to catch his breath. Still stooped over, he waved his wand across Panderflip's feet and pointed at the tree branch over his head.

A rope appeared. One end crawled down the trunk and across the bed of pine needles to Panderflip's boots. Two twists around, a simple knot and the rope snake stilled. Fistlock stepped back. Panderflip's body slid across the needles, rubbing away the top brown layer to expose a trail of dirt underneath. The rope dragged its captive only a short distance before lifting it off the ground. Panderflip swung gently upside down, his head even with Fistlock's shoulders.

"Too much green," Fistlock said. He mumbled something and pine branches around him lurched. Like the sound of crinkling cellophane, green needles crackled, turned brown, and dropped from their branches. Fistlock cursed and brushed the needles off his shoulders. He walked back to the ruins where he watched and waited.

Fistlock's wait was short. Panderflip's mouth turned black and puffed outward, his lips hard like the beak of some large creature. His head twitched and shoulders hunched as he twisted upward to form a hideous letter J. Saliva dripped syrupy at first, quickly thinning into a long thin strand. The creature he had turned into began spinning.

"This part always fascinates me," Fistlock said. He folded his arms and watched as the cocoon formed. He didn't bother to wait the required time, and used magic to speed up the transformation. The wraith wouldn't survive long. Fistlock had to take the risk. Too much time had already slipped past and his chance to catch the book thief could be lost if he didn't hurry.

He whistled an off-key tune while he walked back to the tree. Without a pause, he pulled his dagger and slashed the bottom of the hanging form. Three black globs dripped and pooled on the ground. "Hm..." he said and gave a kick. "Four." The last drop splashed into the others.

Like thick ink, they flowed together and changed shape, first an oval pool, then round-ended fingers stretching outward. One finger touched the tree's shadow and the whole pool moved into it.

Fistlock opened his pewter container while he watched the pool blend until only the tree's shadow remained visible. "I have work for you." He sprinkled a pinch of silvery powder on the pin.

"Yes, Master," the trundle-wraith answered from its hiding place in the tree's shadow.

"Someone stole my book. Track the thief and stick him with this." Fistlock dropped the pinpoint into the shadow. "Go."

Part of the tree's shadow separated and flowed to another shadow cast by a branch. From there the trundle-wraith moved quickly, uncomfortable away from its normal home in the shadows under a bed. Branch, to grass, to stone, to a moving shadow from a cloud, it ran. Fistlock tried to keep it in his sight, but couldn't. Even knowing what it was and what to look for didn't help. He buttoned up his travel cloak and summoned a journey-wind.

ꕥ

Shadows from the big rectangular shapes gave the trundle-wraith some comfort. The forms reminded it of beds, but higher off the ground. They stretched out in a long row that made the traveling easier than in the woods. But something didn't feel right. Thinning and changing to match the darker, then lighter shadows, took too much effort. Thinning was easier. Dark was hard, like matching these shadows. They moved slowly, stopped and then moved again, spaced evenly along a narrow strip of hard black ground. Not far ahead, it could sense the thief. The trundle-wraith felt itself thinning. Would it make it there before wasting away? Would the thief be sleeping and let an arm dangle from the bed?

ꕥ

"Okay, hide it now. They're both inside," Windslow said. "Stick it inside my saddlebag.

"I can't. It's too close to the door."

"Then open it. Quick," he said and twisted the door handle.

Hillary squeezed past him and shoved the door open.

"Come on. Hurry," he urged as she jumped out. He held the bag open while she shoved the book inside.

They both let out a long breath when Hillary slammed the door and jumped back into her seat.

Windslow laughed and drummed his hands against the van's roof. "You did it. Now we can just sit back and enjoy the ride home. Nothing can go wrong from here."

"Shoot," Hillary said.

"What's the matter?"

"Something bit my ankle."

5: Dream Snatched

Back home, neither Windslow nor Hillary had time to give the book much thought. They were busy enough helping unpack from the camping trip and getting things ready for school the next day. Trish looked at the bite on Hillary's ankle and decided it wasn't serious. A dab of antiseptic and a Band-Aid helped stop the itching and took Hillary's mind off the small red spot. They all hoped to get extra sleep that night, knowing tomorrow would likely be a hectic day.

After Windslow's accident, they had swapped bedrooms. Bill and Trish moved into Hillary's bedroom in the walkout basement of their rambler. Nestled into a gentle slope, the house had a path that curved around from front yard to back. Bill paved it with bricks so Windslow could use it with his wheelchair. A wooden ramp gave him access to the front sidewalk, driveway and garage. With little effort, he could wheel himself around the yard, up the ramp and down the hall to his bedroom, just across from Hillary's.

As night settled on the neighborhood, lamps turned off, blinking out yellow squares of light that stretched from windows onto lawns in front of each house. An occasional car drove down the street, sweeping headlights across hedges, young trees and a bicycle someone forgot to put away. Here and there a voice called out about a notebook, lunch money and other things. The voices faded. Darkness took hold, except for thin strips of hazy light that snuck past edges of drawn curtains; one of them from Windslow's room.

He'd gone to bed long ago. The flashlight rested on his blanket, weary batteries barely giving light he no longer needed for the book. It lay open exposing the first page. The cream-colored paper held no visible words, yet showed faint shading where four lines of text waited in its center. Windslow's breathing was slow and regular. The book rose and fell on his chest with each breath as he stepped deeper into sleep. With each step into sleep, the lines darkened. When his dream began, graceful script with swirls and sweeping flourishes stood boldly on the page.

The story in this chance begins,

Found in pages locked within.

Open them with words of care.

What you seek is waiting there.

꧁꧂

He floated downward ever so slowly, rocking first to the left and back to the right. A puff of wind gently lifted him upward. It eased away its support and down he drifted once again. Below him, finger-paint colors played a game of chase, marking multicolor paths with bright greens, blues and yellows. Above and around him clouds gave comfort; silver-gray and brilliant white, they carried him along. He played the shape game, searching out billowy forms that reminded him of animals and buildings. He couldn't call out any names. His voice failed him but he didn't mind.

His feather ride gained speed and the movements lost their gentle sway. He twisted wildly, dipping and rising in a carnival ride of wind. The clouds turned burnt charcoal. Grainy edges scattered into powdery dust, leaving black coal forms with pocks and deep shadows. A delicate hand stretched out toward him, but the clouds and winds sucked it away. There. Again, it reached for him. Someone screamed his name. He knew the voice. Dark shapes wrapped around the arm, struggling to pull it back.

Windslow tried to cry out, "Hillary," but the words choked in his throat. He stretched his hand toward hers. Their fingers touched.

He couldn't grab her hand or see her, yet that small connection between them held. The wind buffeted against the stormy battle that swept them along. He enjoyed the thrill and wonder of it all. He'd had vivid dreams of traveling before. He started having them after the accident. Some had scared him but now he recognized them for what they were. Just dreams. He'd wake up soon to find his chair waiting for him.

A strand of silver brushed past his face and draped across his wrist. He laughed to himself, thinking it looked like a bit of tinsel from a Christmas tree. It wrapped itself around his wrist three times. With each turn, the end tucked under and over itself, weaving in and out until the two ends formed a small clasp. They clicked together to finish the silver bracelet that hung loosely around his wrist.

His fingertips tingled and slipped away from Hillary's. Her fingers retreated back into the boiling clouds that drifted away. The storm calmed. He thought his feather ride would return. It didn't. Whatever held him up abruptly left.

The sensation of falling in a dream always woke him up; even faster after his real fall from the roof. This fall was short and he didn't wake.

Foof... Pa-toof. He landed like he'd flopped into a beanbag chair, but this wasn't like the one Hillary had in her bedroom. It was wood with no arms and a high back, just like the ones in the dining room that he and Hillary weren't supposed to rock back in. And, it was pink; the brightest pink he had ever seen.

ᘛᘚ

"Too bad for you. Wakie up now."

Hillary rubbed her eyes. It couldn't be time for school yet. She felt like she had just gone to sleep.

"Why you here?"

What was that voice? she asked herself, as her sleep haze gave way and she opened her eyes. She blinked and stared, wondering if she should pinch herself like she heard people on TV say when they couldn't believe what they saw. She was in a cell; a cell with iron bars *and* in a dungeon too. Cold stone formed the cell's back wall. On each side, rows of metal bars thrust forward to separate her small space from others on either side of her. Rods set just wide enough to reach a hand through stood sentinel across the front, their even pattern barely broken by the door frame of each cell. Old straw littered the floor and the place smelled like a dog kennel that needed a good wash by a fire hose.

"He get you here. Dream snatchie, betcha."

Hillary turned her head, almost afraid to look where the voice came from. In a corner of the cell next to her huddled a girl, about the same age as Hillary and a little shorter. The girl sat like Hillary, in a corner with her legs pulled up against her chest. She stared back with big round gerbil eyes and smiled.

Hillary took a quick glance at herself. She was wearing her pajamas; the pale yellow cotton ones with the tiny monarch butterfly print. The girl in the next cell wore a plain brown dress that stopped at her knees where blue big polka dot socks continued down and tucked into soft brown boots. Her eyes and hair almost called out a silent command to ignore her clothes and look at her face. Black bristly hair, sticking out in a neatly trimmed circle reminded Hillary of a chimneysweep's brush.

"Hi. I Molly Folly Sallyforth. Who you?"

"I... I'm Hillary. Hillary Windgate-Summerfield.

Where *are* we? How'd I get here?"

"Fistlock's place," the slender girl said as she scooted over to the bars separating their cells. "Told you. Dream snatchie. Woodo voodoo." Molly thrust her arms between the bars and wiggled her fingers. "Magic stuff."

Hillary stayed in her corner. "Who is Fistlock and you didn't tell me where we are."

"Big baddie. Big trouble. He big boss of everything. We here," Molly said and tapped her finger on the stone floor. "Dungeon. Not bad place. Better place than there," she said, pointing upward. "Fistlock up there."

Hillary hoped the strange fast talking girl didn't notice when Hillary slipped an arm down and pinched herself.

"What you make face for? Cause you gonna die? Don't worry. I help you out. Help you escape for ear thing." Molly tugged at her ear and smiled.

"What? You mean my earring?" Hillary asked and touched one of the earrings she wore. It was the only pair she had; tiny diamond studs, so small you could hardly see the stone, but Hillary loved them. Mothers were strange. Trish wouldn't let Hillary wear makeup but had been the one who urged Hillary to get her ears pierced. Hillary saw this as a small battle won in the struggle to convince her mother to give in about the makeup. She wouldn't part with them for both reasons, and besides, this whole thing, this place... That was it. This place, she thought. This is just a dream; just a dream because of that stupid book. "Sorry, Molly. I'm keeping them. I think this is all just a dream."

"Was dream," Molly said. "Not now. Now real, but maybe you safe a bit. Maybe he not kill you before you sleep. Then gone, bye bye. But you be back again. Next dream. You see," she said nodding her head as she spoke. "Where other friend?"

"What friend?"

"Lookie your fingers."

Hillary looked at the back of her hand then turned it over to check her palm. Her fingertips were smudged with silver, as if she had wiped them across glittery eye shadow.

"See. You gotta mark. You come with somebody. He boy. Got boyfriend?"

Hillary curled her fingers into a fist and put her hand behind her back. "What makes you think that?"

"That double dream snatchie mark. Girls gold, boys silver. Girls prettier."

"Windslow," Hillary said softly. She moved over to the bars and held out her hand. "Here, take my earring. We need to have a long talk."

"Not now," Molly said and snatched the earring. "Somebody come."

ജ്ഞ

"This dream is so cool," Windslow said and looked at the three small men dressed in funny clothes standing in front of him. Each man stared and pointed a long, skinny, bark-less twig at him.

"No dream, boy," One of the funny men said. "Hand it over."

"Hand what over?" Windslow answered and looked around, ignoring them. This was the best dream he'd had in a long time and he didn't want to miss anything. Usually his dreams didn't have detailed backgrounds. "This place is great," he said, not really talking to the men as he looked around the old room. Odd shaped beakers sat on wall shelves and dried plants dangled from bits of twine tied to the rafters.

"Give it up or .... Or we'll do something you won't like."

"Sure, sure," Windslow said, still ignoring them, hoping they'd just fade away. He tried to see around them to look for a kitchen. He must have gone to bed hungry because the smell of cinnamon floated to him in-between scents of licorice and root beer. He wondered if the smells might be coming from vapors that floated up from tiny brass pots on the table behind the three misfits from a matinee movie.

"All right, we're going to take it. No funny moves now."

Windslow looked down. The Book of Second Chances lay in his lap. "Whoa, what's this doing in my dream?" He gave the book a shove. It slipped off his pajamas, bounced off his toe and slapped to the wood floor. "Owe!" he yelled. He didn't jerk his leg up but it did move. He saw it. He felt it twitch from the pain throbbing in his big toe. For the first time he looked closely at the three old men. They backed away and stood shoulder to shoulder, still pointing their sticks at him.

He'd never been hurt in a dream before and nothing ever happened below his waist in a dream since his fall. He glanced around the room again; realizing things looked too real, smelled too real, felt too real. "I *am* dreaming?" he asked, this time speaking directly to the three men.

"You were, but not now," the one with the long beard answered. "You dream traveled. Larkstone cast a spell bracelet to intercept you. It's on your wrist. Fistlock has a charm on that book. You're lucky he didn't get you. Now hand it over."

"I didn't know it belonged to anyone," Windslow said and tried to reach the book. He leaned over and stopped; afraid he'd fall out of the chair. "I can't. I'm... I'm paralyzed."

"Check him, Larkstone."

The odd fellow wearing a robe embroidered with fish and seashell shapes took a step forward. Windslow felt a slight tingling sensation move down his body as Larkstone moved his stick in a large oval. Both of Windslow's legs quivered for a second when the tingling reached them. "Could be a lie. Then again, could be the truth. I can't tell," the old fellow said.

"How about this," the third man said. He thrust his stick out at Windslow.

It felt like the time Windslow had been trying to fix his stereo and had touched that red wire. He jerked upright, stood, teetered for a few seconds and fell to the floor.

"Humph. Thought so," the man said. "It's not that he couldn't use his legs, he just doesn't. Something is injured in his back but he could overcome it."

Windslow twisted to his side, grabbed the book and gave it a hard shove. It slid across the floor to the three men. "Take it," he said, fighting back tears. "Just let me go home. I want to wake up."

"I told you," the one with the beard said as he squatted down and put one hand on the book. "You're not dreaming and you won't go home until you fall asleep." He kept his stick pointed at Windslow. "You'll dream-slip back to where you came from. Now that we have the book, you won't be back."

"Look," the one named Larkstone said. "It's unlatched."

The bearded man moved his stare from Windslow to the book. He flipped open the front cover. "He knows how to use it," he said to his companions. "There's already writing on the first page. Now what?"

"It was blank when I fell asleep," Windslow said. "I don't know how to use it or what it's for. It's just a dumb old book. Can I go home now?"

6: Scritched

Hillary heard the footsteps. She stood, moved to the cell door and grabbed the bars. Molly Folly Sallyforth scooted back into a corner. Both girls waited. The large stone room echoed faintly with far off sounds of hard-soled boots on stone. The girls occupied the two cells in the center of a group of four that stretched across a room twice as long and wide as Hillary's garage. She could see nearly everything from where she stood. Big blocks of slate-colored stone and thin strips of gray cement formed the walls and floor. She didn't see any way in or out, except for the door across the room from where the sounds came. They sounded louder.

Hillary looked up at the dark wood planks and thick square beams coated in cobwebs overhead. She'd never be able to reach that high, even by standing on her dad's shoulders. Besides, he wasn't here to save them and Molly was shorter than Windslow. In the center of the room neatly mortared, pumpkin-sized stones formed a three-foot high circle that could be a well. A slightly shorter table sat next to it. The footsteps sounded close.

Torches set in brackets gave off more smoke than light. The smoke drifted along the ceiling like upside down fog to a hole above the well where the smoke curved upward and disappeared. Two possibilities for escape including the door, Hillary concluded. Whatever plan Molly had, made three. The footsteps stopped and Hillary looked toward the door.

The doorframe's mouth opened wide, filled with the shapes of two men, one standing behind the other. One man, short and pudgy, half hid behind the taller one whose skinny body spanned the frame from top to bottom. He wouldn't win any fashion contest. Too skinny for his height, he looked like the classic villain from a late night movie where the actor's lips and words moved out of sync. A long purple robe flowed beneath a slightly shorter and black outer cloak with silver trim. He looked like everlasting Halloween. Hillary wanted to laugh at him until she looked at his eyes. They made her feel creepy. Violet, almost red pupils stared at her.

As the men walked forward, a marshmallow face peeked out from behind the man in front. His long thin nose seemed to point like a stubby finger in the direction it wanted his squinting eyes to look. Small lips completed a set of features that looked spaced too close together for the size of his face. White buttons strained to hold his shirt closed. The yellow cloth stretched wearily across a belly that flowed up over the top of orange pants. There was too much man and not enough cloth. Even his coat sleeves gave up trying to cover him, ending halfway to his wrists.

"You must be Fistlock," Hillary said, tipping her head slightly to the side and looking at the man with the multicolored clothes. "Why are you hiding behind your tall assistant?" She hoped Fistlock got her point. The stubby man's head ducked out of view. Behind her, Molly whimpered.

"I'm Fistlock," violet eyes said. A bit of spittle flew from his lips and clung to his pointed beard that ended just below his chin. "Where's my book?"

"If you mean the one we found, it's not yours. It belongs to the US National Park Service," Hillary said and folded her arms.

"If she's the right one, shouldn't it be with her?" Orange pants asked.

"It should but it's not because that idiot Panderflip made a worse trundle-wraith than a chamberlain," Fistlock said.

"Uncle not idiot. Him smart. Good chamberlain."

Fistlock raised his hand. A slap sounded and Molly tipped to her side. Hillary adjusted her perspective on the situation. Fistlock had never moved his hand. Some force from his hand had slapped her friend. When Molly sat back up, Hillary could see red finger welts on Molly's face.

"She had to be with whoever has the book," Fistlock said and lowered his hand. He never looked at Molly. He kept his gaze focused on Hillary. "Panderflip must have stuck her by mistake. I'll prepare a potion so when she dream-slips back home she'll come back here with whoever does have it. It'll take some time to prepare it. Don't let her fall asleep, Bitterbrun or I'll give you the same promotion I gave to Panderflip. Fetch your bag."

Bitterbrun turned and darted out the doorway. In barely a few seconds, he backed up through the door. He dragged a large canvas bag, grunting with effort as he pulled it to the table. While Fistlock watched, Bitterbrun placed a large leather bound book on the table. He ducked down to his bag and stood back up holding two tall thick yellow candles. He set them in front of the book.

Hillary watched as Fistlock lit the candles without touching them, probably by magic she thought. He mumbled some words. She couldn't hear them all but did hear him say "awake" and "all night." The book opened and the pages turned themselves. When the pages stilled, both Fistlock and Bitterbrun leaned over the book.

"How about this, your Brilliancy?" Bitterbrun asked and pointed at a page. "Attaches to your TV, comes with two controllers and one game. It's some kind of a machine."

"No. It should be something we can feed her. Something reliable. Here," Fistlock said. He jabbed his finger at two spots in the book. "Some of this and some of that. I'll send a scritch."

Fistlock backed away from the table and walked to a shadowy corner of the room. He waited motionless like a stork fishing for frogs in the shallows of a shadow pond. After a quick snatch in the air near the floor, he returned to the table. Fistlock cupped his hands together and twisted and pressed them as if packing a ball of mud. When he opened them, a black ball the size of a plum rested on his palm. He bounced it twice on the floor, caught it and held over the book. "Lower the bell," he said.

Bitterbrun slipped his hand under the table edge. Hillary heard a small click and then the sound of chains and a squeaky wheel. A large tarnished brass bell, nearly three feet across, lowered from the hole in the ceiling. She heard another click and the bell stopped, suspended two feet above the well.

"When the scritch comes back, feed the girl and keep her awake." Fistlock moved the ball close to his lips, said something to it and then tossed it in the well. Without another word, he turned and walked out the door. Bitterbrun hopped up on the side of the table facing Hillary. He put his hands behind him and let his feet dangle as he looked at her.

Hillary stared back for a while, then eased back away from the door, moving over to the bars that separated her cell from Molly's. "What are they planning?" she asked in a low voice. "What's a scritch?"

Molly scooted against the bars. "They scritchy things. Steal. Put it down and look away. All gone. Scritch take it. Move fast. Can't see."

"Why did Fistlock throw it in the well?"

"Do spelly, welly thing. Send scritch to your world."

"For what?"

"Something. We find out, I betcha."

Hillary didn't need to wait long. She heard a "whoosh," the bell rang, and Bitterbrun hopped off the table. Zip.

Whoosh. Zip, zip. The ball bounced around the room; too fast to see except for a black blur and only if you were looking in the right place. With one final "zip-boing," it sat still on the table next to a package of coffee and large bag of chocolates.

Bitterbrun brushed the ball off the table. A boing and zip later it disappeared.

"What are those for?" Molly asked and moved back to the front bars of her cell.

"To keep you awake. Dinnertime," he said and opened the two packages. He sniffed the coffee grounds first, and then the chocolate. "Wish I had to stay awake."

"Well, don't you?" Hillary asked. "I bet Fistlock would give you that promotion he mentioned if you fall asleep. Eating just one of those little brown squares in the big bag would help you. There will be plenty left to keep me awake for a week."

Bitterbrun's eyes widened at the mention of a promotion and nodded as he listened. He sniffed the bag of chocolates again and picked out one square, holding it gingerly in his fingers. He sniffed it again after unwrapping it and took a tiny bite off one corner. The rest he shoved into his mouth. He unwrapped another and sent it in after the first one.

"Don't forget me," Hillary said as a pile of small foil wrappers began to pile up in front of Bitterbrun.

He popped one more chocolate into his mouth, grabbed both bags and walked to her. "Here," he said and shoved the packages through the bars.

"I can't eat this," Hillary said, holding open the bag of coffee grounds. "It's for a drink. You need to put this stuff in hot water. It's like tea or an herbed drink."

Bitterbrun looked back over both shoulders, as if by looking, he would somehow discover a kettle on a stove.

Hillary let out an exaggerated sigh. "You better go fetch a pot for me to make this in. Bring a cup too."

"I'm supposed to watch you," Bitterbrun said. He stepped back a pace and folded his arms across his chest.

"And you're not supposed to let me fall asleep until your string-bean boss comes back. Here, I'll help you out." Hillary unwrapped and ate two pieces of chocolate. She tossed the bag to Molly. "There, that should keep me awake. See? Don't you feel better now? More confident?"

Bitterbrun relaxed his arms and nodded.

"The chocolate will only work for awhile, though. Then you'll worry won't you?"

Bitterbrun nodded again. The smile faded from his lips.

"You don't want that, do you?"

He shook his head back and forth this time.

"You're lucky that I'll be wide awake long enough for you to run for some hot water. Make sure it's really hot. Simmer it for at least ten minutes. Can you remember that?"

Bitterbrun raised his eyebrows and smiled as he shook his head.

"You better get going. Quick now. You have things to do. Why are you standing here?"

Bitterbrun's eyes widened. He pivoted around and ran for the door.

"That takes care of him, for awhile anyway," Hillary said and glanced at Molly. "Maybe I can pick this lock."

"Scritch key. Get scritch. He do it."

"That ball thing? It's gone."

"Not gone. Always around." Molly crawled to the front of her cell and placed a small morsel of chocolate on the floor just outside the bars. She looked away and then back. The floor was bare. She backed away from the door and held out her open palm. Another bit of chocolate rested in her hand. When she looked away, she grabbed tight. "Gotcha." She held the black ball firmly in her hand. "You want more chocla? Then go scritch cell key from Bitterbrun." She stuck her arm through the cell bars and threw.

Hillary saw the ball fly, but it disappeared with a "zip" in midair. She watched anxiously.

"Here chocla. Good scritch," Molly said behind her.

Hillary turned around. Molly stood at the bars between their cells. She held out a big iron ring full of skeleton keys.

"Scritch fast. Have to be. Otherwise not scritch."

Hillary gave a little laugh and took the keys from her new friend. "Molly you're wonderful. Let's get out of here."

Hillary knelt in front of the lock. When she held up the key ring, she noticed the keys were identical, except for symbols stamped into the end of each one. They all had the same words along their pencil thick shafts. 'Forge-Twiddler Key Works.' "They're all the same," she said to Molly.

"Not same. Different key, different lock. Look end to pick right one. Same wordy on lock."

Hillary shrugged and sorted through the keys to find the one with matching symbols. She fumbled and the key ring clanged to the floor; the sound they made followed by a zip-wiff. When she looked down, they were gone. "Shoot," Hillary said. "They were scritched. Molly, give me a piece of chocolate." Hillary turned her head.

Molly held the empty bag upside down. A chocolate smudge ringed her lips.

ഗ്ര

"It's no use," Haggerwolf said. "The book just isn't going to close unless you use it or figure out how to do it."

"We could..." Fernbark said, his words trailing off. "Well, someone could. I wouldn't."

"What? Kill him and be just like Fistlock. No. I think... Well... Well, just no."

"Take the book the way it is," Windslow said and held it out to them. "I don't want it. Really!"

"I wish we knew how it worked," Haggerwolf said. He grabbed the edge of the book and gently guided it back into Windslow's lap.

"What?" Windslow said. "You're kidding."

"It's true," Larkstone said. "Biffendear was the only one besides Fistlock who figured out how the book works. He was the one who scritched it from Fistlock."

"Then why not... yawn... ask... Biffendear?" Windslow asked and rubbed his eye with the back of his hand.

"He got eaten," Larkstone said and shrugged his shoulders.

Haggerwolf opened a steel-banded oak chest at the side of the room. He rummaged around, tossing several things on the floor as he muttered to himself.

"What are you looking for?" Fernbark asked.

"A dream snatch stopper. That magic bracelet you made kept Fistlock from snatching him on this dream, but it won't work for the next. The boy's getting sleepy. He'll be dream-slipping home any minute."

"I've got one," Larkstone said. He moved his wand up and down in the air, and stuffed the stick back inside a pocket in his robe. In the air where he had waved his stick, a large shiny zipper, two feet long and six inches wide, hovered in the air. The sight made Windslow sit up straight in his chair. There was no cloth, only metal that looked like chrome. The wide triangular pull had words painted in gold. 'Forge-Twiddler Storage, Inc.'

"Bet you'd like one of these... ah... What's your name, son," Larkstone asked.

"Windslow Summerfield, and what is that thing?"

"Ever get tired of cleaning up your room? You know. You mother hollers at you and you shove everything in the closet?"

"Yeah. My real mom was that way. Trish, she's my step-mom, doesn't get on me too much anymore because—"

"Because you quit walking?"

"No! Because I can't walk."

"If you say so," Larkstone said. He grabbed the zipper pull and drew it down. The two sides of the zipper parted. He shoved his arm through, up to his elbow, moving and twisting as he felt inside.

Windslow opened his eyes wide. He expected to see Larkstone's arm stick out the back side, but it didn't.

While Larkstone fished inside his zipper, he looked back over his shoulder at Windslow. "My mother made this for me. It's like that closet you dump everything into. But this one never fills up, you always have it with you and everything is within reach just inside. "Got it," he said and took his arm out. With his other hand, he zipped up the opening, gave the pull a flip and the whole thing disappeared. A rubber band dangled on the end of his finger.

"I'm surprised you had one," Haggerwolf said and took the rubber band. "I wish they weren't so rare. I'd give you one for your sister if I had another one."

"Windslow?" Fernbark said softly. No one paid any attention to him.

"Wear this when you go to sleep," Haggerwolf said as he slipped the quarter inch wide rubber band over Windslow's hand. "It's made from a rare plant. No one can dream snatch you if you're wearing one."

"Winds low?" Fernbark whispered again.

"You're... yawn... kidding, right?" Windslow asked and gave the band a tiny snap. "In my... yawn... world... yawn...

"Windslow," Fernbark asked loudly, this time. "You wouldn't happen to have a sister, would you?"

"Oh... yeah, I... do..." Windslow's eyelids fluttered and closed. He began to fade.

Fernbark grabbed the can of pink paint they had used for the chair and set it in Windslow's lap. "What's her name!" he yelled as loud as he could.

"Hill... Hillary Windgate-Summerfield..." He was gone.

"Fernbark?" Haggerwolf asked. His friend stood in front of the empty chair, staring at the seat. "Fernbark!"

"Hm... Oh, sorry."

"What was that all about?"

"His name," Fernbark answered. He tested the paint to see if it was dry and sat down in the chair. "That's why he could open the book. He and his sister were supposed to."

"I don't understand," Larkstone and Haggerwolf both said at the same time.

"Windslow Summerfield. Winds low, summer field. Hillary Windgate-Summerfield. Hill airy, wind gate, summer field. Hillary and Windslow, son of the summer storm and daughter of the mountain breeze, the children mentioned by the oricle.

7: Second Chances

Hillary looked at the empty bag and Molly's face. Shaking her head, she knelt down in front of the cell lock, closed one eye, and tried to look into the mechanism. "Do you have anything metal, like a belt buckle or thick hairpin?" She asked Molly.

"Nope. Only got key."

"What?" Hillary said and spun around.

Molly held a loop of string circling her neck. A key like the one on Bitterbrun's key ring, dangled from the cord just below her fingertips. "This key for my room. Not for that lock. Different words on end."

Hillary took the key, gave it a quick look and tried it in the lock. When she turned the key, the lock sounded a solid, "click."

"Molly, are all the keys the same? The same on this end?" she asked and held the key up as she opened her cell and moved to Molly's door.

Molly nodded. "Forge-Twiddler make alla keys and lock. Alla same."

"What's your escape plan?" Hillary asked and unlocked Molly's door.

"Plan is wait for sisters. Wanna wait? They sneakie here tomorrow."

"No." Hillary said, loud enough that Molly took a step back. "We're getting out of here now! What's outside the door to this room?"

"Big long hall. Turns this-a-way and that. Then soldier room, then outside. Maybe we run fast like scritch. Soldier not see Molly and Hillre."

Hillary leaned over the well and looked down into darkness. "How about down there; the way the scritch went?"

"No, no. That nota way. Go that way and you gonna die. Better run fast like scritch past soldier."

Hillary looked up past the bell, following the chain it hung from. She couldn't see very far from her position and climbed up on top of the table. Carefully she stepped to the stone wall that circled the well. "Maybe this is our way out. Climb on the other side."

When Molly stood with her on the wall, Hillary moved around until she was directly opposite Molly and the bell hung between them. "We have to get up on top of the bell. See up there? I think those metal loops sticking out of the wall in the shaft are like a ladder. Maybe the shaft... yawn... goes somewhere."

Hillary had to stretch as far as she could to grab the big brass ring at the top of the bell. She knew Molly was too short to reach it on her side. Hillary was worried. If they didn't balance when they climbed on the bell, they might ring it and alert the soldiers. She was worried about Bitterbrun too. He could be back at any minute. She grabbed the ring and began pulling herself up when the bell lurched and swung back and forth. Hillary froze and held her breath, listening for the clapper to bang against the inside.

"What Hillre wait for?" Molly asked, looking down at Hillary from the top of the bell. "Grab hand."

Hillary let Molly help her up. The chain links were big enough to use as toe and hand holds. They climbed four feet of chain to reach the metal loops stuck in the side of the bell chamber walls. With Hillary leading, they climbed. The smoke from the torches down in the room curled up past them. It burned Hillary's eyes and almost made her sneeze. She felt herself getting sleepy, but if she fell asleep now, she'd fall past the bell and into the well. She kept climbing.

She wasn't sure how far they had climbed, and couldn't see the bell through the smoke anymore. A bit higher, she could see a small door with a keyhole. When she was level with it, she read the black letters painted on the smoke stained wood. "Bell Works Maintenance Room." The lock had symbols, but Hillary ignored them. She saw what she was looking for stamped just under the keyhole. "Forge-Twiddler, Inc." She tried Molly's key. The lock clicked, and a small push opened the two-foot square door. The girls squirmed through and shut the panel behind them.

Enough dusty sunlight pushed through a small, octagon shaped window to let them see. It was above Hillary's reach and looked too small for them to squeeze through. Gears taller than Hillary crowded the eight-foot square room. A chain like the one the bell hung from, came down through a small hole in the ceiling and wrapped around a big drum. Across the room waited another wooden access panel and keyhole. The sign above it read, "Drawbridge."

The space inside this passageway reminded Hillary of a big wooden air duct. The passage was barely three feet wide and tall, so they had to crawl. This passage connected to others, and soon they were lost in the maze.

"I'm falling asleep, Molly," Hillary said and stopped. "What's going to happen?"

"Here Eat chocola." Molly's tiny hand pushed up near Hillary's face.

"I thought you said we were out of chocolate?"

"Nope. Not say that. Say nothing. Chocola bag empty. Got some in pocket. Eat so stay awake."

"Molly, that won't keep... yawn... me awake."

"Then bye bye. Back home you go. Next dream you go back to cell. I get-cha out. Come back with sisters. You see."

"I'm not going... yawn... to let him... yawn... get..."

"She gone. Guess I gota eat it," Molly said and put the chocolate in her mouth.

ꕥ

Windslow popped his eyes open and blinked. Using the hand rails fastened to the wall his bed sat against, he pulled himself up into a sitting position. "Oh, no," he said as he twisted his shoulders and pulled at his pajamas.

"Windslow!" Hillary said, bursting into his room. "You're never going to believe... Windslow? What happened to you? You've got pink paint all over your pajamas."

"Did you... did... Did you have a really, really weird dream last night?"

"Maybe I did...we did. A dream I mean. Oh crud! Give me that can."

"Can?" Windslow twisted around to look behind him where the two walls of his room formed the corner his bed nestled into. Propped up by a pillow sat a can of pink paint with a brush sticking out of the open top.

"Does it say 'Forge-Twiddler' on the label?"

"Yeah. Right here," Windslow said and handed the can to her.

"Hey, you two. Ready for an early start?" Windslow's father called from down the hallway.

"Double crud," Hillary cursed. She grabbed the book, dropped in on the floor and kicked it under the bed.

Windslow's dad stopped halfway through the open doorway. "What in the...? I can't believe this. Look at you, Windslow. And you, Hillary! What's going on? This is... This is... You're grounded. Both of you! For a month unless your mother thinks it should be for a year. Neither one of you move. Not an inch! I want her to see you just like you are now." He turned and left.

"Did you hear that, Hillary? Woo hoo, I'm grounded. This is fantastic. Finally I got punished for something. Do you know how cool that is? It makes me almost normal. None of that 'poor kid in a wheelchair' this time."

"Yeah, really great. Just the same old thing for me." She sat down on the bed and cradled the paint can in her hands. "Thanks a bunch."

"Give me that," Windslow said. Not waiting, he grabbed the paint can from her and looked at the label. "Forge-Twiddler Reversible Paint."

"Reversible? How?"

"I'm reading—I'm reading."

"Hurry up!"

"To remove paint, seal can with lid upside down," Windslow read from the label.

"Where is it? Where's the lid?" Hillary asked as she leaned over her brother and shoved pillows out of the way.

Hillary crawled off him and held the lid in her hand. Windslow grabbed it. He shoved the brush underneath his pillow, flipped the lid upside down and pressed it on to the can. He watched as the pink quickly faded from his pajamas and arms. "What about my back?" he asked as he leaned forward.

"Clean. What'll we do with the can?

"We can—" Before he could finish, the can vanished.

"All right, you two. What's this I hear about pink paint?" his stepmother asked. She stood in the doorway; one hand on her hip, the other on Bill's shoulder.

"We, ah..." Windslow stammered.

"Where'd it go?" Bill asked and pushed past his wife. He bent over Windslow, moved pillows, lifted blankets and then stepped back, scratching his head. "I swear, Trish. I came in here and Hillary was holding a paint can, and Windslow was covered in pink. He... They... I..."

"Bill, do you need some coffee?" Windslow's step mom asked with a playful sound to her voice.

"I'm sorry, Bill. We were playing a joke on you," Hillary said.

Windslow winced. His father wanted Hillary to call him dad, but she didn't like to call him that.

Still scratching his head, Bill took another look around the room. "Okay," he said. "The laugh is on me. But how'd you do it?"

Windslow and Hillary stared at each other for a few seconds before Windslow blurted out, "Magic. It was special paint. All you do is put the lid back on the can upside down. The paint disappears, can and all."

"Ha," Trish said and laughed. "You'll have to show us how you did it, but not now. I'll start breakfast. Hillary, I think some of that lipstick you've been hiding would look nice on you today. Bill, you get Windslow ready and we'll all meet for pancakes and sausage in ten minutes. Bill, don't put any of Windslow's clothes on him upside down." Trish started giggling. Windslow could hear her snickering all the way down the hall.

ꕥ

They didn't have time to talk that morning. They hurried to get ready, had breakfast and loaded into the van. Bill headed for work, and Trish drove them to school. While Hillary wheeled him into school, Windslow told her to meet him for lunch if she could. At lunch, he couldn't get rid of his friends. It didn't look like Hillary could get rid of hers either. Windslow waved at her and blushed when some of her friends waved back. In class, he tried to concentrate on lessons, but his thoughts kept wandering back to the book, the three wizards, and whatever world his dream had carried him too. He thought about Hillary's comments that morning. Her hand reaching out to him in the first part of his dream-slip must have been real. He snapped the rubber band on his wrist several times as a way to keep himself from daydreaming. He wondered if you could daydream-slip.

The bell rang at the same time he snapped the rubber band for about the tenth time this period. Everyone hurried for their lockers, anxious to end the day. Windslow waited for the room to empty to make it easier for him to navigate with his chair.

"Windslow," Miss Christensen asked, "how are you and your new mom doing?"

He hoped he wasn't blushing. After his real mom died, Miss Christensen had helped him a lot; more than the school counselor. He had been in the nurse's office two years ago. Miss Christensen came in looking for a Band-Aid. The nurse wasn't ready to see Windslow yet and he and Miss Christensen just began talking. After that, he stopped by her room a couple times after school just to talk. After his accident, she helped him again. She was easy to talk to and pretty.

"Windslow?"

"I was thinking about something. I'm sorry," he said.

"Is everything all right at home? How about you and Hillary? I bet it's fun having a sister."

"Oh, she's real cool; almost like my best friend."

"I'm glad to hear that. I hope being in my class this year won't stop you from talking with me once in awhile."

"No, I like doing that." He gave the rubber band another snap. "Can I ask you a dumb question? If you had a chance, a second chance to do something, what would it be?"

"That's quite a question. In fact, I don't know how to answer it. Hm... a second chance at something."

Windslow sat quietly and watched her turn toward the window and bite on her bottom lip. Finally she looked back at him.

"I'm only telling you this, Windslow, because we've shared a lot in our conversations the last two years. My second chance would be about a boy I knew once."

"A boy? Really?"

"Yes, really," she said and smiled. "I had a boyfriend in high school. He was more than a boyfriend, he was my best friend. We graduated, and I went off to college. He couldn't afford college and joined the Navy.

"So you never saw each other again?"

"No, but we had planned to. We promised to keep in touch. For almost a year we wrote back and forth and called each other when we could. Then we wrote less and stopped calling. Finally the letters stopped too."

"Which one of you stopped?" he asked.

"I don't know if it was me or him or both of us. It just happened."

"So if you had a second chance, it would be to start writing again?"

"In a way," she said. Her smile broadened, and she glanced back out the window.

"If I had a second chance," she said looking back at him with soft eyes, "it would be a second chance at being boyfriend and girlfriend. That probably sounds silly to you, but that's what it would be."

"Why don't you just look up his phone number and call him?"

"Where would I start? He might even be living in Europe and is probably married."

"Search the internet," Windslow said and hung his backpack on his wheelchair. "I bet you could find him or his family or something and call."

"So why the question? Is there something you want a second chance at?"

"Only about a thousand things right now. I... I have to do a paper on it. I keep thinking about stuff like, if you had a magic second chance book, how would you make it work?"

"I think you answered your own question. We teachers give assignments because we want you to think. Look at your answer. You told me to just look up my old friend and give him a call. The only magic I'd need for that is a magic phonebook. You'll do fine with your assignment."

"Thanks, Miss Christensen," he said and began rolling his chair toward the door. "I better go. My dad's probably waiting for me."

"Bye, and don't forget. We discuss pages 7-14 tomorrow. My assignments get equal attention."

Windslow grinned, and headed for the parking lot.

ꙮ

After dinner Hillary and Windslow finally had time to talk more while they were supposed to be doing homework. Hillary told Windslow all about Molly Folly Sallyforth, Bitterbrun, and Fistlock. Windslow told her about the wizards and how only someone named Biffendear and Fistlock knew how the book worked.

"Look here," Windslow said and showed her the book. "It's got words now, and you can turn the first page."

Hillary read the words that had formed after Windslow fell asleep last night.

Chapter I.

The story in this chance begins,

Found in pages locked within.

Open them with words of care.

What you seek is waiting there.

"You can turn another page," she said.

"That wasn't there when I was with the wizards or this afternoon. I looked at it when we had library time."

Hillary read the new words to him.

Something lost in time long pas,t

Chancing love she thought would last.

You helped her think of what to do,

A link once cut she now renews.

"This isn't making any sense," she said. "Maybe it's a puzzle?"

"I'll tell you what it is," Windslow said. "It's spooky."

8: Gorge-gobbler

Just before bedtime, they met in Windslow's room. They both had backpacks they hoped would travel with them if they dream-slipped tonight. Windslow had a camp saw, hammer, compass, flashlight, rope, slingshot, pepper spray, a handful of nails, and his music player and earphones. Hillary had bug spray, toilet paper, a tablet and pencils, safety pins, scotch tape, needle and thread, extra socks, moist towelettes, flashlight, and *her* music player and earphones.

"Well, your stuff is just as dumb," Windslow said to his sister, trying to keep his voice low. "I need this stuff so I can rescue you. I'm getting you out of Fistlock's place."

"Windslow, the shaft where I left Molly is barely big enough to crawl through and... and you don't even have a wheel chair there. Do you even know where I am in that world? I don't. You don't even know where *you* are."

"The wizards know. They'll help me. I know they will. If I could just figure out how to close this stupid thing..." he said and pressed his thumb against the book latch without success. "Maybe I could trade the book for you? Fistlock is supposed to know how it works."

"I don't think we should trust him," Molly said and buckled the straps on her backpack. "We need to find a way to stop going there in our dreams. And not sleeping won't work. Find out everything you can if you dream-slip there tonight. No rescue. Promise me?"

"I could..."

"Windslow!"

"Okay. I promise, but here." He pulled the rubber band off his wrist and handed it to her. "Wear this. It's supposed to keep Fistlock from dream snatching you."

"If the book travels with you, Windslow, and you end up in the cell, then we're both in big trouble."

"The wizards said it's made from a rare plant. I cut this one from an old bicycle tire. It's real rubber, not that fake stuff," he said and held up a black rubber band nearly identical to the one he offered Hillary.

"I'll wear the fake one," Hillary said and grabbed it from her brother.

They talked more that night. When Bill hollered, 'lights out.' They both headed for bed.

ꕤ

Fistlock gave the bell another shove. Bitterbrun's shoulders banged against the brass, giving off a muffled ring. He hung upside down inside the bell, his head just poking out past the bottom. He had to turn his face so the clapper wouldn't hit him in the face again.

"The men searched everywhere, your Ruthlessness. The girls couldn't have gone far. I wasn't away that long."

Fistlock shoved again. This time a small, foil wrapped square fell from Bitterbrun's clothes and landed on the wooden boards covering the opening to the well.

"What's this?" Fistlock asked and unwrapped the foil.

"The chocolate you sent the scritch for. I even made her eat a bunch to keep her awake. I don't think she dream-slipped yet."

Fistlock touched his tongue to the corner of the chocolate, then sniffed it. "You're sure she ate some of this?"

"I watched her eat it."

"Distinctive smell," Fistlock said and flicked his wrist.

Bitterbrun dropped in a heap on the well cover. He quickly rolled off and tumbled to the floor just before the planks faded and disappeared.

"I'd turn you into a gorge-gobbler, but I don't have the time. Fetch me one." Fistlock rested his elbows on the table while he waited. Bitterbrun ran from the room and came back quickly, holding a long pole out at an angle in front of him. A large birdcage hung from the end. The room filled with snarls and growls.

"Where do you want it?" he asked, straining to keep the cage suspended off the floor.

A ball of black shiny fur filled the inside of the two foot round cage. The hairs bristled and stuck out from the bars as the creature twisted, exposing two bright green eyes, a double row of needle teeth and ivory claws that scraped across the cage bottom. Fistlock held the chocolate between the tips of his finger and thumb, barely grasping one corner. His hand shook as he slowly moved the chocolate closer to the cage. The gorge-gobbler snarled and lurched. The cage swung and Fistlock jerked his hand back.

"Hold it steady!" He yelled at Bitterbrun. "If that thing nips me, you both go down the well together!"

Carefully he moved the chocolate forward again. The beast held still and sniffed, its pink nose puffing aside the hair that covered it. It began clawing toward the top of its cage. Fistlock helped Bitterbrun hold the pole.

"They went up there," Fistlock said. A grin spread across his thin lips. "Let it out."

Fistlock took the pole and held the cage up toward the bell while Bitterbrun pulled a long set of tongs out of his back pocket and climbed up on the table.

"Ready, your Smartness?" Bitterbrun asked.

Fistlock nodded and held the pole steady.

Bitterbrun leaned over and used the tongs to unclasp the birdcage door. The hairy creature leaped to the bell and climbed.

When the snarls faded, Fistlock looked up the shaft. Bright brass gleamed through claw scratches in the tarnished surface of the bell. The gorge-gobbler was gone.

"But it if kills the girl," Bitterbrun said as he jumped down, "you won't get any information from her."

"No need to," Fistlock answered. "She doesn't have the book. I'll send some of her body parts as a message to whoever does. There's a link between them. I don't need her alive to use it."

ꟷꟷ

There was no 'ka-plunk.' Windslow opened his eyes. He was sitting in the pink chair, facing three shoring wizards. "Haggerwolf, Lark—"

Windslow had to duck under the burst of light that shot from Fernbark's wand. All three wizards jumped to their feet and pointed their magic sticks at him.

"Don't sneak up on us like that, boy!" Haggerwolf grumbled.

"Sorry," Fernbark said and put his wand inside his robe.

"I didn't sneak," Windslow said. "One minute I was no place and the next minute here. What am I supposed to do, ring a bell or something?"

"No need to be ornery," Haggerwolf said.

"Yes there is," Windslow said and checked for his backpack. It wasn't there. "My sister is here too. Fistlock has her."

Windslow told them everything he could remember

about the dungeon, and passages. He also showed them his improvised rubber band, cut from an inner tube. He was proud of himself for fooling Hillary. He thought she would take the copy and had switched them. She took the real rubber band. Larkstone warned Windslow about taking that kind of a risk. He agreed with Hillary about what would happen if Fistlock got Windslow and the book. The wizards weren't too happy to learn about Hillary's companion, but wouldn't say anything more.

"Did you have those things I asked you to make for me?" Windslow asked.

"We had the Forge-Twiddlers make them," Fernbark answered. "They're the only ones who could do it in a day."

"Where are they?"

"I have them." Fernbark reached into his vest pocket and took out something that he held between his thumb and finger. "Here they are," he said and handed two perfectly crafted, inch and a half long crutches to Windslow.

"I can't use these. They're supposed to be bigger and long; from my armpit to the floor."

"Hm... seems we jotted down the 'under your armpit' part but not the dimensions. The Forge-Twiddlers worked from your sketch."

"See, they're perfect," Larkstone said. He took one of the crutches and placed it on top of the sketch. "An exact match. Don't worry about it. We can fix them. Now let me take a look at your back."

Windslow was both worried and excited about what Fernbark was going to try with his magic. Haggerwolf had assured Windslow that Fernbark was a skilled healer. It wasn't the reassurance that convinced Windslow to let them try. It was the thought that they couldn't do much more damage. Whatever Fernbark did made Windslow's legs burn. They jerked and quivered, but it was good to feel pain; to feel anything in them again.

"It's just kind of a patch," Fernbark said when he was done. "I still don't know what's wrong. I just made what's there a bit stronger. It's magic, so it won't travel back with you. It should help. Ready to try?"

Windslow nodded as Haggerwolf and Larkstone helped him to his feet. Fernbark used more magic to fix the size of the crutches and adjusted them when they were in place under Windslow's arms. Fernbark mixed ground herbs into a cup of water for Windslow to drink. Fernbark claimed the brew would help Windslow's muscles strengthen. He gave him the pouch of pungent smelling dried plants and told him to drink a cup of the brew every day in both worlds.

Ready and nervous, Windslow took his first step in two years. It was shaky, and his legs burned, but he stepped.

ജ്ഞ

"Wakie up. You back."

Hillary opened her eyes. Waking up here was just like waking up back at home. It took her a moment to adjust to the dim light. She was relieved the fake rubber band had worked, not wanting to think about starting all over again from the dungeon. She probably wouldn't get a second chance to escape from there. "Why did you wait for me, Molly? You could have gone on without me."

"Not wait. Go explore. Just places where itty-bitty light. Not spooky dark place. No way out. No got key. Gota go quick. Scratchie thing at door," she said and pointed at the wooden access panel just behind Hillary.

Hillary looked back over her shoulder. She heard clawing and a muffled snarl. Something unpleasant was on the other side of that door and she didn't want to wait and find out want it was. She reached for her backpack and skinned her knuckles on the rough stone wall. Her backpack didn't dream-slip with her. She rose up enough from her laying position to peek at her clothes. That night she went to bed in the jeans and the flannel shirt she wore camping. She was still wearing them. "Let's get out of here and check the spooky places," she said and pulled a candle and matchbook from her pocket. Twenty feet ahead, the floor turned to stone, eliminating any chance for light to filter into the passage.

They paused long enough to light the candle. Each time Hillary held a match close to the wick, a small puff of wind blew the tiny flame out. Down to her last match, Hillary struck a flame while Molly sheltered it with cupped hands. Far behind them, both girls heard the faint sound of splintering wood. They crawled faster and moved through two more rooms full of wooden wheels and gears. Each time they closed and locked the wooden access doors behind them. Each time they heard snarling and clawing on the other side of the doors.

Not far past the last room, the passage branched. Nothing obstructed the right branch. A wire grillwork set in a heavy rod frame guarded access to the left. It had only been a few seconds since Hillary had clearly heard splintering wood and very loud snarls.

"This way," Hillary said. She unlocked the wire grate and pressed back against the passage wall to make room for Molly to wiggle past. "Hurry!" she said. She gave her friend the candle and pushed on Molly's boots to help shove her past the opening.

The snarling made Hillary's heart race and she could hear what sounded like nails scraping on stone. Halfway through the opening, something grabbed her tennis shoe.

The hairy creature held the bottom of her tennis shoe in its spiky teeth. Wild green eyes looked at her as the beast violently shook its head like a dog. Both girls screamed. Hillary kicked hard with her other foot with no effect.

Molly grabbed Hillary's hands and pulled while Hillary kicked again and again, hoping her shoe would come off. She twisted her hand away from Molly's grip and reached for her back pocket. She had nearly forgotten about the can of pepper spray she took from her brother's pack.

"Close your eyes!" She screamed at Molly. Hillary directed the pepper spray at the creature's eyes. It didn't blink but did stop shaking her foot and stopped snarling. A little pink nose puffed away the hair that covered it and sniffed the air. The teeth let go of her shoe and a long red tongue with grey patches curled upward and licked across the beast's eyes. It sniffed again and began licking the floors and walls.

Hillary scrambled through the opening and clanged the grate shut. Her hand shook as she reached back with the key. The creature watched her but kept licking pepper spray.

"Great, it likes the stuff; like beastie salsa," she said as the lock clicked. The slurping stopped and the tongue disappeared back into the mass of hair.

She flinched when the creature jumped at the grate. Long claws stuck though the grill, shaking and rattling the wires as the beast lurched, shook and pulled at the door. Foamy saliva ringed the creature's mouth, and big droplets spattered through the screen. The girls crawled as fast as they could. The snarling faded as they moved farther away.

Hillary led, brushing away spider webs as they took another side branch. They couldn't see more than a couple feet ahead or behind with only the candle for light. Only an inch of candle remained below the flame and Hillary could feel the heat on her fingers. Twice, hot wax burned her. She nearly dropped the candle both times.

"There's an opening up ahead, Molly," Hillary whispered over her shoulder to her spiky haired friend. "Maybe it's another room."

It was a room, but not what Hillary expected. The light from her candle didn't reveal much. The shaft opened high up the wall of a long narrow space. Wood panels formed the far wall and she didn't have enough light to see the ceiling. She could make out the shape of a normal size doorway just at the edge of her candlelight.

"Take a look, Molly," Hillary said and squeezed herself against the passage wall so Molly could slide up beside her. "Anything look familiar? Do you know where we are?"

"This good way out," Molly said. "We be safe. Better place than back thata way. Hear scratchy sounds and metal bang. Big rat thing again."

"Are you sure? If we go down there, we won't be able to get back up. This passage is too high."

"Good door. No lock, that one. Close to outside place. Nobody see us."

Hillary twisted around and slid out the passage, feet first. She dangled from her fingertips, took a breath and let go, landing quietly on the stone floor. She had Molly wait while she explored as far as she dared.

"Hold the candle down as low as you can," Hillary said. She'd found a torch sticking from the wall just past the doorway. Stretching on her tiptoes, she reached up to light the torch with the candle. The first two times she tried, the candle flame bent to the side from a soft wind that came from nowhere, nearly puffing out the candle.

"Go way," Molly said.

"What?"

"Not Hillre," Molly said. "Flame-fluffer again. Shadow beastie. Blow stuff out." She held out her doubled up fist. "Go way. Got biggie magic from Hillre world. Shoo." She opened her hand and threw. Coffee grounds sprinkled down on Hillary's head.

"What are you doing," Hillary said, louder than she should have.

"Get rida fluffers. Try torch again."

Hillary shook grounds out of her hair and stretched again. This time the candle flame stayed steady while it dripped hot wax to the passage floor and spread itself to the torch. After helping Molly down, Hillary saved the candle stub and used the torch to examine the door.

"Molly, there's no latch. How do we open it and what's on the other side?"

"Don't know. Magic maybe. Not been here before."

"I thought you said—"

"This away out, betcha," Molly said and moved past the door toward the darkness.

Hillary stood still for a moment and listened, then held the torch up and followed after Molly.

Back the way the girls had come, a small pink nose sniffed at the tiny puddle of cooled wax.

9: Crystal Mountain

Walking hurt, but Windslow didn't care about the pain, either in his legs or from the crutches rubbing his underarms almost raw. The wizards stayed close to him in case he faltered as he moved from Haggerwolf's laboratory to the porch. Getting him down from the tree abode took a bit of work. A pulley, stout rope, and a basket became the solution but it took the weight and strength of all three wizards to lower him to the ground.

"I almost wish I had my chair," Windslow said as they helped him out of the basket. "How long is the walk to Biffendear's home? Is his place a tree house too?"

"Oh, it's much too far to walk," Haggerwolf said. "Biffendear was a Leaper."

"Strange place," Larkstone added. "All the Leapers live at the edge of Grisly-grim. It's a big swamp about two days walk in that direction."

Windslow looked in the direction Larkstone pointed. "How do we get there before I fall asleep again?"

"We fly," Haggerwolf answered. "We'll use hippograffs."

"Wow, really? I mean, they exist here in your world? They're just mythical creatures on earth."

"More than a myth here," Fernbark said. "Common mode of transportation."

"But aren't they dangerous?" Windslow asked. "They have wings and big claws, the head of a griffin and the body of a horse."

"What does?" Haggerwolf asked.

"Hippogriffs," Windslow answered and twisted around watching the sparse stand of trees for any movement.

"Here they come now," Larkstone said and pointed up. "But they're hippograffs."

Windslow could see four shapes high over the trees. They were still too far away to make out clearly but were growing larger as they flew closer. He wondered why he couldn't at least see their wings flapping. When they flew closer, their shapes didn't look right. A few minutes later he saw why when the first one landed.

"It's a hippopotamus," Windslow said. "A hippo with dragonfly wings."

The hippo belched, and folded its wings back against its bulging sides. It belched again and slimmed a bit. "Whew, its breath stinks." Three more hippograffs landed with large thuds behind the first one.

"True enough," Fernbark said. "They're like cows. They have a bunch of stomachs. We feed them broccoli. It sits in one stomach, makes gas that puffs up the other ones, and helps them fly. To land, they just burp a bit out and hardly ever crash. Climb on one. Fernbark has something to lash your crutches with."

Windslow mounted a small hippo, about the size of a large pig. He straddled it, just behind its head and let his legs dangle in front of its wings. Double wings on each side of the hippo looked too frail to hold up such a beast. They shimmered, made of small individual gossamer octagons that seemed to change from pastel blue to pink and back when the sun reflected from their surface.

"Here," Fernbark said and crisscrossed a length of yellow rope across Windslow's back and chest. "Just hold your crutches behind your back and say 'lash.' Say 'release' when you want them loose again. You'll need this too." He looped the long cloth handle of a canvas book-bag over Windslow's head, letting the bottom of the pouch rest against Windslow's leg. "Stick your book in that and see what happens."

Windslow slipped the Book of Second Chances inside the bag and watched as both bag and book shrunk until only a six-inch square cloth sack hung at his side.

"Just stick a finger inside and it'll get big again," Fernbark said.

Haggerwolf nudged his heels against the sides of his hippo. Its wings fluttered, then blurred, giving off a buzzing sound like a hive of bees, as it rose three feet off the ground and hovered. Windslow nudged his hippo the same way and it raised level with Haggerwolf's. Haggerwolf reached back and patted his hippo; it moved higher and steadily forward. Windslow was about to pat his, but it suddenly lifted and followed behind the leader.

There was nothing to hold on to except the thick folds of skin at the back of the hippo's neck. After a few minutes Windslow let go but kept his hands ready, just in case. The ride was gentle and swift. They didn't fly high, staying just above the treetops. Windslow had hoped to see more of the land. From this low flight he couldn't see much, except for rolling broad leaf forest. The air didn't feel like fall. The tree leaves had lost their color and were shades of brown; none of the yellows, orange or amber he expected. "What season is it?" Windslow yelled to Larkstone, who flew at his side.

"Late spring. Why?"

"Shouldn't the trees have new leaves? Green ones?"

"Those are new," Larkstone yelled back. "Fistlock hates green. Follow the darker browns to your east."

Windslow looked where Larkstone pointed. The tree leaves turned darker shades of brown as they stretched to the east. They were nearly black where the land started to rise. He saw the mountain. Not a mountain range, just a single mountain, thrust up like a huge jagged cone. When they had flown a few more miles, Windslow got another surprise when he looked back at the mountain. A rainbow circled it, except for one black spot near the summit on the north side."

"What makes it light up like that?" Windslow asked.

"It's Crystal Mountain. Made of glass," Fernbark said from Windslow's other side. "The black spot is Fistlock's castle. That's where your sister is."

Windslow kicked at his hippo's side, trying to turn the fat beast. It stayed on course, ignoring Windslow's blows.

"You're wasting your time," Larkstone called. "Haggerwolf is riding the herd leader. The other hippos won't do anything but follow her. I wouldn't worry about your sister. Fistlock would be crazy to do anything to harm her until he has the book. As long as you keep the book safe and away from him, Hillary won't be in any real danger."

ഗ്ര

Not far down the hallway Hillary and Molly came to another door; this one clad in copper turned green with age and covered in strange raised marks and symbols. Hillary couldn't find a lock.

"Hair ball!" Molly screamed. "Gimme torch." She didn't wait for Hillary to hand it to her. "Look for shiny spot!" Molly yelled and shoved the flames at the Gorge-gobbler. Smoke curled up, giving off the stench of burned hair. The gobbler tumbled backward, rolling to snuff out any sparks that remained. It danced from side to side, snarling and gnashing its teeth with a clattering sound.

Hillary searched the door and saw what Molly meant. Two of the symbols reflected bright copper in the torchlight. Hillary pressed them.

"It's unlocked," she yelled and shoved hard. The door slammed open and banged when it hit the wall in the next room. Hillary held the door while Molly backed up, keeping the torch between her and the Gorge-gobbler.

"Now!" Molly shouted and threw the torch at the gobbler.

Hillary slammed the door shut and braced herself against it. "This side is just wood. I don't see any way to latch it."

"Oh, oh," Molly said. "This not good place. Maybe fight hairball instead of go here."

Hillary turned around and braced her back against the door. The gobbler pushed and clawed on the other side.

"Molly, what is this place?"

"Very bad. Very, very bad. This Crystal Mountain."

On their camping trip to the mountains, Hillary's family had driven past a big billboard and painted arrow that read, 'Turn left for Crystal Cave.' They didn't make the turn but Hillary knew that Crystal Cave on earth couldn't be anything like this place.

The cavern that surrounded them had stalagmites and stalactites, but not ones formed over thousands of years from dripping water. These were evenly spaced glass spikes and polished flat edges that sent rainbows of light dancing around the cavern. Everything was glass except for the granite wall with the door she held closed and the dark pool one hundred feet ahead. The glass floor sloped downward. Where it neared the pool the floor leveled for the last three feet and stopped at a waist-high brass railing. It ringed the bubbling oily liquid like some sort of safety rail for a tourist attraction. High overhead a jumble of geometric glass shapes glittered like a huge diamonds. Light that streamed down to the black pond glittered on a lacework pattern of crackling pale-blue electricity.

"It's beautiful," Hillary said. As she looked around, she lost her concentration. The door shoved open an inch and ivory claws pushed through the gap.

"This Gorlon place," Molly said and pushed her shoulder against the door to help Hillary. "Now we really gona die."

"Quit saying that. What's a Gorlon?"

"Him biggest baddie. Bigger than Fistlock. Make gobbler look like cute chipmunk. Gorlon kill alla armies. That why Fistlock win big war.

"Where is it? Is this cave its home?

"No. Live outside-a cave. Big magic chain. See? Lookie other side pond. Fistlock got key."

Hillary looked. A black chain, with links bigger round than her arm, rose from the pond and disappeared down a glass corridor.

Wood splintered when the gobbler raked its claws up the side of the door.

"One beast at a time," Hillary said. "Any ideas about how to stop this one?" She kicked at the claws, but her effort didn't dislodge them.

"Good shoe for glass. Boot slippery," Molly said, first looking at Hillary's tennis shoes and then at her own soft leather boots. "Got idea, but trade first."

"Molly, I already gave you an earring."

"Not trade like that. Need shoe for plan."

"All right," Hillary said and kicked off her tennis.

Molly sat down and changed shoes. When she stood, she dug into her skirt pocket and pulled out her doubled up fist. "I give signal. Open door fast and stay outa way." Molly ran down the sloping floor and stopped just in front of where it leveled out. She waved her hands over her head.

"Now what?" Hillary called.

"That signal," Molly said and lowered her hands. "Try again. Ready?"

Hillary rolled her eyes and nodded.

When Molly waved her hands, Hillary pulled the door open. The gorge-gobbler raced toward the small girl. Molly swung her arm like she was sowing seeds in a garden. When the gobbler reached her, Molly stepped to the side. The gobbler's claws sounded like fingernails on a chalkboard as it tried to stop on the glass. It slid under the brass rail and plopped into the pool. A small crackle sounded and a short burst of sparks arched upward, then settled back into the black bubbling liquid.

"One dead gobbler," Molly said and dusted off her hands.

Hillary came running down to her and slipped, falling backward. She used her hands and feet to stop sliding. She was about to ask how Molly had made the floor so slippery when she figured it out herself. She looked at her own hand. "Coffee grounds," Hillary said and gave Molly a big smile.

"Yep. Molly use biggie magic from Hillre world."

"Molly, I'm getting sleepy. We need to find a place to hide."

"We go that-a way," Molly said and pointed.

"Why that way?" Hillary asked, remembering the other times that Molly claimed to know the way.

"Cause only two ways. That other way got Gorlon."

Hillary couldn't argue with Molly's logic. A few hundred feet into the twisting crystal passage, Hillary sat down, her eyelids drooping. Molly snuggled up against her but only for a minute. Hillary vanished, dream-slipping back home.

ꕥ

They flew for about an hour, with Haggerwolf in the lead, Windslow just behind him and Larkstone and Fernbark to his sides. The treetops had been fairly level, copying the terrain of the rolling ground. Just ahead, the trees reached nearly twice as high, as if the land took a fifty foot high step upwards. Deep hued green foliage contrasted with the browns Windslow had become used to. The high canopy stretched as far as he could see. Above the treetops, the air shimmered.

"Charm-wood Forest," Fernbark yelled at him. "There's something magic about the place. We can't fly over it and Fistlock hasn't been able to turn it brown. We have to go through it. You'll need to keep your head low and hang on."

Windslow leaned forward and held onto a ridge of thick wrinkled skin at the hippo's neck. Following Haggerwolf's flight path, Windslow's hippo dove and leaned hard to the left, then leveled again. They entered the trees.

They flew beneath the canopy yet high above the ground. Windslow's hippo dropped down six feet, almost as if falling and darted forward again. Just over Windslow's head, a silky spider web stretched between the trees for thirty feet in every direction. It drooped slightly in the middle, hanging like a safety net for the trapeze artists at the circus. Windslow looked down and saw another web below him. The hippos darted up, down. They twisted and turned at sharp angles to stay between the webs that layered themselves at different levels in the woods. Windslow only saw one spider; hairy like a tarantula and bigger than a sheepdog.

Windslow craned his neck, trying to spot another one when he jerked to a stop and dangled in the air. His hippo kept flying. A web waited below him. Windslow looked up. Strapped to his back, his crutches stuck up higher than his head. A snarl of gray spider silk wrapped around the ends of his crutches at the edge of a large hole they had ripped in the web. The gaping hole tore again, abruptly dropping Windslow until he jerked to a stop, three feet lower. The web jiggled from the quick stride of a spider moving toward him.

Hairy legs reached down through the opening. As if probing, they felt along his crutches, feeling their way toward the back of Windslow's neck. He jerked and fell as the damaged web ripped loose. The next layer of webbing stopped his fall. The sticky silk stuck to his back but bounced him up, slamming him into the spider that fell with him. Their combined weight was too much for the net. It silently tore and dropped them both to the ground.

"Release!" Windslow yelled and grabbed his crutches from behind his back. The fallen spider lay on its back; eight hairy legs wiggling in the air as it twisted its body, trying to right itself. Windslow backed away. He steadied himself with one crutch, held the other up like a club, and waited.

10: Fibbing

A long tangle of silk floated down from the lowest web. The upside-down spider snagged it with its legs, pulled, and in seconds righted itself. Two more spiders worked their way downward from damaged webs at higher levels up in the branches. Windslow heard buzzing and saw a flash. A spider up above curled up its legs and fell through the layers of webs, tearing even larger holes in them.

Riding his hippograff, Haggerwolf hovered over the top web. He pointed his magic wand. A long blue spark crackled out and struck the closest spider, sending up a curl of smoke that smelled like burnt rubber. The spider turned around and lowered its front legs. A silk filament shot toward the hippo and tangled in its wings. The buzzing stopped and the hippo plummeted. Haggerwolf slashed with his wand. Free of silk, the hippo's wings buzzed again. It stopped its fall but lost its rider. Haggerwolf fell through the web layers and landed five feet to Windslow's side. The spider on the ground charged.

Windslow hobbled forward a step and smashed his crutch over the spider's head. The spider reared back, paused and lurched at him. With a sidearm swing, Windslow smashed his crutch into the spider's legs. It dipped forward and Windslow kicked as hard as he could. The spider backed away and turned around.

"Duck!" Haggerwolf yelled.

Windslow fell to one side. A sticky mass of spider silk flew past him and tangled in the undergrowth. Haggerwolf pointed his wand, the air sizzled, and the spider shuddered.

Its legs began to shake and gave way, letting the lifeless body flop to the ground.

Larkstone and Fernbark flew down on their hippos; both wizards sending out jagged streaks of blue magic from their wands to clear a path ahead of them.

"Darn near lost you," Haggerwolf said, as he dusted himself off. "Are you all right, Windslow?"

"I have a bruise, or two, but I'm fine," Windslow said and wrinkled his nose from the smell. "Is my hippo okay? Where did it go?"

"Flew off," Larkstone said as he dismounted. "We'll have to go on foot. We better start soon before more spiders come."

"Can't I just double up and fly with one of you?"

"Not that simple," Fernbark said. He gave his hippo a pat and both hippograffs flew off. "They're out of gas. They build up enough to carry a load. In order for them to land for us, they burped out the excess. Now they only have enough to get themselves back up in the air."

"Which way," Haggerwolf asked.

Fernbark hurried to a round clump of dark green ferns. Leaning close to them, he lifted several of the drooping fronds up to his face. After closing his eyes, he hummed softly. The remaining fronds lifted as if a wind had fluffed them up, and settled, all pointing in one direction. "That way," he said. "But we'll have to find a way through Dreadmoor. There's no other choice."

Haggerwolf must have seen the look on Windslow's face. "He has a way with plants," Haggerwolf explained. "Larkstone is good with birds and earth. Me, I can tune into some animals' thoughts."

Windslow closed his mouth and looked at Haggerwolf. "I wasn't thinking about the plants. What's Dreadmoor? Some kind of swamp?"

"No. A temple, carved out of a cliff. One entrance at the bottom, another at the top. No one has been able to get through it in the last two hundred years. It's haunted."

"There are no such things as ghosts," Windslow said and hobbled after Haggerwolf who followed the other two wizards into the undergrowth.

ꕥ

They walked for nearly an hour, moving as fast as Windslow could manage on his crutches. More spider webs loomed over them. Tree trunks, bigger around than a pickup truck and plants with leaves like giant green fans, gave the feel of a jungle. Windslow half expected to hear strange bird calls or even a lion roar. The only sounds were muted rustlings as things unseen scurried away across the decaying leaves and sticks on the ground.

Twice they stopped to rest and Fernbark had Windslow drink more of the ground herbs mixed into the last of their water. Whatever the mixture was, Windslow could feel it strengthen his leg muscles. Thick tree roots snaked up out of the ground and twisted across the musky smelling earth. Windslow's heart raced the first time he tried to step over one, holding his crutches out to the side for balance. The more he used his legs the stronger they felt.

Windslow didn't see the cliff until it loomed in front of them. Vines wove a green pattern up the limestone rock, letting patches of tan and sand colored stone peek through. The wizards tore the smaller vines away and used magic from their wands to cut the thicker ones. Windslow had expected something larger looming from the cliff. The wizards cleared a space about half the size of a garage door. Two-foot wide and six-foot high pillars, carved from natural stone, framed an entrance. A flat beam of stone spanned the pillar tops and deep carved letters spelled the word 'DREADMOOR.'

"That's all there is? Just an open doorway?" Windslow asked and yawned.

"It won't be open for long," Haggerwolf said, looking back over his shoulder. "Let's go. Keep close together. How about some light, Fernbark?"

Fernbark nodded. From a small cloth pouch, he sprinkled dried moss onto his palm and rolled it into four bean-sized balls. "Here," he said and handed one to each of his companions. "We're out of water. Spit on them yourselves."

Windslow watched the wizards and copied them. He spit on his clump of moss and rolled it between his fingers. Fernbark sprinkled each damp moss-ball with orange power and all four lit up, casting off yellow-green light.

"Use it this way to keep your hands free," Fernbark told Windslow.

Windslow pressed the light against his forehead like it was a wad of chewed gum and followed the wizards through the door. When they were inside, Windslow heard the sound of stone scraping stone. He turned and watched a thick slab of rock slide down from above to seal the doorway.

Windslow swept the magic glow from his moss around the room. Four bare walls and a high ceiling carved out of the cliff showed themselves. Larkstone stood at another open doorway in the wall across from the entrance. When they stepped through it, the doorway closed, just as the entrance had.

Their combined lights couldn't reach the end of this space, more a cavern than a room. The walls curved upward to become the ceiling far overhead. In front of them stretched a series of three-foot thick walls set in a tangle of right angles.

"If one of you lets me stand on your shoulders, I could see over the tops," Windslow said and yawned. "I could check to see if there is a trap or something."

"No need," Fernbark said. "We're already in the trap. It's a maze. We'll have to discover a way through it and find a place where you can sleep."

"I'll be okay," Windslow said and yawned again. "This part looks like it could be fun."

"We'd have a better chance if you knew how to work that blasted Book of Second Chances," Haggerwolf said and began walking. "Let's go."

It took another half-hour to find the route through the maze that led them to another wall and doorway. When they stepped through it, the door sealed, just like before. Ahead, another maze waited. Windslow felt sleepy but didn't say anything to the wizards. One part of him hoped he would see a ghost; another part was glad they didn't see anything. It was the sounds he didn't like. He looked up and searched with his light each time he heard the sounds. Larkstone said it was probably rats, but the sounds came from the sides of the cavern and high up. If the scratching and shuffling was from rats, Windslow figured they must have wings.

"This could work," Haggerwolf said when they came to a collapsed section.

The builders had used rectangular stone blocks stacked on top of each other to make the walls. In front of Haggerwolf, half the stones for a wall had fallen into a pile, leaving a ragged edge like a set of rock steps. "We can pile some of them up and make an enclosure for him, like a little cave."

"You're talking about me, aren't you?" Windslow asked.

"We're not even close to getting out of here," Haggerwolf answered and used his wand to help Fernbark and Larkstone move the heavy stones. "You're close to dream-slipping. I think it would be best if we hid you until you dream your way back."

The wizards struggled with the blocks, moving them into place by hand. Larkstone had used his magic wand to move the second stone. He lifted another and the blue thread of magic between the end of his wand and the block, sputtered and went out.

"Shouldn't the magic be stronger in here?" Haggerwolf asked. "We're underground."

Larkstone pressed his ear against the floor, then brushed the dust from another spot and licked his finger. "There's no living rock in here. It's all dead stone because of the mining."

"What's the matter?" Windslow asked.

Larkstone wiped his hands on his robe and looked at Windslow. "Magic gets weaker every year. It's been that way since Fistlock took over. No one knows why. Magic comes from the earth. Our wands and spells just scoop it up and concentrate it."

"We better move the rest by hand," Haggerwolf said and picked up another block. "Too bad we don't have any water. I could use a drink right now."

"That book bag will dream travel," Fernbark said to Windslow and settled a stone into place. "If you don't mind, could you bring back some food and water when you dream-slip?"

"There's other stuff I could bring," Windslow said and yawned as Haggerwolf guided him forward.

The wizards stacked the stones against the wall to make a slender, covered, rectangular space that Windslow slid into. "What could we use?" he asked from inside his hiding place. "A compass? How about... yawn... a..."

ണ്ണ

"...or a shovel," Windslow mumbled.

"For what? Digging treasure?" His dad asked. "Must have been a good dream. You were talking in your sleep when I came in. You overslept."

"We were—" Windslow hesitated and felt for the bag. "... doing something. Could you get me a glass of water?"

"Sure," his dad said and ruffled Windslow's hair. "I never remember my dreams."

When his father turned to grab the water bottle from the nightstand, Windslow slipped the bag strap off his shoulder and pushed himself up. "Is Hillary up already?"

"She overslept too," his dad answered. He handed Windslow the water bottle and a handful of tissues. "You better wipe that booger off your forehead. How'd you manage that?"

"What? Oh," Windslow said and used the tissues. He had forgotten about the wad of moss.

"I'd holler at both of you for sleeping late, but I know it was because you were up studying. I guess that's a valid excuse. Come on, I'll get you dressed. Your mom's making something you can eat in the van."

ഗ്ഗ

On the ride to school, all Hillary and Windslow could do was exchange glances at each other. Hillary did say that studying together helped. She winked at Windslow when she asked if he wanted to study together again tonight. She wanted to go over the new chapters. Windslow was pretty sure he knew what she meant and said he wanted to start right after school so he could get some extra sleep. That comment drew a funny look from his dad, who gave a chuckle and said he was tempted to take them both to a doctor. Then being serious, he told them he was proud of the attention they were paying to schoolwork this year. Hillary blushed. Windslow slouched down in his chair. He'd done his homework for his morning classes and would need to find time in school to finish the rest.

Talking with his sister at lunch proved impossible again and Windslow used the time to finish his homework. He hoped Miss Christensen didn't notice he only skimmed the pages she had assigned for the day. Thankfully, she didn't call on him to answer any questions but did ask to talk to him after class. His friends snickered when she asked him.

"Thank you for staying, Windslow," Miss Christensen said. She walked over to his wheelchair and sat in the desk next to him. "I won't keep you long. I want to thank you."

"Thank me?" He said.

"Yes," she answered and put her hand on his. "Thank you for the second chance."

Unconsciously he moved his hand to his backpack where he kept the magic bag and Book of Second Chances.

"I took your advice last night, and guess what?"

Windslow just shrugged.

"I found that friend of mine I told you about and called him. He lives in Cedarbrook."

"That's not very far from here, is it?" Windslow asked. "Their soccer team is playing ours this year."

"It's about a half-hour drive. I'm going there this afternoon for coffee and maybe dinner."

"With who? Oh..." Windslow said and blushed.

"Yes. With that old friend of mine. There's another surprise, too. He's a teacher there."

"Is he married?"

Miss Christensen laughed. She squeezed Windslow's hand before she stood and answered his question. Her friend wasn't married and they had talked for two hours on the phone the night before. Several times she mentioned second chances as she told Windslow more about their conversation. She noticed Windslow glance at the wall clock and apologized for keeping him longer than she had intended. She pushed him to his locker, the short ride fast and wild. He laughed and she giggled when she banged his chair into a recycle bin in the hallway, sending the plastic container spinning. Hillary was waiting for him.

"Teacher's pet," Hillary teased as she wheeled him to the van.

"No. I think I gave her a second chance. The book works."

ꙮ

Back home they rushed through chores, not even arguing while they washed and dried the dishes. Both Bill and Trish made comments about that. Windslow wondered what they'd think if they knew it was only because Hillary and he were anxious about having time to plan for tonight's dreams. After chores, they both worked furiously on their homework and met in Windslow's room after Bill dressed him for bed.

"Finally," Windslow said. "I like them helping with homework, but did they have to pick tonight to spend so much time with us?"

"I know," Hillary said as she sat on the end of Windslow's bed. "I kept telling both mom and Bill I was doing fine. Mom was driving me crazy. She kept looking at my work and telling me how pleased she was that I was working so hard at school."

"Dad was worse. He kept telling me stories about when he was my age. You're lucky. You haven't heard them a hundred times." Windslow looked at Hillary and grinned. "At least yet," he added.

"What did you figure out about the book?"

"I told you about Miss Christensen. She found her old boyfriend and they're meeting tonight. She thinks I gave her the chance. Grab that little canvas bag out of my backpack."

"Where'd you get this?" Hillary asked and held up the tan bag. "It looks like a purse with a long strap."

"Watch." Windslow slipped one finger inside the bag. It expanded back to its larger size. He pulled out the Book of Second Chances and opened it. "Look," he said flipping through the pages. "There's more writing, and there's a new chapter."

Hillary scooted up beside him. "Wait. Flip back. I want to read from the beginning."

Together they studied the writing. Each page held only four lines, hand written with large scrolling letters in the center of the cream-colored sheets.

Chapter I.

The story in this chance begins,

Found in pages locked within.

Open them with words of care.

What you seek is waiting there.

Something lost in time long past,

Chancing love she thought would last,

You helped her think of what to do.

A link once cut she now renews.

A second chance you granted them.

Teachers reach for hope again.

The first of four you did not waste,

Although you granted it in haste.

Chapter II.

Chapter two this lesson learn,

Do not ask for what you yearn.

Magic does not come from here.

It comes from those who lose their fear.

"This is really spooky," Windslow said. "The words don't show up until something happens. And this isn't just coincidence. It can't be."

"It fits too good, doesn't it?" Hillary said, agreeing with him. "I think this means," she said, pointing at the text, "that you get four second chances."

"And we have three left before we can get rid of this book. But what about Chapter II? What's that mean? I don't think I started a second chance for someone else." Windslow closed the book and put it back in the canvas bag. When he took his hand out, the bag shrunk. Hillary jumped.

"Wow, cool," she said.

They compared notes from their last dream-slips. Windslow's voice filled with excitement when he told Hillary about how he could walk using crutches. He showed her the little bag of herbs, too. He smiled and nodded when Hillary told him that she and Molly stopped the gorge-gobbler.

He almost forgot about bringing back food and water. Hillary offered to help but Trish found her in the kitchen. A few minutes later Trish came into his room with two plates. Windslow nibbled on a pickle and took one bite of an apple while Trish chitchatted with them. Hillary did the same with her plate. When his stepmother finally left, Windslow wrapped the sandwiches and brownies in paper napkins, but finished the pickle.

"Will you get my windbreaker jacket from the hall closet?" He asked his sister. "And grab some bottles of water."

"What do you need the jacket for? Is it cold in the maze?"

"No. I need pockets. I want you to take the bag."

"No way," Hillary answered. "I can shove everything I need in my jeans. If Bill comes in to dress you and finds you wearing a jacket, how are you going to explain it to him? Besides you need the bag for the food. I'll go get the water."

After Hillary left to go to bed, Windslow thought about what his sister had said about being out of danger. He didn't know if he should believe her. She hesitated too much when she answered him. She didn't usually have trouble finding words or talking a mile a minute. He hadn't told her all the details about Dreadmoor. He only told her that he and the wizards had to figure out an easy maze to get through the temple and continue on to the Leaper colony. With the magic book bag slung around his shoulder, he fell asleep.

11: Dreadmoor Temple

"Got more Chocola?" Molly asked as she shook Hillary.

"What? No," Hillary said and rubbed her eyes. "But here's some water." She pulled the plastic bottle from her pocket and handed it to Molly. "No! Don't bite it. Here." She twisted the cap off and handed it back to Molly.

"That pretty good thing," Molly said. She twisted the cap on, and off, and back on again. "Find way out while Hillre sleep. Find way past Gorlon. It not see us."

"Molly, you're a dear." Hillary gave the tiny girl a big hug. "No chocolate, but I did bring you a peanut butter sandwich. It's a bit squished, I'm afraid."

Molly snatched the bread from Hillary's hand and took a big bite. "Squish butter good," she said between chews. "We go this-a-way."

"Just a minute," Hillary said. "I want to do something first." Hillary pulled a disposable camera from her back pocket and held it up to her eye.

"What that-a-thing? More Hillre big magic thing?"

"It's called a camera," Hillary said. "Stand by that glass pillar. Don't worry. Get rid of that scowl and give me a smile. This box has good magic that paints a picture. You'll see a flash of light but it won't hurt you. Ready?" Hillary pressed the camera button. Nothing happened. She pressed it again. "Never mind," she said and put the camera back in her pocket. "Let's get out of here."

Molly led her through a labyrinth of passages. Hillary laughed at the smears of peanut butter that Molly's hands left on the glass each time they turned a corner. *Glad I don't have to clean this place,* she thought as they walked. At the next turn Molly stopped. Both girls looked out at blue sky, bright sun, and an expanse of black-leaved trees not far below.

"This is like a cave in the side of a glass mountain," Hillary said. She kept one hand on the glass behind her as she stepped out onto a wide ledge. "It must be beautiful in the spring when everything is green."

"Is spring," Molly said and licked the last of the peanut butter from the side of her mouth.

"Spring? Then why are the—" Hillary stopped in mid-sentence when she heard the growl. She looked down to her left at the base of the mountain and saw a loop of chain just outside a large cave entrance. The growl sounded again. The glass under her hand vibrated. The chain moved.

"What's that?" Hillary asked and moved back a step.

ജ൦ൽ

Winslow woke in darkness at Dreadmoor. He lifted his head and bumped it on the stone that covered his little hiding tunnel. "Ow," he said. "Can one of you shine your light in here?"

No one answered.

When Windslow shifted to his side, his crutches clattered against the stone. The noise startled him. After taking a deep breath, he put his finger in the book bag to expand it. He reached inside and felt for the flashlight he'd packed. When he found it he clicked the switch but nothing happened. He gave it a shake and tried again.

"Great," he mumbled. *Those batteries are brand new. Maybe the bulb is bad,* he thought. When he started to crawl out, he felt something soft with his hand and jerked away at first, then felt again. *Moss,* he said to himself. He spit in the darkness and a green glow spread from his palm. Using the light, he crawled out and looked for the wizards. He was alone.

"Haggerwolf?" he called softly. "Fernbark? Larkstone?"

Windslow pressed the glowing moss against his forehead and unscrewed the top of his flashlight. The batteries had two spots you could press to check their condition. He pushed hard but nothing showed on the little power indicators. *Hmm... maybe it was on inside the bag,* he thought. He was about to put the flashlight away when he had an idea and unscrewed the front lens. He took the bulb out and replaced it with the moss. A few seconds later a bright green light beamed from the flashlight. He grabbed his crutches and moved through the maze.

He took only two turns through the maze before coming to the exit. His palms began to sweat and his heart raced when he saw the stone slab that sealed the door shut. He listened for the scurrying sounds they had heard before. The only sound he heard was his crutches on the stone floor as he found his way back to his hiding place and sat down.

Now what? he thought. Not coming up with any ideas, he looked at the crumbled wall he sat against. Because of the missing blocks, the remaining wall section formed big steps, nearly to the top of the wall it connected to. The wall stones were just wide enough for him to step on if he balanced with one crutch. Before he started his climb, he mixed the muscle strengthening herbs into a water bottle and took a big drink.

His first few steps were shaky, more because he was nervous about only using one crutch than for the climb. And, he was worried about falling. He tried not to think back to his accident when he had fallen from the roof. Each step was only about two feet high. One step up and two steps ahead took him to the next block. Finally at the top, he swept his glowing flashlight over the top of the maze.

Ready to climb down, he noticed a shadow his light cast against the far left wall above the maze. Tracing a route of connecting wall tops with his light, he hobbled ahead. At the sidewall, he found the reason for the shadow; a narrow opening. He ducked through.

His light showed a straight narrow hallway that ran parallel to the maze wall. He moved forward. Every ten paces, he passed small square holes cut at eyelevel. Holding his flashlight close to his head, he looked through one of them. He had a clear view of the maze. At the end of the hallway, he saw another opening, tall and wide enough for him to squeeze through.

ꙮ

"That Gorlon howl," Molly said. "Big trouble now. Better slip-slide fast. Chain pretty long." Molly sat down, dangled her legs over the ledge and pushed.

"Whee..." her voice trailed off as she slid down the sloped glass and landed on another ledge fifty feet below.

Still in the doorway, Hillary sat down and eased herself forward a little bit at a time until her legs hung over the ledge. When the Gorlon growled again, she pushed.

The slide wasn't as fast as Hillary had feared. She used her tennis shoes for control. They squeaked against the slick glass as she slid. She ended up sitting next to Molly, halfway down to the forest floor.

Molly cupped her hands around her mouth and gave a long trilling call, almost like a whistle. The Gorlon growled. Hillary heard its chain clinking on stone where the glass ended just outside the monster's cave.

"If you're trying to let him know we're here, you're doing a good job," Hillary said and grabbed Molly's arm.

"Call birds." Molly said and pulled her arm away from Hillary's hand. "Slide more. Birds not come up here. Afraid."

Molly pushed off. Hillary looked over the ledge and watched until her friend landed safely on the forest floor. She took a glance at the Gorlon's cave and slid. Before Hillary reached the bottom, Molly was already trilling again.

"Gota hurry now," Molly said. "Gorlon see us."

Hillary looked toward the cave. Inside the black opening in the crystal, she saw two orange colored eyes staring out. She ran to catch up with Molly.

They dashed through the tall trees. Molly didn't stop to search for a path. She ducked under branches and hopped over fallen logs. Hillary had a hard time keeping up, but didn't want to stop. She wondered how long and how strong the Gorlon's chain was. She almost fell over Molly when the young girl stopped in the middle of a clearing.

"I don't think we should rest yet," Hillary said, even though she was glad to have a chance to catch her breath.

"Not rest," Molly said and pointed.

Hillary looked up and saw two large birds circling overhead. Molly trilled again and the birds spiraled downward, circling the clearing, but still high above the tree tops.

Hillary wondered what the birds carried in their talons. She found out before she could ask. Two small tangles of leather crashed into the brush at the clearing's edge. Molly ran to them.

"Here," Molly said and handed one of the tangles to Hillary. "Do like this."

Hillary watched as Molly buckled up a harness of leather straps that wrapped around her waist, across her back and chest, and under her arms. A big loop of stiff leather, thicker than the straps, stuck up behind Molly's head.

"What are we doing?" Hillary asked as Molly helped her get into the second harness.

"We gettin' outa here." Molly said. "Go find sisters. They help. Stand like this."

Hillary stretched her arms out to the side, like Molly did. They stood side by side in the middle of the clearing with their fingertips barely touching.

The jerk made Hillary scream. Before her scream ended, she was over the treetops. She closed her eyes. She didn't need to look to see what just happened. She could feel the wing beats from each blast of air that twirled past her.

"Open eyes. Good fun," she heard Molly yell.

Hillary opened first one eye and then the other. She looked down, but only for a heartbeat and closed her eyes again. This time she kept her gaze level and looked to the side. Molly swung gently in her harness and waved. A huge brown eagle carried her, its talons wrapped around the leather loop above Molly's head.

"We alla safe now," Molly yelled. "Maybe harness break. Not think so. Not today." She gave another trill, held out her arms and flapped them, as if she herself were flying. "Got more squishy butter?" she called.

Hillary closed her eyes and ignored her.

ᘘᘙ

Windslow peeked through the opening, exploring first with his flashlight. He expected another large room and maze. That's not what he saw. This room had a ceiling low enough that he could almost touch it by holding up one of his crutches. What caught his attention was the staircase across the room. Halfway up the steps he heard squeaking and rustling.

He sunk down to his hands and knees and held his crutches at his side. He hoped his legs were strong enough to let him crawl up the rest of the steps. His knees wobbled. Pajama bottoms didn't provide much padding and the stone steps hurt his skin. Close to the top, he sat up. By stretching he could see over the last step. He kept his flashlight inside the book bag hanging at his side.

Four candles, thicker than his arm, sat in tall brass stands at the corners of the big room. The flames didn't flood the whole space. Flickering light spread flat across the floor and clawed up the wall in a circle behind each stand. The place stunk.

Windslow stood and moved into the room. He listened to the rustling. All around him, dark smelly sludge lay in heaps inside neatly formed rectangles edged with foot high stones; like strange gardens waiting for planting. The sixteen rectangles filled the room, four across and four deep, with five-foot wide paths between them. At the far side of the room, another opening marked a stairway like the one he had just climbed. It stretched down into darkness. Six feet past the stairway opening, a large mass of stone hung down just behind a bench or low table.

"It's a bat," Windslow said softly as he swept his light across the hanging stone. The carving hung upside down, just as a ten-foot high real bat would, but with its wings extended wide. Whoever had carved it included all the details. Windslow used his light to trace the wing bones, carved to look like they were just beneath thin stretched skin. When he walked closer, he could see fine hairs chiseled into the body. Other than being big and tan like the temple stones, it looked lifelike.

Windslow moved to the bench in front of the hanging statue. Cut from the same stone as everything else, it seemed out of place. *Who would want to sit here with that statue staring at your back*, Windslow asked himself and turned around. He looked at the eyes, or at least where they eyes should be. The empty sockets looked like they might have held something once. Two holes where the eyes should be in the statue let him look through to the back wall, just a few feet behind the carving. Through the holes, he saw narrow steps going up.

When he stood, rustling sounded loud and movement caught his attention. Windslow pointed his light straight up. The whole ceiling came alive. Black wings fluttered and a large mass of bats flew in crazy crisscrossing patterns just over his head. He held his hand over the end of his flashlight and the bats began to settle. All the bats returned to the high ceiling; most of them to perch again. The rest flew to the back corner of the room and disappeared out a small opening where the ceiling and wall met. Windslow could see a faint glow of light that filtered in to reveal the top two steps of the stairway cut into the back wall. He moved behind the statue to investigate.

Uncovering his flashlight, he moved his light up the steps. Barely a foot wide, the steps started at the floor directly behind the statue. They angled up in a straight line to the opening. Windslow tried to stand on the first step, but there wasn't room for his foot and a crutch. He nearly fell. It was then that he heard the chanting.

ꕥ

Fistlock gathered his long robes up in one arm and squatted down near the brass railing circling the pond inside Crystal Mountain. "What's this?" He slid his hand across the smooth floor.

Bitterbrun got down on one knee and used his hands to sweep together a small pile of the brown flecks. He pinched a tiny bit between his thumb and finger and brought it to his tongue. "Coffee, your Splendid-ness."

Fistlock rose and dusted off his hands. "I didn't think they'd get this far. Either they fell into the pool or the Gorlon got them. But whoever has the book is still out there. Captain," he said and turned around.

"Yes, my Lord," a tall man dressed in shiny silver colored armor answered from the doorway.

"Pull your men out of the cities. You have a day to get them back into the castle before I set the Gorlon free."

The Captain gave a short salute, turned and walked out of the room.

12: Eldervale

"Which way is Dreadmoor Temple?" Hillary called to Molly.

"That-a-way," Molly called back, pointing to her left, away from Hillary.

"Can your eagles fly us there?"

"No way! Bad stuff in Temple place. Bad stuff lota place. But not this place. Get feet ready."

Molly lifted her knees up.

Hillary looked ahead. The ground came up fast as the eagles headed straight for a crowd of people standing in the center of a town square. Hillary held her legs like Molly, but when the eagle let go, Hillary tumbled forward.

"Supposed to run on ground when land. Not roll," Molly said. She offered a hand to help Hillary up.

Hillary reached out, but Molly's hand disappeared in a rush of people.

"Hi. Dimbleshoot, here."

"I'll get you some soup. Call me Lizzybud or just grandma."

"I'm gramps."

"Me too."

"Bildernick, at your service, sweetheart."

"I'm granny Gilderbun."

Bodies pressed against Hillary, moving her backward until more grannies and grandpas crushed her from behind. "Molly! Help!"

"Give her room," someone hollered and began shoving people back. "Let the girl breathe." An elderly couple, both with gray hair and age wrinkle skin, started clearing room around Hillary. Molly squeezed through from between a pair of stubby legs and knobby knees. She crawled to Hillary.

"Molly, where have you brought us?"

"Eldervale. Granny Grandpa place. Alla people here want Hillre be their granddaughter. Want Molly too. Go way. Shoo," Molly said and flipped her hands in the air like she was brushing crumbs from a tablecloth.

"You two come with us," the woman who had helped clear the crowd said and extended her hand. When neither girl took it, the woman fussed with a pink ribbon in her thinning sliver hair, as if that's what she meant to do all along. "Follow Dimbleshoot. I'm his wife, Gilderbun," she said and smoothed her blue checkered dress.

Dimbleshoot bowed, and swept his arm in front of his chest in a grand exaggerated gesture. His green vest hung open. "Welcome, my dear ladies. This way to our humble little hut. Are you hungry?" he asked and quickly buttoned up his vest while his wife scowled at him.

"Of course they are," Gilderbun said, and ushered them forward, holding her apron out as if herding a flock of geese.

Dimbleshoot turned and led the way. Behind Hillary, people still called out.

"We get them for breakfast."

"I call lunch."

"Dinner and story time."

"Nursery rhyme and tucking in for us."

Dimbleshoot walked slowly using his cane. Two steps forward. Stop. Move cane. Two steps forward. Stop... Twice he stopped completely, turned around and asked the same question; were they hungry. Both times Hillary said no. She wanted to hurry past him and walk faster until she realized she didn't know where they were and really had no place to go, unless one of the senior citizens knew the way to Dreadmoor. She simply accepted Dimbleshoot's pace, yet found she had to concentrate to walk that slow and not step on his heels.

The village wasn't large and looked a bit like an out of the way tourist spot shown on the travel channel at home. All the buildings looked stooped over like most of the citizens. Whitewashed single story homes and peaked thatched roofs lined up along each side of the central town square. Behind each row of buildings Hillary could see another row, and another; everything arranged as if the builder used a gigantic ruler.

"Where are they taking us?" Hillary whispered to Molly.

Molly shrugged. "Don't know. Not my granny. Not yet. Use big Hillre magic and find out."

It seemed like five minutes had passed before they reached Dimbleshoot and Gilderbun's house in the second row of buildings. Hillary checked her wristwatch and wasn't surprised to see it didn't work. *Battery operated*, she thought to herself and nodded.

"Why nod head?" Molly asked. "Hillre like granny place?"

"Molly," Hillary said. She put her arm around Molly's shoulders, leaned close and spoke softly. "You said you called the eagles so you could find your sisters. Are your sisters here someplace?"

"Tickle ear you talk close like that," Molly said, pulling her head away and not bothering to lower her voice. "Sisters not here. Eagle get them. They be here soon, betcha."

"Are you hungry," Dimbleshoot asked again as he held the brightly colored door open. Painted daisies on a green background made the door look inviting. The floral pattern matched painted strips of wood nailed around twin windows with lace curtains. The interior looked cozy and smelled like pumpkin and spice. Gilderbun gave a quick tour. Two simple bedrooms formed the back of the house, each furnished with a bed, night stand, and pegs on the wall for hanging clothes. Hillary liked the kitchen which took up the whole front of the house. Gilderbun smiled her approval when Hillary asked if she could try the red hand-pump fastened to the counter. Hillary cranked the handle up and down. On the third squeaky pump, cool water splashed into a bowl under the spout.

"Are you hungry?" Dimbleshoot asked again and sat down in one of the four ladder-back chairs at the kitchen table covered in a blue and white checkered tablecloth.

"You've asked us that before," Hillary said. "Several times now," she added, her voice a bit louder.

Molly scattered a small handful of coffee grounds across the floor. "Go way, tellagains. No belong here. Leave granny grampa place."

Hillary watched Molly sprinkle more grounds near the windows. Molly stomped a foot, the curtains fluttered outward and drifted back into place. "They gone. He not ask again."

"Are you girls thirsty?" Dimbleshoot asked.

"Not same thing. Is different," Molly said before Hillary could say anything.

"A cup of water would be nice," Hillary said to Dimbleshoot. He smiled at her and nodded his head.

"Big thirsty! Take water!" Molly yelled. She looked at Hillary. "Make voice big. Granny grampa not hear tiny words."

Gilderbun filled two mugs with ice-cold water and handed them to the girls. "It's so nice that you could visit," she said and sat in a chair next to her husband. "Just the other day I was telling Dimbleshoot that we should get things ready for visitors. He thought I should bake some cookies. Well just the other day I... I... Oh dear. What was I talking about?"

"Cookies," Hillary said. Gilderbun didn't say anything. She and Dimbleshoot stared out the window in silence, their faces showing a faint hint of sadness.

"What's wrong with them?" Hillary asked, her voice low again. "Did you do something to them? What did you shoo out the window? "

"Chase away alla tellagains. Shadow beasties. Make grampa tell same thing over and over. Ponder-glitch take granny's words. Steal thoughts like scritch. Granny grampa watch memory place inside head now," Molly said and put both hands up to her eyes. She made exaggerated movements like she was unscrewing her eyeballs. "Live happy thought in here." She pointed a finger at the side of her head.

"Granny Gilderbun?" Hillary asked loudly. "Granny!" Neither Gilderbun nor Dimbleshoot looked at her. "It's like a trance," she said to Molly who just shrugged.

"Now what?"

"Wait for sisters."

While they waited, Hillary asked more questions and Molly answered those she could. Fistlock hated families. He broke them apart and sent children to live in one place, parents in another and grandparents in places like this village, Eldervale. Fistlock had villages for overweight people, cities for short people and even isolated lodges for people with warts. The more Hillary learned about Fistlock, the more determined she became to use the Book of Second Chances to help these people. She told Molly that's why she wanted to go to Dreadmoor; to find Windslow and get the Book.

"Book of Second Chances?" Dimbleshoot said and looked at Hillary when she mentioned it.

"You have the Book?" Gilderbun asked.

Hillary shrunk back a bit, startled by the way they snapped out of their trance. "My brother has it," she said softly. They had no trouble hearing her this time.

ꙮ

Windslow put his crutches behind his back and whispered "lash" to bind them. The chanting grew louder. He ducked down behind the hanging statue to hide. A two foot gap separated the bottom of the statue from the floor. From where he squatted he could see the bench, and just past it, the top of the wide staircase where the sounds came from. A long column of hooded figures, standing four across, moved up the steps; their backs toward Windslow. When the lead group reached the top step, Windslow spotted his three wizard friends several rows back.

Windslow searched the back of the statue. At the bottom he felt a fist-sized piece of rock that he hoped stuck out far enough for him to stand on. He put his foot on it and felt for handholds higher up. Where the wings joined the body he found solid spots he could grab, and pulled himself up. He worried about how long he could hang. His leg wasn't very strong so he used his arms as much as he could to hold himself up out of sight. From the sound of the voices chanting, he knew there were more than just the twenty or so figures he'd seen coming up the steps.

He didn't hang long before his leg started to shake and his arms burned. Silently he lowered himself back down. When he looked through the space under the statue, he didn't see what he expected. The three wizards sat on the bench. Thin rope bound their hands behind their backs. The wizards blocked Windslow's view of the hooded figures. But they also kept anyone from seeing him.

Fernbark squirmed on the bench. His movement opened a small gap between his arm and Larkstone sitting next to him, giving Windslow his first peek at one of the hooded figures. He nearly cried out when he saw its face.

A long pointed mouth and jaw, sharp teeth and black nose thrust out from under the hood. With its pointed ears, the man-sized face looked like a hairless rat. Its deep set pink eyes looked watery. A red tongue licked up, curling around the creature's snout before ducking back behind its teeth.

Windslow watched long slender fingers, ending in claws, expose themselves. They poked through the gap running down the front of the creature's black robe.

Windslow unlashed his crutches and quietly put one of them on the floor. He extended the second one toward Fernbark's back. He could barely reach the bench with it. Leaning as far forward as he dared, he slipped the end between Fernbark and Larkstone. Windslow gave his crutch a wiggle.

Fernbark looked down. He looked back up but gave his head a very slow, almost imperceptible nod.

With a jerk, the creature pulled open its cloak. It kept hold of the cloth and spread its bony arms wide. It stood silently for a moment, its chest bare, showing pink wrinkled skin. Tight pants, like black long underwear, covered its bony legs. *It looks like a shaved bat,* Windslow thought to himself, *with a cape for wings.*

Windslow pulled the crutch back, opened his Swiss army knife and pressed the blade into the end of his crutch. He stretched it forward again, aiming for Fernbark's bound hands.

"Whizzzz-ards," the creature hissed in a windy voice. "Whizzzz-ards claimed us. Whizzzz-ards changed us. See what Whizzzz-ards made us." The creature let its robe settle back around its body and took a step closer to the three wizards.

The army knife touched Fernbark's hands. The wizard wiggled his fingers, trying to grasp the knife. He curled two fingers around the handle and wiggled the knife loose. When he tried to reposition the knife it clattered on the floor. At the same time, Fernbark coughed loud.

Windslow flattened himself on the floor and closed his eyes for an instant. Nothing changed.

The creature took another step forward. "Now learn how we change whizzzz-ards," it hissed and took another step. This time it stretched its arms forward and flexed its fingers, drawing attention to its claws.

Windslow slid under the hanging statue and grabbed his knife. Quickly he sawed through the rope around Fernbark's hands, then cut the other the other two wizards loose.

Windslow took a quick breath and jumped up behind the wizards. "Hey! Yeah!" he yelled as loud as he could and pulled out his flashlight. Stepping to the side, he yelled again and pointed the flashlight at the ceiling. "Double crrud," he muttered. "No light."

The creature stepped backward several paces and tripped. Other hooded figures jumped to their feet. The wizards stood and rushed next to Windslow.

"Stay back," Windslow yelled at the creatures. He pointed the dark flashlight at them. "This is wizard magic. If I open it, the magic will destroy this whole place." He looked at Fernbark. In a softer voice, he said, "I need some of that moss you spit on."

Fernbark began searching his pockets. The creatures stared. Several in the front row edged forward. The wizards eased back, while Windslow stood his ground and unscrewed the flashlight lens.

"Here," Fernbark said. He took half a step forward and handed Windslow a wad of moss. Windslow spit and shoved the damp moss into the flashlight's bulb socket. Green light streamed from the end.

"Steps. Behind the statue," Windslow half shouted as he swept the light back and forth across the ceiling. The creatures ducked. The ceiling came alive. Thousands of bats took flight, dipping, diving, and swerving as the room filled with the sound of fluttering wings and screaming creatures. "Run," he said and had to push Haggerwolf to get him moving.

"What's wrong with you guys?" Windslow asked, frustrated that the wizards weren't moving very fast. "You could do something to help or use you magic or something."

"We don't have any magic left," Haggerwolf said. "My wand was the last one to fizzle out when they captured us. Without magic, we aren't wizards. We're just three old men."

One of the creatures darted around the statue. It crouched low and bared its claws. The wizards pressed back against the wall. Windslow stuck his finger in the book bag to expand it and swung hard, smashing the bag against the creature. Two more creatures came around the other side of the statue. Windslow grabbed his crutches and began swinging.

"Do something!" Windslow yelled.

More creatures crowded together at both sides of the statue. Windslow pointed the flashlight at them. The creatures grinned. One reached for Windslow.

Windslow pulled the book from his bag and held it up. "Go ahead," he yelled. "Do whatever you want, but I have the Book of Second Chances. I know how to use it. With one of my chances I'll beat you. I'll use them all if I have to."

The creatures froze. Red tongues slurped out of sight. On the other side of the statue creatures began chanting. "He hassss the book," one of them close to Windslow hissed. They all moved back.

"You know how to use it?" Haggerwolf asked and moved to Windslow's side.

"I've got it figured out. I already used one chance back home."

"Larkstone," Haggerwolf yelled. "Get us some weapons."

"From where?" Larkstone asked.

"Your closet, idiot."

"Of course. Why didn't I think of that before?" Larkstone said. "I have enough magic for that." He wiggled a finger and his shiny zipper-closet appeared, suspended in midair in front of him. He reached in, rummaged for a second and pulled out three short swords. Haggerwolf and Fernbark each grabbed one.

"I think there's a way out up those steps," Windslow told them. "They're too narrow for me to climb with my crutches. You three can make it. Maybe I can hold these bat people off until you get some help. Or is there some other way out? I'm getting really sleepy."

"Now that you can work the book, we all have a chance; several if we need them," Haggerwolf said. "Larkstone, can you scrape together enough magic for one last spell?"

"If he can't, I can," Fernbark said.

"You better hurry then," Windslow said. His arms were getting tired from holding the book up over his head, and he couldn't stop yawning. The creatures had backed away but still watched as if waiting for something to happen. *Or not happen,* Windslow thought.

"I'll chant a spell to fix the steps," Fernbark said. "When I start, Windslow, put the book in your bag and move to the steps. When I say the third line in my spell, run. We'll follow you and hold them off with our swords until you're safe. Ready?"

"Do it," Windslow said and lowered the book.

"Four need freedom from this lair," Fernbark recited.

Windslow shoved the book inside his bag and moved to the bottom step. The creatures started forward.

"Escape be made by wider stair."

The wall rumbled. More bats flew and the creatures stopped.

"Let none else change but... but..."

"Finish it," Haggerwolf yelled.

"Let none else change but facial hair!"

The stairway widened. The ground shook. The bat statue broke loose from the ceiling and crumbled into a pile of rubble. Windslow hobbled up the steps as fast as he could. He glanced back. The three wizards were close behind him. Larkstone was at the back and slashed his sword at the creatures that followed him.

At the top step, Windslow threw his crutches out a round opening and pulled himself through. He turned around on his hands and knees and helped pull the wizards up. When Larkstone was out, Windslow grabbed a crutch and held it over his shoulder, ready to smack the first creature that stuck its head up.

"They aren't following us. That last bit of spell worked out in our favor," Larkstone said and laughed. "They started growing hair. I'd say they're all more than a little confused right now."

The three wizards began laughing. Windslow started to chuckle too, but not because of the creatures. "Your spell worked too well," he said and grinned. "Feel your chin," Haggerwolf.

Haggerwolf stopped laughing and grabbed for a beard that wasn't there. He ran his hand over a smooth hairless cheek. "Not my beard!" Haggerwolf cried.

"My hair," Fernbark said and snatched off his hat."

Windslow laughed harder.

"Mine too," Larkstone said, "But there wasn't much there to start with."

"You all look so different," Windslow said. He yawned and laughed again.

"I don't know what you're laughing about," Haggerwolf said to Windslow. "Feel your face."

"Oh, crud," Windslow said as he felt his new beard and moustache. "This isn't... yawn... going to be... yawn... perm..." He didn't finish his sentence. Windslow curled up and vanished.

13: Close Shave

"If the Gorlon seeks out the miserable soldiers and mercenaries the people used to have, what's left for it to find?" Bitterbrun asked as he walked behind Fistlock into the pond chamber inside Crystal Mountain. "The last Gorlon killed them all."

"That's true," Fistlock said. "I built the urge to find and destroy armies into the magic that forms the Gorlons. Last night I put together a little bit of this, and a little bit of that, and came up with something to change the Gorlon so it will seek out anyone who has touched the book."

"Begging enlightenment, your Smartness, how can a dumb creature like the Gorlon figure out something like that?"

"With this," Fistlock said and touched one finger to his nose, tapping very lightly.

"Ah, yes. Of course. With your nose, my Greatness."

"Not mine, idiot!" Fistlock said and stopped at the brass railing surrounding the pool. Fistlock opened his small container of needle points and plucked one out. Carefully he fitted the needle into the small hole at the tip of his wand. "Let me demonstrate." He took a small amber bottle from another pocket and pulled out the cork stopper. "Just a little dip in digested blood from the stomach of a leech." Fistlock held up the dipped needle for Bitterbrun to see.

"For seeking out hidden things?" Bitterbrun asked.

"Yes. For once you got something right." Fistlock put the bottle away and took out a small packet of turquoise glitter. "Now a dab of powdered gristle-ghast stomach."

"But they're extinct; all hunted down for their hides. A book covered in gristle-ghast leather lasts forever. The Book of Second Chances is bound in gristle-ghast leather."

"Yes, my inquisitive little Chamberlain. That's true. It is a bit rare and I hate to waste it but—" Fistlock jabbed the needle into Bitterbrun's arm.

"My Lord?" Bitterbrun grabbed his arm where Fistlock had stuck him. "I... I've served you faithfully. Well, except the time I snuck into your... your..." Bitterbrun stopped and sniffed the air. He dropped down on all fours and began sniffing, first up toward the entrance, then down to one of the passages.

"Get back here!" Fistlock yelled.

"But I... I... I can smell it. The book... Faint..." sniff, sniff, "I want to..."

"Now!"

Bitterbrun stood and tucked his shirt back in. He looked one more time down the passage and walked back to Fistlock.

"Good. It works," Fistlock said and began preparing another needle. "I didn't want to have a monster wandering around doing nothing. Go fetch the key while I prepare the Gorlon."

Bitterbrun kept looking over his shoulder and sniffing as he walked to a glass pillar. On the way, he unwrapped another square of chocolate. He had trouble with the wrapper. It was his last piece and it had melted a bit in his pocket. After licking the paper he stuffed it out of sight.

"Hurry up with that key," Fistlock yelled.

Bitterbrun spread his fingers wide against the glass. He had to move two fingers a little to the side to get the pattern correct. When he did, a click sounded and the glass turned to stone. A rectangular door panel swung open. He pulled out a long metal rod with a T handle across the top;

the other end was hammered flat and formed into a miniature profile of Fistlock's head.

Fistlock knelt down by a large padlock that joined two sections of chain. One section draped over the pond and disappeared into the tar colored fluid. The other length of chain stretched out through the crystal passage leading to the Gorlon's cave. Woven through the links and lock, a tendril of blackness stretched from the pool and followed the chain's path. Fistlock jabbed his barbed wand into the black strand. A howl echoed through the crystal chamber. The chain jerked, sending ripples across the black pond.

Bitterbrun dragged the T-bar across the floor. Fistlock helped lift the heavy rod and hold it over the padlock. When the end with Fistlock's profile settled into the lock's keyhole, both men twisted the handle. The lock clicked and opened. The chain and black cord disappeared.

"I wouldn't take a walk in the garden until much later this afternoon," Fistlock said to Bitterbrun. "The Gorlon should be on the book's trail before sundown."

"Ah, we don't have a garden, your Cleverness."

"That was a joke," Fistlock said. "I always feel in a good mood when I set one of these loose. Have some shadow beasties follow it and report back to me. And next time, laugh."

"Yes, your Humorness. Of course..." Sniff, sniff. "Ha.. ah-ha-ha,"

ꕥ

Windslow bolted upright in bed and looked at his alarm clock. "Crud. Eight minutes maybe." He slipped the book bag off his shoulder and pushed his blankets back. Grabbing the handle of the canvas bag, he flipped the small bag over the back of his wheel chair and pulled. The first time the bag slipped off. The second time he pulled slower and the chair began rolling. He hoped his legs would work like they did when he dream-slipped. They didn't. His muscles looked firmer and he was sure they had more bulk but still no feeling. He struggled, using his arms to half drape himself into the chair and almost fell. Finally he was in the chair and lifted his legs into place.

He backed up to the door, twisted the knob and got the door open. With a bit of maneuvering he rolled into the hall, and sighed a breath of relief when he saw the open bathroom door.

ꕥ

"Windslow?" his dad called and knocked on the bathroom door.

"I'm okay," Windslow called back. He put the scissors in the vanity drawer, and wadded up the hair in his lap along with the towel he had used to catch it.

"Want some help? How'd you get into your chair by yourself?" His dad called and rattled the doorknob.

"I want to do more myself," Windslow said and smeared shaving cream all over his face. "I'll holler if I need help."

"I'll just hang around outside the door... just in case."

"Crud-o," Windslow said under his breath. One small spot of white shaving foam began turning red. He couldn't reach the sink to rinse the lather off his dad's razor so he wiped it with toilet paper and tossed the wad into the trash can. He winced and pulled the razor across his tender face again.

The door handle twisted and clicked. "Are you all right, honey?" Trish asked and opened the door. "Your dad said—"

"Can't a guy have some privacy in this house?" Windslow complained. He didn't look at his step-mom. He just waited for her to scold him for talking to her that way.

"Oops. Excuse me," she said and backed out of the doorway. "Bill, I think this a guy thing. I'll go start breakfast."

"What's going on?" Hillary asked and peeked her head around the corner of the door frame.

"It's stare at Windslow day," Windslow said. "Got a good enough look? Everybody else has."

"Haven't you seen a man shave before?" Bill asked. He nudged Hillary back into the hallway, stepped into the bathroom and closed the door. "You should have told me you wanted to try shaving. Let me look," he said and cupped Windslow's chin in his hand. He turned Windslow's face, left and then right. "Nice job. The first time I shaved I cut myself about six times. Here, stick a little corner of tissue on the cut. It'll stop bleeding in a minute."

"Dad, I..."

"You don't need to say anything. I felt funny about shaving the first time. I snuck down to the basement and shaved there. I don't think you'll need to shave more than... hmm..." He looked at Windslow's face again. "Once a month for a while, anyway. Say. Why don't you and I go shopping this weekend and I'll buy you your own razor? We could make a day of it."

"Sure, Dad. But I was going to say I didn't mean to snap at Trish that way. I was kind of embarrassed."

"Don't worry about Trish. You could do us both a favor though and call her mom once in awhile. She'd like that. She's worried about you and Hillary both feeling like we're a whole family."

"Oh, I do. I mean, sometimes I really miss mom and wish she was alive. But it's like I only have one mom name in my head. So if I call them both mom, they'll get all mixed up. And don't worry about Hillary. She thinks you're pretty cool, Dad. But she's only got one dad name in her head, too."

"My son gets wiser and starts shaving all in one day. Pretty soon I'll have to start hiding the van keys."

"No way," Windslow said. "You and Trish get the van when we start driving. Hillary and I get a sports car."

ꕥ

At school, Miss Christensen chatted briefly with Windslow after class. He had noticed her yawn twice during class and half expected to see her fall asleep and dream-slip away someplace. She told him how she had met her friend for coffee and then went to dinner with him. She said they had a wonderful evening but lost track of time. She didn't get home until after midnight and still had to prepare her lesson plans for today's class.

She gave Windslow a small pat on his shoulder. At his locker, Windslow's friends teased him about the lipstick smear. He teased back but secretly liked having the red mark and turned his head to the side, hoping some of the cute girls would notice it. He scrubbed it off with a paper towel when Hillary came to get him.

ꕥ

While they worked on their homework, Windslow thanked his sister for getting rid of the, "shaving evidence" from the morning. They talked about how they were both really safe, at least for now. Windslow didn't like what Hillary told him about Fistlock. He agreed with Hillary that they should use two of the remaining chances to help get rid of Fistlock. Windslow was glad that Hillary was the one who suggested they save the last chance to try and do something about Windslow's back. He wanted to save one chance for that, but felt too guilty and selfish to say anything about it himself.

"Okay," Windslow said. "Tonight we try to meet up at Biffendear's home at the edge of Grisly-grim. Do you think Molly and her sisters will take you there?"

Hillary laughed. "Molly's sweet. I really like her. I think her eagles can take me about anywhere. I'm bringing her chocolate peanut butter candy and I've got a little hanky for granny Gilderbun." Hillary held up a folded piece of pink paper. "I couldn't think of anything for Dimbleshoot so I made him a card."

"Is it their birthdays or something?" Windslow asked.

"Just like a boy," Hillary said. "When you're a guest in someone's home, mom says it's polite to give them a little present. Besides, I feel sorry for them... for all of the grandparents in Eldervale. It must be sad not to see your family."

"Hillary."

"What?"

"I just want to say thanks for being my sister. My grandparents were in the car with mom when..." Windslow turned his head away.

Hillary put her hand on his arm and stayed silent.

"Get the brown shoebox out of my closet, will you?" Windslow asked. He sniffed and wiped his arm across his face.

"Sure. What's in it," Hillary asked and found the box.

"Give this to grandpa Dimbleshoot," Windslow said and pulled an unopened package of hard candy from the shoebox. My grandpa used to give me a bag of these all the time. I never liked them but never said that to gramps. They're butterscotch. I saved the last package he gave me before he... Well, anyway. Give them to Dimbleshoot for me. Tell him he can give them to his grandkids when we get rid of Fistlock."

Hillary took the bag and gave Windslow a kiss on the cheek. It wasn't like Miss Christensen's kiss and Windslow pulled his head away and rubbed his hand on his cheek.

"Feeling for whiskers?" Hillary asked and laughed.

"Geeze, I almost forgot about that," Windslow said and felt both sides of his face. "They're not growing back, are they?"

"I don't think so," Hillary said. "The Forge-Twiddlers probably had something to do with the magic or spell. I'd like to meet them someday. Nothing they build works very well. I'm glad we don't need to rely on anything they make."

"They made my crutches. I can almost walk without them when I'm in... in..."

"Gabendoor," Hillary said. "That's what they call their world. Gabendoor. Molly told me."

"If I can walk in Gabendoor, then maybe I'll be able to walk here in our world, and we can use the last chance against Fistlock if we need to," Windslow said. "Help me up. I want to see if I can at least stand yet."

Hillary helped him up, but only for a few seconds. They both knew he would fall if she let go. Windslow tried to smile. He didn't want Hillary to know how he felt. *We've got to save everyone and only use two chances,* he told himself. *If I hadn't wasted one on Miss Christensen...* Windslow scolded himself for even having that thought. He felt the familiar burden of guilt pushing down on him again.

"Hello. Hello!" Hillary said, louder the second time. "Earth to Windslow. For a minute there I thought we had a ponder-glitch in the room."

"A what?" Windslow asked.

"Ponder-glitch. One of Fistlock's shadow beasties. They steal away your train of thought."

"Ha." Windslow laughed. "Trish has one of those following her all the time."

"And Bill has a tellagains with him. I see what you mean about your dad telling the same stories over and over again."

They both laughed and began naming other relatives and the kind of Gabendoor shadow beasties that haunted them. Soon they were both scribbling ideas on sheets of paper as they tried to make sense of words in the Book of Second Chances. They had agreed to use the book to free Gabendoor, but still didn't know how the book really worked.

Chapter I.

The story in this chance begins,

Found in pages locked within.

Open them with words of care.

What you seek is waiting there.

Something lost in time long past,

Chancing love she thought would last

You helped her think of what to do.

A link once cut she now renews.

A second chance you granted them.

Teachers reach for hope again.

The first of four you did not waste,

Although you formed the chance in haste.

Chapter II.

Chapter two this lesson learn,

Do not ask for what you yearn.

Magic does not come from here.

It comes from those who lose their fear

Chances hide when first you look
Seek your answers from this book
The words placed here for you to see
Come from what you made them be

There is no magic where you thought.
It came from things its bearer brought
These pages put you to the test
You've learned to plan and do your best.

14: Two Triplets

"Hillre, wake-ie up. I here."

"Me not here."

"Are too!"

"Am not."

"I not here."

Hillary rubbed her eyes and sat up. She was still inside the cottage, but on a bed in the back room and covered with a mountain of hand stitched quilts. She blinked her eyes, rubbed them again, and stared. In front of her waited three Mollies; all identical except for their hair color. Each girl wore the same plain brown dress that stopped at their knees where blue polka dot socks continued down to tuck into soft boots. Three sets of big black gerbil eyes stared back. Hillary recognized Molly from her bristly black hair. Next to Molly stood an identical copy with green hair, and next to her a girl with orange hair.

"Bout time. Hillre wake up. Sisters here," Molly said.

"Hi. I Tillie Truly Sallyforth," the girl with green hair said and gave a little curtsey.

"I not Nelly Never Sallyforth," the orange haired girl said and gave an identical curtsy.

"You're triplets," Hillary said. She shoved the quilts off her legs and twisted around to put her feet on the floor.

"Not triplets," Molly said. "They twins."

"But you're all alike," Hillary said with wrinkles forming on her brow. "That makes you triplets."

"See," Molly said and pointed at her sisters. "One, two. They look alla like, so they twins."

"They twins too," Tillie Truly said and pointed at Molly Folly and Nelly Never. "One, two. They alla like."

"Them alla like, Nelly Never said. "So they not twins."

"But you're *all alike.* That means... oh, never mind," Hillary said and stood up. "I'm Hillre... *Hillary.* I'm glad you came to help. Is there some way you can take me to a house owned by a wizard named Biffendear at the edge of Gristly-Grim swamp?"

"Nope," Nelly Never answered. "Pretty nice place. I like-a go there, alla time.

"Molly call eagles for us," Tillie said. "We help. You betcha. You gota big Book Second Chances. Got alla chance we need to getcha there."

"You four dears aren't going anywhere without a proper breakfast," Gilderbun called from the kitchen. "Dimbleshoot, you set the table for six, and I'll start baking some biscuits. I think I have some gippleberry jam here somewhere," she said and began rummaging through a shelf full of multi-colored jars near the corner of her kitchen.

"Sorry, granny Gilderbun," Hillary said as she walked into the kitchen. She gave the elderly lady a kiss on the cheek. "Here," she said, turning to Dimbleshoot, who was busy placing wooden plates and spoons around the table. She handed him the bag of butterscotch candies Windslow had sent. "These are from my brother. His grandpa used to give them out to all his grandchildren. Windslow and I are going to use the Book of Second chances to defeat Fistlock. We'll free all the families. And this is for you," she said and handed the hanky to Gilderbun.

Gilderbun didn't say anything. She looked at the hanky and nearly crushed Hillary with a big hug.

"Thank you, sweetheart," Dimbleshoot said as he looked at the package of butterscotch candy. "I remember when Fistlock first tried to split us up. All the soldiers from all the lands banded together to fight him. I gave our son some candy in case he got hungry marching off to battle. Then the Gorlon came. It... it..." Both Dimbleshoot and Gilderbun stared off into the distance, their expressions blank.

"Granny grampa watch memory place inside head again," Molly said. "They better that way. We stay inside and I call eagles back."

Hillary nodded. It surprised her when Molly, Tillie, and Nelly all marched out the door.

"Better come," Tillie called back over her shoulder. "Eagles be here quick."

Hillary ran after the triplets and all four girls began strapping on the leather harnesses piled just outside the door.

ꕥ

When Windslow woke, the first thing he did was rub his hand across his chin.

"Only temporary," Haggerwolf said. The three wizards sat on the ground near the opening they had used to escape from Dreadmoor Temple. "My beard's back better than ever. Grew about two inches an hour."

Windslow smiled and watched the old wizard stroke the fine white whiskers that stretched down nearly to his belt buckle.

"I think I have a little more hair up top," Fernbark said and ran a hand over his nearly bald head. Windslow couldn't really see any difference. Larkstone's small goatee and moustache looked a bit fuller. Windslow had to work hard at not grinning. Larkstone looked like the colonel guy that did the fried bucket of chicken commercials on TV.

"We don't have far to walk from here," Larkstone said. "We can reach Biffendear's place in about half an hour. Let's get moving," he said and began walking through the trees.

Windslow followed, with the other two wizards behind him. The trees looked like the ones back home. Here the leaves showed their bright spring colors and the air smelled fresh, compared to the browner forests they had flown over before. Oaks and willows stretch their branches upward. Birds sang off in the distance, and Windslow heard the sounds of small animals rustling in the undergrowth. Once he even saw a rabbit and pointed it out to the wizards. Larkstone just "harrumphed." Several times Fernbark stopped to touch a tree or plant and even spoke softly, in mumbled words, to several big mushrooms.

It wasn't long before the path and forest started to change. The ground turned soft. Instead of hard ground littered with small twigs and fallen leaves, they walked on a carpet of dark green moss that spread in every direction. Some of the moss crept up the sides of trees. Farther down the path, more moss hung in long dripping clumps from bent limbs. The trees changed to towering pines of some sort, with thinly spaced needles and small spurs that stuck from the branches. Windslow looked back and saw his footprints in the moss fill with green water. He knew this must be the start of Gristly-Grim swamp.

The smells reminded Windslow of how he and his mom would search behind the garage for angleworms. His mother would tip over a rock or piece of board. Underneath them moist ground and dead grass gave off the same smell as the swamp did now. His mom used a shovel to dig up the ground and Windslow would sift through it for worms. When his dad came home from work they would go fishing down by the stream behind his house. Windslow missed his old house, but agreed with his dad that it held too many painful memories. He wondered if Trish and Hillary liked to fish.

"Hold up," Larkstone said. The wizard stopped suddenly. Windslow almost ran into him. "Stay on the path," Larkstone instructed. "The swamp won't like it if we disturb any of the Leapers."

Windslow looked up ahead. Pale green water replaced the moss carpet. It looked like pictures of the Everglades. Tall grasses grew in clumps from the water near some of the trees. Here and there a log floated in the water, and Windslow could see ripples and V's of water made by things moving underneath the surface.

The sounds caught his attention. He still heard birds, but not the soft chirps he had heard earlier back in the forest. Long calls sounded and he heard wings flutter. He wasn't quick enough to catch sight of the birds that made the sounds. Crickets called. He recognized their sound. *Kree..ket, kree..ket,* they sounded. The *gurlump... gurlump,* must be from frogs. He thought he remembered his mother telling him what made the *pee-d-peep, pee-d-peep, pee-d-peep,* sound, but wasn't sure.

"That pee-d-peep, sound," he asked, trying his best to mimic it. "Do things called spring peepers make it?"

"That's the sound of magic, boy," Fernbark said. "Magic is silent in the daytime. At night it comes out. When you are in special places, like this, you can hear it. The louder it sounds, the closer you are. Watch."

Crack!

Fernbark snapped a dead branch in half over his knee. "Hear that?" he asked Windslow.

"I don't hear anything," Windslow said.

"The magic went back into hiding. That's why you never see it. You only feel it. Sometimes when the wind and the moon are just right, listen to the peepers. Walk soft and slow. Follow their song. If you're lucky, and try hard, you might see a little glow off in the distance. If you do, it's magic. Few people are lucky enough to see it. It looks like fog or mist that floats just above the ground. Magic is timid and flows all around us. It's powerful if it lets you use it, but it's too shy to show itself in its normal form. Come on. Don't fall off the planks."

Skinny planks held in place by bark-less poles sticking out of the water, started at the solid ground and continued out across the water. They formed a walkway of twisted angles that disappeared into the trees. The planks sagged in the middle when Windslow and the wizards walked too close together. They spaced themselves a bit farther apart so none of them would get their feet wet. Windslow saw more ripples in the water and even heard splashes. When he looked close, he could see pairs of big round eyes poking up just above the water's surface. Whenever he got close to them they disappeared, leaving telltale rings that spread out across the water.

"There's Biffendear's place," Larkstone said and pointed up ahead.

Where he pointed, the trees spread to border a wide pond formed by a narrow waterfall that tumbled down the face of a tall cliff. Fine mist from the falling water danced with rainbow colors and sent tiny waves across the pond. Bright green lily pads with white flowers rocked gently as the rippling water passed underneath them. Frogs blinked and dove from the floating pads to the water. Soft *plunks* and louder *ga-blunks* sounded each time one jumped, adding to the gurgling sound from the falls.

"Leapers," Windslow said and began to laugh. "This is the Leaper Colony."

"What did you think it would be?" Haggerwolf asked.

Windslow didn't answer. He looked at the house, built on stilts at the back of the pond and far enough to one side of the waterfall to keep dry. The small house was one story high. Raw wood planks, fit tightly together, formed the walls and a little porch. Two windows, one on each side of the center door had amber colored glass. Split wood shingles, with tinges of moss, covered the roof that sloped gently down from the cliff to the front porch. Windslow was about to look away when he spotted the thin ropes and cross steps that stretched up the cliff from the cottage roof. *A stepladder,* he said to himself and traced the ropes up through the tangle of vines and ivy that clung to the rock.

He first thought about how fun it would be to climb the ladder, but the feeling didn't last. His hands began to sweat and his legs shook. He shoved his crutches under his arms to steady himself. A couple of deep breaths helped him push away the feelings that came with his memory of falling off the roof back home.

"You'll need to step carefully," Haggerwolf said. "Put a foot on the wrong lily pad and you sink to the bottom."

"Don't worry," Fernbark said. "It's not deep. Maybe up to your waist."

"I'll have to do this without crutches," Windslow said and took another deep breath as he bound his crutches to his back. While they had walked thought the forest and swamp, he tried not to use his crutches unless he really needed them. His legs still burned and he had fallen and skinned one knee, but the thrill of walking again had encouraged him. He was ready to try his first non-crutch challenge, even if he did still feel shaky from his memory of the accident.

"I'll go first," Haggerwolf said and put one foot on the closest lily pad. Ten steps and ten lily pads later, he was halfway across the pond. Windslow followed, making sure he stepped on the same plants.

"Windslow!" Hillary yelled as she ran out the doorway and onto the porch. "I made it!"

"Me too."

"Not me."

"I maybe."

Three curses sounded. All three cut short, covered by the sound of big splashes. Windslow teetered and held his arms out as he balanced on one foot. Up in front of him, Haggerwolf thrashed the water as he got to his feet.

"Don't scare leapers!" Molly yelled. She and her sisters lined up beside Hillary.

"What are they doing here?" Larkstone yelled as he shook his head, trying to shake some of the water out of his hair.

Windslow got his balance. There were only ten more lily pads between him and the porch. There wasn't any place else to step and he carefully made his way to the porch. The wizards didn't bother climbing back on the stepping-pads. They waded through the waist-high water toward Biffendear's home.

"Wizards like-a be mean sometimes," Molly Folly said. She turned around and stomped her boots on the plank floor as she disappeared inside the cottage.

"They my big friends," Nelly Never said. She turned and stomped even harder as she went inside.

"They alla time mad at us," Tillie Truly said and stomped away, even louder.

"You're really walking," Hillary said, ignoring the three Sallyforth girls, for now, as she stretched her hand out to her stepbrother to help him up on the porch. "Molly and her sisters helped me get here. We flew, dangling from eagles, just like I told you we did before. The birds dropped us on the roof and we climbed down a trapdoor. We were only here a minute before I saw you."

Hillary let go of Windslow's hand and watched the first wizard climb up onto the porch. "Hi. I'm Hillary. I bet you're Haggerwolf," she said and stepped back as he shook himself.

"I know who you are," Haggerwolf grumbled and began checking his pockets. "Larkstone!" he yelled. "Grab my wand. It's floating right behind you." He mumbled something else that Hillary couldn't make out. "What are you doing with the Sallyforth girls?" Haggerwolf asked. "You should have got rid of the first one after she helped you out of Fistlock's castle."

"They're nothing but trouble," Larkstone said and handed Haggerwolf's wand up before climbing onto the porch.

"Hi. I'm Fernbark," the third wizard said as he climbed up. He smiled at Hillary, but looked away when his face began to turn red. He peeked back at her for a second and his blush spread to his ears.

"Don't mind him," Haggerwolf said. "He's been excited to meet you ever since the oracle spoke to him."

"What oracle?" Hillary asked and turned to look at Windslow.

He shrugged and looked at the wizards.

"Um... didn't we mention that?" Larkstone asked. "I thought we had. Well, maybe we should sit down and Fernbark can tell you."

"Why don't we go inside so you three can dry off and Molly and her sisters can hear too?" Hillary said. "Come on, Windslow."

"What? Inside with those three?" Haggerwolf said and folded his arms. "Never!"

Fernbark waved his wand down along his body. As the stick moved, water streamed from his clothes, leaving them dry. “The oracle did mention them too,” he said and used his wand to dry his friends.

“The Sallyforth girls?” Haggerwolf asked, his voice loud. “Impossible!”

15: Biffendear's

Hillary and Windslow ignored the wizards' protests and stepped inside Biffendear's cottage. Molly, Tillie and Nelly sat side by side on a table in the center of the room. Three scowling faces and three pairs of folded arms greeted Hillary and Windslow. Nelly deepened her scowl, pinched her lips together and turned her head.

Molly stared at Hillary, but her face softened when she looked at Windslow.

"No like-a wizards," Tillie said and picked up two glass beakers that sat next to her. "Big bully mosa time. Alla time." She poured the blue liquid from one beaker into the pink liquid in the other and set both bottles down.

"It okay, though," Molly said. "Hillre and Windso nice. We help anyway, but not wizard."

"It's Windslow," Windslow said. "And we're all going to need to work together. I've got a feeling it might take more than just us to fix things around here. Nelly, I don't think you should be playing with that stuff."

"She not Nelly, she Tillie," Molly said. "Tillie twin with orange hair. Tillie that one," she said and pointed to her sister who jumped down from the table and skipped across the floor to a broad desk bounded by shelves at the end of the room.

The desk drawers stood half open and overstuffed. Papers, books, big and small clay pots, bits of bone and things Windslow couldn't identify littered the top. Multi-colored jars, some with liquids, some with coarse powder, others with chunky things suspended in fluid, filled the shelves. Tillie grabbed an orange jar that matched the color of her hair and unscrewed the lid.

"Ah, Tillie," Windslow said, but gave up. The girl started dropping pinches of different colored powders into the jar.

"I think we should just leave everything alone," Hillary said. "Windslow, keep an eye on things. I'll go get your wizards."

"They're not mine," Windslow said over his shoulder as his sister walked back out the door.

Windslow ignored the girls, except for an occasional glance he gave to Molly who stayed on the workbench and kept staring at him. He had always wanted a chemistry set. The tools and glass beakers on the table intrigued him too. He walked around the table and poked at a couple pots, lifted the lid from a carved wooden box and twisted the knob of a brass tube that looked like a gas burner. He followed the rubber hose to a copper tank under the table. Stamped into the bright metal were the words, "Hippograff Gas".

A small bed, littered with more papers, and wadded up blankets sat against the back wall, close to the middle of the wall where a wooden ladder stretched up to a trap door in the ceiling. Windslow figured that must have been the door Hillary mentioned.

Something moved under one of the blankets and Windslow took a step back.

"That just-a leaper," Molly said.

Windslow looked over his shoulder. He felt a bit uneasy knowing she was still watching him. Carefully Windslow pulled the blanket back and a large bullfrog jumped off the small bed. Two more hops and it disappeared out a three inch square opening cut in the back wall. Windslow heard the "plop" when the frog landed into the water.

He looked carefully and saw more little openings cut at regular intervals all around the cottage.

Tillie put the cover back on the jar she had been playing with and shook it up. When she put the jar back on a shelf, a salamander scooted out of the way, dropped to the desk, then to the floor and scurried out a hole.

A rustling overhead caught Windslow's attention. Two long beams and a couple of square planks held up the roof. Small bags, bigger pouches and bundles of dried plants hung from them. One moved and Windslow watched a toad wiggle under a nest of wet moss on one of the beams. A rubber tube ran from the nest up to the roof. Windslow wondered if mist from the falls could reach far enough to drip water down and keep the moss damp. He saw more tubes at other spots in both the ceiling and walls. They all led to small dishes, some half full of water, others filled with moss like the nest on the roof beams.

Ka-Blang!

Windslow jumped and spun around.

"Windso kind-a cute," Molly said, looking at Nelly. Molly held a wooden ladle. A copper pot hinging above her head rocked back and forth. She gave it another small tap.

"He mostly ugly," Nelly answered back. "You get him."

"No way," Molly protested. "He mine."

"Now!" Hillary's voice sounded from the doorway.

Windslow and the three Sallyforth sisters all turned their heads.

"They're impossible," Hillary said and shook her head as she marched back inside the cottage. The three Wizards walked single file, close behind her. Hillary looked at her brother and shot glances at all three girls. "And leave all that stuff alone!" She hollered.

Even Windslow jumped. The triplets put down whatever they were holding and folded their hands.

"Now," Hillary continued. "We are going to work together. Aren't we," she said and looked at the three wizards. Haggerwolf nodded, Fernbark blushed and Larkstone studied his boots. "Agreed?" she said, just as loud and looked at each of the triplets.

Molly nodded and grinned. "Yep. I biggest friend of Hillre."

"Me too," Tillie said.

"I not work-a them no matter what," Nelly said.

"Nelly," Hillary said, her voice very stern. "I mean all of us."

"I be big problem. And, that no promise," Nelly said. She shrunk down, as if trying to be a turtle and pull her head out of sight.

"She gave you her word," Haggerwolf said. He moved to a pile of books stacked under one of the amber-glass windows and used them as a stool.

"She's lying," Larkstone said and sat cross-legged on the floor under the other window.

"No lies," Hillary said and looked back at Nelly.

"You don't understand," Fernbark said and sat down between the other two wizards. "That's what's so hard about working with them; among other things."

Windslow checked the bed before sitting down. "I don't have a clue about what any of you are saying."

"It easy, Windso," Molly said and gave Windslow a wink that made him blush. "I Molly Folly. She Tillie Truly," she said pointing at her orange haired sister. "And she Nelly Never. We alla Sallyforth."

"What she's saying," Haggerwolf said, "is one of them always tells the truth. One sometimes tells the truth but not all the time. The other one always lies."

"You always lie," Hillary said. She stepped close to Nelly Never and squeezed the girl's hand.

"I not try help you much," Nelly said and squeezed back.

"And you always tell the truth," Hillary said looking over at Tillie.

"And you," Hillary said and gave Molly a big hug. "That explains a lot of things about you knowing and not knowing the way out of Fistlock's dungeon."

"Yep. I alla time biggest help. Bigger than ever-body else," Molly said. "Now I help Windso too."

"Wow, cool," Windslow said, then shut up when all three wizards rolled their eyes.

"It's more than just that," Haggerwolf said. "There's also-"

"We don't need to go into that," Hillary said, cutting Haggerwolf off. She boosted herself up on the workbench next to Molly. "Now one of you was going to tell us about the oracle. Who wants to start," she said and looked at Haggerwolf.

"Well, it was this way," he began.

All three wizards jumped in at different times to tell about how the combined armies couldn't stop the last Gorlon. It was unstoppable, with weapons or magic. The wizards' council consulted the mountain oracle several times, but the number of questions the oracle would answer had a limit. While the generals prepared for the final attack, the wizards met with the oracle to ask their last question. Haggerwolf had led the group and gave instructions as the last surviving wizards assembled around the pond the oracle appeared from.

"I told them all to think of what our last question might be and just how we could phrase it," Haggerwolf said as he looked at Fernbark. "The wording is very important. You have to ask a single question and the oracle answers. I said that one of us must think of a question that would lead to a way to stop the Gorlon."

"Your exact words," Larkstone said, "were, 'there must be a way to stop it.' Fernbark mumbled something under his breath. The next thing we saw was him stiffen up and turn all silvery. The oracle settled back into the pond and Fernbark collapsed."

Haggerwolf interrupted. "The idiot had asked a question without even thinking about the consequences. The oracle took it as our last one and gave him an answer directly into his brain."

"I think Molly is right," Hillary scolded. "You especially, Haggerwolf, are rude and cranky."

"So what did you say and what was the message, Larkstone?" Windslow asked.

"It wasn't much of a message, really," Larkstone answered. "I just muttered that I wished I knew someone that could save us. I got my answer. We kept going over it and over it again, trying to figure it out. The oracle said:

False hopes unsealed,

The truth revealed,

Uncertainty that yields.

With these three, the son of the summer storm and daughter of the mountain breeze will restore Gabendoor.

"The first part has to be those three," Haggerwolf said as he pointed at the Sallyforth triplets.

"Son of the summer storm has got to be you," he said pointing at Windslow. "And Hillary is the daughter of the mountain breeze. It all came together when you found the Book of Second Chances."

"We gonna help save ever-body," all three sisters said at the same time.

Hillary started to laugh but stopped when the flask Tillie had been playing with began to bubble. The air filled with the smell of sauerkraut and purple smoke streamed up from the bottle.

"Duck!" Fernbark yelled.

The girls jumped from the table and scooted back under it, just as the three wizards dove for the same spot. Heads clunked together and curses mixed in with screaming. Tillie ducked under the desk. Windslow tried to crawl under the bed, but the space was full of wood crates and more clay pots. He grabbed the biggest crock and held it over his head.

"Ka-boom!"

Windslow's ears rang and he yanked the crock off his head. Frogs jumped, salamanders slithered and toads hopped everywhere; each leaper heading for the nearest escape. Tillie's hair stuck out at even odder angles than before. Haggerwolf stood up and slapped at his smoldering whiskers. Hillary,

Molly, Nelly, and the other two wizards crawled out from under the table.

Other than purple soot that fell like tiny snowflakes, Haggerwolf's beard, and Tillie's hair, everything looked undamaged.

"That's what I was talking about outside!" Haggerwolf said. "I told you— Duck!" He yelled again. Everyone scrambled back to where they took shelter before. Windslow grabbed another pot, thought about his last experience and just spread himself flat on the floor. The jar Tillie had mixed and shook up, began rattling on the shelf above the desk. It pulsed with greenish light as if it held a thousand angry fireflies. The metal lid unscrewed and flung itself across the room like a wild Frisbee and clanged against the far wall. A grapefruit smell filled the room as yellow confetti blasted from the jar. Each tiny piece of paper turned into a pink butterfly and in a steady flutter of wings they flew out the door.

Haggerwolf poked his head up. "Did anyone fool with anything else?" he half shouted.

Two no's and one yep, were the answers he was looking for from the Sallyforth triplets.

"I bang a pot," Molly said as she stood. "But that don't count."

Everyone else slowly got back up. Hillary flinched when Windslow kicked a piece of broken pot. "That was so cool," he said softly.

Hillary shot him a stern look which didn't last. She started a giggle that turned into an all-out laugh. Windslow and the sisters joined in. Even Larkstone and Fernbark began laughing. Haggerwolf just "harrumphed," but the corners of his mouth curled up. He turned around and began adjusting his cloak.

"All right," Hillary said and dusted off a spot on the workbench. She boosted herself back up and everyone else sat down as they had before the Sallyforth excitement. "The first thing we need to do is figure out how the book... yawn... works.

"What?" Haggerwolf said and spun around. "But I thought... I thought—"

"You used it to give us a second chance in Dreadmoor Temple," Larkstone said and got to his feet. "You said you knew how to use it, Windslow."

"I'm sorry," Windslow said. "I was bluffing to keep those creatures back. It was the magic you three worked that saved us. I know I've worked the book and used a couple chances up already but I really don't know how I did, yawn... it. We thought you... yawn... wanted to come here because Biffendear figured out how to use the book before he died."

"That's why we wanted to come here in the first place," Haggerwolf said. "But then we thought you figured it out. Biffendear died just before he could tell us what he discovered."

"This is horrible," Larkstone said and put his head in his hands. "We're no farther than when we started."

"Not really," Hillary said. She slid down from the table and walked around to sit on the bed beside her brother. "Tell us what happened to Biffendear and maybe it will be a piece of the puzzle that makes the other parts fit... yawn... together better."

"There's not much to tell," Fernbark said as he scratched his head. "Biffendear stole the book from Fistlock about fifty years ago. Biffendear discovered that Fistlock must have used up all his chances because the book was latched. Biffendear opened it and began experimenting. He cast some sort of leaper spell on the book so Fistlock couldn't track him."

"Do you know the... yawn... spell?" Hillary asked. "We could use it to keep Fistlock from finding us."

"Biffendear was secretive about most of his work," Haggerwolf said. "We don't know what he did. He did get words to show up in the book, like you have, Windslow."

"I was here the night he discovered how the book works; the same night he died," Larkstone said. "Biffendear was at his desk, where Tillie's sitting now. I was standing by the doorway, just about where I am now."

"What happened?" Hillary asked and yawned.

"Biffendear jumped up from his desk and slammed the Book of second chances shut. 'I've got it!' he yelled and began dancing around. He said, 'I've got it... the three lines. You open the book. Learn the lesson and everything becomes clear.' Just about then, it happened."

"What happen Biff wizard?" Molly asked.

"Well," Haggerwolf continued. "You know he's a leaper. He had a potion to save him from spending all his time catching crickets to feed to his toads and frogs. He'd catch a fish and put one little drop on it. The fish would turn into a hundred crickets. He could get five or six crickets out of a big earthworm. He was dancing like mad and the bottle holding his potion fell off the shelf, bounced on the desk and splashed on him."

"You don't mean..." Hillary said. She squeezed her eyes shut and turned her head away.

"Yep," Haggerwolf said. "One second he was standing there. The next second, sticky tongues were flicking out. Toads, frogs, salamanders and creatures I've never seen before were all chasing crickets. A minute later he was gone, along with whatever he had discovered."

"Yuck," Windslow said and shuddered.

"Him bug food," Molly said. She was the only one who looked up when a small chirp sounded from outside.

"Gone pretty quick with alla leapers here," Tillie added.

"Bed pretty full," Nelly said. "Not any room for alla us to sleep."

Haggerwolf turned and looked at the empty bed.

A bluebird chirped, louder this time. In a blur of blue wings the bluebird flew through the open cottage door and landed on Molly's shoulder. Almost as quickly as it had perched, it flew back out the door, buzzing close enough to Haggerwolf's head that he ducked.

"Good thing Hillre, Windso fall-a sleep an dream-slip home. Gorlon come."

"What?" Haggerwolf said as all three wizards stood. "How long, Molly?"

"Come now; maybe later. Birdie not know. Fistlock set

big Gorlon free. No more chain."

16: The Gorlon

Hillary bolted upright in bed and brushed wildly at her clothes. She stopped when she realized it had just been a short dream. It was the first time she remembered having a real dream mixed in with dream-slipping back and forth between here and Gabendoor.

She looked over at her alarm clock and shut it off so its annoying buzz wouldn't start in a couple of minutes. "Ick," she said and made a face. "Death by crickets."

Hillary heard a noise that sounded like a door open and shut and figured that Bill was offering to help Windslow. After his 'hair adventure,' Windslow wanted to do more to get himself ready in the morning. Bill usually stood by, just in case Windslow needed some help. *At least* that book is helping someone, Hillary thought as she took off the jeans and flannel shirt that had become her regular dream-slipping clothes. *Windslow is almost acting like he did before the accident. I wonder how he'll feel when we save Gabendoor and we don't dream-slip there anymore? I hope we can figure out a way to help him here. I don't want him to be disappointed*, she thought and stared at the disposable camera on her dresser. *How many things from here, don't work there? How many things from there, won't work here*? she wondered. She shoved the camera into a drawer, pulled on pajamas and a robe, and headed for the bathroom.

The hallway was empty, and she didn't hear the familiar sounds of Trish working in the kitchen, getting breakfast ready or making school lunches.

"Crapo," she said softly and slapped her palm against her forehead. "It's Saturday." She considered going back to sleep, but changed her mind and snuck into Windslow's room. She wasn't surprised when she saw him sitting up in bed.

"I thought it was Friday," Hillary said to her stepbrother. "I don't think I can get back to sleep, so I was going to borrow the book and see if I could figure out any of the puzzle."

"Yeah, I woke up too. I keep thinking about crickets."

"Me, too," Hillary said and laughed as she sat on the side of Windslow's bed. "I wonder what mom and Bill have planned for us today. Not the zoo again, I hope."

"They're going out with some friends this afternoon and then dinner later," Windslow said. "I forgot to tell you. Dad told me that Alexis is coming to baby-sit us."

"A babysitter? We're too old for that. I bet Alexis isn't much older than we are."

"Lighten up, Hillary. Alexis goes to college."

"Oh, her. The artist. I remember now. She's the babysitter you have the crush on."

"I do not," Windslow said and swung a pillow at Hillary.

She ducked his swing and leaned over to grab another pillow to fight back with.

"Ouch, ow! You're on my leg," Windslow yelled. "Be care..."

Hillary stood up from the bed. She didn't say anything. Neither did Windslow. They both stared at his legs, outlined by the blankets covering them.

"Pinch it," Winslow said.

Hillary reached out, pinched his leg through the blankets, and quickly pulled her hand away.

"Harder."

She pinched him again.

"Twist it. Hit it or something," Windslow said and pounded his fist against his leg. As far down as he could reach, he hit himself again. Hillary grabbed his hand and stopped him.

"Don't hurt yourself," she said. "You're going to have bruises."

"Any new bruises will just blend into the others I already have. Dad thinks I'm bumping myself when I get into my chair alone. That's not what they're from. They're from checking my legs. I felt something, Hillary. I really did. It was a sharp pain, but there's nothing now. I miss walking and running. Why do my legs only work in Gabendoor?"

"The wizards made some kind of temporary fix to your back. You know it's hard to get things to dream-slip. Your flashlight didn't work there, and neither did my camera. Even if we figure out how to work the Book of Second Chances, it might..."

Windslow flopped back down and pulled the pillow over his face.

"Maybe... maybe you..." Hillary sighed.

Windslow hugged the pillow even tighter.

"We'll figure out that book," she said and eased backward toward the door. "Maybe we should both try to go back to sleep."

Hillary turned and walked back to her room. She lay on her bed and stared at the ceiling. *I wonder if I'll dream-slip if I take a nap,* she thought and sat back up.

ꟷ

That afternoon, Trish made Hillary and Windslow go over a list of telephone numbers and instructions. The list had "911" marked in big red numbers across the top. Underneath were more telephone numbers for all the places Bill and Trish would be, plus numbers for doctors, hospitals, police and the fire department. Finally Alexis came and their parents left. Hillary and Windslow wanted to work on the riddle in the book, but Alexis insisted they all work on activities together. It wasn't long before they forgot about the riddle, but not Gabendoor. Alexis had her art materials with her. Windslow and Hillary made up a story about making puppets for a school project and ideas they had for the faces. By dinner time, Alexis had sketched the three wizards and the Sallyforth sisters from Windslow's and Hillary's descriptions. After dinner, Alexis began watching a movie on TV, finally giving Windslow and Hillary a chance to be alone.

"Did you hear what Alexis said about Miss Christensen?" Hillary asked. "Why didn't you tell me? Didn't she say anything to you? I think it's so cool."

"You don't even know if it's true," Winslow said and took the Book of Second chances out of his bag. "Alexis heard it from a friend, who heard it from a friend, who heard it from a friend. So big deal if Miss Christensen is engaged."

"Windslow, you idiot! Miss Christensen has only known the guy for a week."

"She's known him longer than that. She knew him in high school," Windslow said and flipped the book open. "If you want to gossip, go talk to Alexis. I'm going to figure out this book."

"Boys!" Hillary said and turned Windslow's wheelchair around to face his desk. She pulled a tall stool up beside him and watched as he turned the pages.

Chapter I.

The story in this chance begins,

Found in pages locked within.

Open them with words of care.

What you seek is waiting there.

"This first part is some kind of warning," Windslow said as he read the words aloud.

"I think you're right about that," Hillary said. "It's telling us to be careful how we use our chances. We know the next section is about Miss Christensen. I just wish I knew how you granted her a second chance."

"Maybe it's magic or something. I don't remember if I wished she had a second chance. I think I just kind of told her to take one. So some kind of magic made it happen."

"Well, dah... We know it's a magic book."

Windslow used his shoulder to give his sister a shove, nearly pushing her off the stool. "If you're so smart, then you figure out the rest."

Something lost in time long past,

Chancing love she thought would last

You helped her think of what to do.

A link once cut she now renews.

A second chance you granted them.

Teachers reach for hope again.

The first of four you did not waste,

Although you formed the chance in haste.

"Okay, we know about Miss Christensen and we both think we get four second chances from the book. What about chapter two?" Hillary asked and then read the lines.

Chapter II.

Chapter two this lesson learn,

Do not ask for what you yearn.

Magic does not come from here.

It comes from those who lose their fear

Chances hide when first you look

Seek your answers from this book

The words placed here for you to see

Come from what you made them be

There is no magic where you thought.

It came from things its bearer brought

These pages put you to the test

You've learned to plan and do your best.

"This happened after you got out of that bat place," she said.

"Yeah, but it almost seems too simple," Windslow said. "It can't be right. The wizards were scared because they were out of magic. I hollered at them and pretended to use the book. When they weren't scared anymore, they used magic. So the magic that saved us didn't come from the book. The wizards had it all the time."

"But it says the magic came from the bearer. You had the book. That means the magic came from you."

"If I had magic, I'd be walking," Windslow said softly. "Look," he said and pointed to the book. "We can turn another page." He watched as Hillary turned the ancient parchment.

Chapter III.

The Gorlon comes, it brings a chance

For one who takes a special stance.

If puzzled out one wish will come.

A prize for something that you've done.

"The Gorlon," they both said together.

"I don't like this, Hillary. What did the thing... the Gorlon, look like?"

"I told you before. I didn't really see it. It was inside its cave. If these words come true then... then..."

"Then it's bringing us a second chance," Windslow said. "Maybe the Gorlon isn't really bad and wants to be on our side? Maybe it's going to help us because we have the book, or because it wants to get away from Fistlock."

"Yeah, and Alexis is going to win the lottery and share it with us. Maybe it means that we get a second chance to defeat the Gorlon if we take a stance."

"But what about the puzzle? Maybe we'll have to solve one like I did in the maze?"

"I don't know," Hillary said and closed the book. "Somehow I don't think it's going to be that easy. Start getting ready. I'll tell Alexis we're going to bed." Hillary stopped at the door and turned back to her brother. "Why don't you sleep in your clothes tonight? Just tell Bill you fell asleep in them. If we're going to face a Gorlon, I don't want my teammate to be wearing pajamas."

"I'm bringing my slingshot too," Windslow said and wheeled his chair over to his bed.

Hillary rolled her eyes and headed for the living room to find Alexis.

ഗ്ര

The three wizards and the Sallyforth sisters stood on the porch of Biffendear's cottage. They watched the forest at the far side of the pond. Far off in the distance, birds flew from the treetops. The small flocks spiraled up and away, squawking and chattering.

"Birds run from Gorlon," Molly said. "Windso and Hillre better go sleepy-time quick, back in earth place."

Another flock of startled birds leapt upward in flight from the trees.

"I'll wait for Windslow and Hillary inside the house," Haggerwolf said. "Fernbark, check the rope ladder. Make sure it's clear of vines all the way up the cliff. The rest of you get up on the roof and wait there."

While the others ran to follow his instructions, Haggerwolf looked back across the pond. He could hear the faint thumps from the Gorlon's steps. The treetops, just across the pond, quivered in time to the dull thuds. The water sent extra ripples across its surface, making the lily pads jump with each pounding step that brought the Gorlon closer to the cottage.

"I see it," Fernbark called. Halfway up the rope ladder, he held on with one hand and used the other to shade his eyes from the morning sun. "We're out of time."

The trees shook and parted on the far pond shore.

"Get up the cliff!" Haggerwolf yelled. "I'll wait until the last moment!"

Fernbark and Larkstone started climbing the rope ladder that looked too frail to hold more than two people at a time. Tillie and Nelly Sallyforth waited until the two wizards were close to the top of the high cliff before they grabbed for the ladder. Haggerwolf scrambled up though the trap door in the cottage roof. He didn't head for the ladder. He turned around and lay down on his belly so he could watch through the opening for Windslow and Hillary to appear.

"I wait. Big Gorlon no scare me so much," Molly said. She stepped in the middle of Haggerwolf's back, to get over and past him. Before he could say anything, she jumped through the opening in the roof, grabbed the lip and dangled for a second before dropping down onto the bed below. "You pretty fat wizard," she called up. "Better start climbing. Tell sisters to call birds for help."

Haggerwolf ran to the ladder and climbed. "Molly said to call the birds!" He yelled up to the Sallyforth sisters.

Tillie and Nelly both stuck fingers between their lips and let out shrill whistles. Some of the birds that circled high overhead, turned in flight; more fluttered up from the trees. They formed a long, wide formation in the sky, like a twisting ribbon of multicolored wings. The leaders snaked back and forth through the sky, leading the others downward. They swooped at the side of the pond, heading for a gravelly beach. Without stopping, each bird skimmed the ground and snatched up a pebble.

"What good will stones do?" Larkstone asked, and helped Haggerwolf climb onto the shelf of rock at the top of the cliff.

"They do more than wizards do," Tillie said.

"Wizards pretty much big help right now," Nelly said and wiggled her fingers in the air. "Glad you not using magic."

"A thousand wizards died trying to stop the last Gorlon," Fernbark said. "There's nothing we can do."

"Wizard got good attitude," Nelly said and pushed past them so she could stand at the cliff's edge. "It gone," she said.

The trees stopped moving. The pond stilled. The slight morning breeze paused. The birds stopped chirping. Only the waterfall dared make sounds, but even it seemed muted. The open space between the trees across the water filled with blackness.

17: A Second Chance

"Hillre! Wake-e up. Up quick. Gorlon here!" Molly shouted and shook Hillary's shoulders.

"What?" Hillary asked and pushed Molly's arms away. "Where's Windslow?" she asked and turned around.

"He not here yet. Just you. Quick! Up ladder. I wait for Windso."

Hillary ran up the staircase leading to the roof. Molly dashed to the door, took a quick look and hurried back to wait by the bed where Windslow had fallen asleep the night before. An image began to shimmer and within seconds, Windslow appeared.

"Big danger!" Molly hollered. She took his hand and pulled him up. "Gorlon outside. He big meanie, but him don't climb good. Up steps. Quick!"

Windslow hurried up the steps with Molly pushing him from behind. Up on the roof, he stayed on his hands and knees. Where the cliff rose at the back of the house, Hillary waited, holding the rope ladder in her hands.

"Look!" she said and pointed.

Windslow turned around.

Blackness filled the space between the trees that the Gorlon had pushed aside. It was as if something blocked the light from reaching that single spot. Rectangular wisps of blackness flew outward like silk scarves. Some floated to the ground, joined together, and turned to a shadowy fog. Others flew upward, filling the sky to form a shield between the sun and ground. The pond, the forest, and the swamp, took on the look they showed on a night of a full moon. Colors turned to gray and shadows claimed a grip on every shape. Two orange eyes glowed through the darkness.

"Climb quick!" Molly called to Hillary. "Get to top, fast. Ladder only hold two biggies like you. Windso, you go too! Start now!"

Windslow eased himself around and crawled toward the ladder.

"Stand up! Run quick," Molly said and grabbed Windslow's arm, trying unsuccessfully to pull him to his feet.

Finally at the ladder, Windslow looked up. Far above him he could see Hillary reaching upward for someone's hand. In seconds she was out of sight. He grabbed the ladder's bottom rung and pulled himself to his feet.

"Go! Go up, Windso!" Molly yelled at him. She put her tiny hand in the middle of his back and shoved. Windslow closed his eyes and hung on tight to the ropes.

"Hurry, Windslow!" Hillary called down from up above. Windslow opened his eyes. He could see his sister's head poking out over the top of the ladder. "You'll be all right. It's easy. Just don't look down!"

Windslow's heart thumped hard inside his chest. His mouth felt dry and his hands shook.

"I show you how!" Molly yelled. She pushed beside him, jumped and grabbed the rung just above his head. Windslow didn't move when her foot hit his face as she climbed up the ladder. Halfway up the cliff, Molly stopped and called down. "See? Climb easy. More easy than fighting big baddie."

Windslow didn't hear her. He stared across the pond at the Gorlon.

A twisted, black, form stepped from the darkness. Twice as tall as the cottage, the Gorlon took another step forward. Massive arms, with oily black, bulging muscles, gripped two crutches. The Gorlon lifted the crutches and moved them forward another pace. He swung two withered and misshaped legs forward. His eyes glowed as he stared at Windslow. Bright white fangs showed as the monster grinned.

ꙮ

"Windslow!" Hillary yelled again, but he ignored her. She glanced at the trees and saw the darkness swirl. A large black horse pawed the air as it rose up on its hind legs. The ground shook when its hooves slammed down. The rider's black cloak blew in a wind that wasn't there. The rider's hood hid its face, but Hillary knew from the glowing orange eyes that it was the Gorlon. Its arm stretched out and exposed silver-grey bones with no flesh. The Gorlon raised a tarnished sword and pointed it at her.

"Signal birds!" Molly yelled from the rope ladder.

Tillie and Nelly whistled.

The birds flew down through the shadows and dove for the Gorlon. Pebbles rained down as the birds dropped their small weapons.

Hillary watched as the Gorlon's sword and arms shrank, sucking back toward its body. The horse began to change its shape, like some blow-up doll loosing air. In seconds there was nothing left that she could recognize. The black glob bulged and twisted. Thick puffy arms formed and swatted at the hail of tiny stones. A round lump took form around the glowing eyes and overstuffed legs lifted the bulk of the Gorlon up from the ground.

A veil of crackling blue electricity danced across the Gorlon's oily skin, as if the beast had walked through a forest of colored electric spider webs. Its arm muscles puffed. When they seemed ready to burst, they shrunk back again. Its legs puffed and quivered as it took another step. The ground shook.

"It's like he's made out of black water balloons," Hillary said and looked back over her shoulder at the wizards.

"He looks like whatever you think he will," Haggerwolf said. "He's a shadow beast. He's part fear, part imagination, all nightmare, and unstoppable. Get your brother up here and fast! The Sallyforth's trick made the Gorlon take its true form for all of us, but the danger is real."

"Windslow!" Hillary yelled again. "Crud!" she cursed. "He's afraid of heights and especially afraid of roofs. We've got to do something."

The Gorlon lumbered forward, sending up big splashes from the pond with each step. Frogs jumped out of the way. The water churned muddy. Windslow didn't move.

Molly looped one arm through the ladder so she could let go with both hands. She stuck her fingers in her mouth and whistled. A small flock of birds scooped up pebbles and flew toward the cabin roof. When they were over Windslow, they dropped their stones.

Windslow let go of the ladder. He fell to his hands and knees while he held his book bag over his head to shelter himself from the raining pebbles. With wild eyes he looked up at Molly.

"Use book magic! Use second chance! Send Gorlon away!"

Windslow didn't say anything, but he did nod. He set the magic bag on the roof and pulled out the Book of Second Chances. Holding the book open, he turned it so the pages faced the Gorlon. With shaking arms he held the book up in front of his own face, to block out the vision of the monster. Windslow squeezed his eyes shut and turned his head when the Gorlon was close enough that Windslow could smell its breath; a sickening odor of motor oil and mildew.

ᘐᘓ

"Windslow!" Hillary watched in horror as the Gorlon pressed its fat belly up against the edge of the cottage roof. Its thick fingers reached toward her brother. The fingers thinned and stretched like rubber. As thin as snakes, they wrapped around Windslow, binding him like black serpents. He snapped out of his trance and began screaming and kicking. He wiggled wildly and managed to close the book. He looked up at Molly and held the book out as if to throw it to her. The roof collapsed as the Gorlon lifted Windslow up. Windslow pulled the book back and held it tight to his chest as the Gorlon's legs demolished the cottage. The Gorlon looked up and saw Hillary and the others at the top of the cliff.

"Molly!" Hillary screamed. With one swipe of its free hand, the Gorlon shredded the rope ladder, sending bits of rock, rope and vines tumbling into the rubble of the cottage. Molly jumped to the side and now clung to a small bush growing from the rock face.

The Gorlon turned and sent small geysers of water flying as it stepped back toward the trees.

"Do something!" Hillary yelled to the wizards.

"I save him!" Molly called.

Hillary watched the tiny girl take a deep breath as she braced her legs against the cliff. Hillary screamed when Molly jumped. Her arms spread wide, Molly sailed downward, landing on the Gorlon's back.

The blue web of electricity cracked and sparked where Molly landed. The black haired girl screamed and fell limp, stuck to the Gorlon's back like a butterfly caught in fresh tar. The Gorlon reached a hand behind his back and brushed her off. Molly's small body landed in a tangle of vines in the shallow water at the pond's edge.

"You not hurt our sister!" Tillie cried.

"You be happy bout what we do now, big meanie," Nelly screamed.

Both girls ran along the cliff until they were close to the waterfall. They backed up several paces.

"No!" Haggerwolf yelled and ran toward them. "We're too high. The water's not deep enough."

His yell was too late and he wasn't fast enough to reach them. The two sisters ran and dove from the cliff.

Hillary looked for Molly. The same vines Molly had landed in were twisted around the Gorlon's leg. As it stepped through the path it had cleared in the trees, its leg jerked the trailing vines, dragging Molly behind it. In seconds, the Gorlon, Windslow and Molly were gone.

Tears ran down Hillary's face as she anxiously watched the churning water at the bottom of the falls. The black fog thinned and disappeared. The sunlight bathed the water and the trees. The water turned blue and the lily pads green. The white lilies bobbed back to the surface, but there was no sign of the Sallyforth sisters.

"We have to go after them," Hillary said between tears. "We've got to save them. How do we get down?"

"We can't," Haggerwolf said and put his arm around Hillary.

"It's about a two week walk to get off the plateau," Larkstone said.

"And then another three weeks to walk to Crystal Mountain," Fernbark added.

Hillary sniffed and used her shirtsleeve to wipe her face and nose. "We can't wait that long. Can't you use magic or something?"

"There's no spell for flying," Haggerwolf said. "If there was a way to use magic, we wouldn't hesitate to use it."

"Then think!" she said and sat on the ground.

"I'll get you a hanky," Larkstone said. "I have some in my closet." He waved his wand and the shiny zipper entrance to his magic closet appeared, hovering in front of him, just above the ground.

For the next several hours Hillary and the wizards sat, trying to think of ways to get off the plateau. Larkstone pulled chairs and two jars of canned peaches out of his closet. Too upset to eat, Hillary paced back and forth in front of Larkstone's zipper closet, while she racked her brains for ideas.

"Can I look in your closet?" she asked Larkstone. "Maybe something in there will give me an idea."

"Sure," Larkstone answered. "Just think of what you need and then feel around inside."

Hillary pulled the zipper to open the closet. She couldn't think of anything specific to look for, so she pulled the shiny sides farther apart and stuck her head inside.

Haggerwolf played with the end of his beard as he watched Hillary reach in farther. He stood up when she leaned in past her waist. "Larkstone," he asked. "Should she be doing that?"

"Doing what?"

"That."

All three wizards turned toward Larkstone's closet. Hillary wiggled forward. Her feet lifted off the ground as she squirmed farther inside.

"Hillary!" Haggerwolf shouted when her feet slipped out of sight. Before he could stand up, the closet zipped shut and disappeared with a single loud "poof."

The Gorlon comes, it brings a chance
For one who takes a special stance.
If puzzled out one wish will come.
A prize for something that you've done.

Chances do not guarantee.
Results are what you make them be.
You took no chance to win or fail.
A chance is lost if not availed.

You made your choice when two fears came.
Repeated steps work out the same.
Something different, something new.
Is what a second chance gives to you.

18: The Oracle

Hillary was still on her hands and knees inside Larkstone's magic closet when she heard the zipper closing behind her. The narrow beam of sunlight from outside got smaller and smaller. It blinked out when the zipper closed, surrounding her in darkness. She stood up and bonked her head on something. Whatever she hit fell loose, bounced off her shoulder and rolled across the floor, with a metallic clunking sound.

Hillary carefully turned around, stretched her arms straight out and felt her way toward the zipper door. After ten steps without feeling anything, she angled slightly to the side and felt her way forward again. She took three steps and fell over something large and square, setting off a series of sounds like boxes and cartons tumbling down from a pile.

"Great!" she said, louder than she needed to. "How am I supposed to find the door in the dark! Crud-o. I need light."

She felt a strong breeze and heard loud clunks and bangs that startled her. She jumped when a lit candle appeared in her hand. She nearly dropped it. Another clunk sounded and Hillary spun around. Four small lanterns, in different sizes from large to small, formed a square around her. She had to back up when a brick fireplace slid out of the dark and stopped where she had been standing. With a whoosh, flames jumped up, flooding the closet with even more light. She took another step backward and nearly tripped over a dozen more candles that began appearing on the floor. "Enough light!" she yelled. "I just need one of the lanterns."

Poof, pop, whoosh. As quickly as the fireplace, candles and lanterns had appeared, they disappeared, leaving one medium sized lantern burning just to Hillary's side. She held it up and looked around.

All about her, stacked in teetering piles were boxes, crates, jumbles of clothes, some folded and some in piles, pots and pans, ladders, chairs, dishes, books, tables and even a small rowboat with a hole in its side. "And Trish thinks my closet is bad," Hillary muttered as she searched again for the zipper door.

"Argh!" she screamed after a half hour of searching through the clutter. "This place is impossible." She had tried calling out for a door. She nearly got crushed from the wood doors, metal doors, barn doors, trap doors and oven doors that began piling up in front of her. She had yelled for help, and was buried by a small pile of books. She had even asked for "just one adult sized bed," hoping she could fall asleep, wake up back at home and find out if Windslow was all right. The bed came, but she wasn't sleepy, so she kept wandering through the clutter.

"I need to talk to someone, anyone, who has answers," she said softly and plopped down on the floor. Before she had her legs crossed, the room began to swirl around her. The small spot where she sat stayed motionless, but everything else spun, shapes blended together, colors turned to brown then grey. With a poof, the swirling shapes disappeared.

ꕥ

At first, Windslow kicked and screamed. He beat his hands against the Gorlon's broad fist and thick fingers. The Gorlon held him snug in its black oily hand; tight enough that Windslow couldn't free himself, but not tight enough to hurt him. The Gorlon's sticky skin was like day old chewing gum. Windslow knew that if his punching didn't hurt his own hand, then the Gorlon probably didn't even feel the blows.

As soon as the monster stepped from the pond, it shifted Windslow, tossing him over its shoulder. The stickiness held Windslow in place at first. The dancing web of blue magic strands changed their pattern, crisscrossing Windslow's back to hold him snugly in place. It was then that Windslow saw Molly Sallyforth being dragged behind. Each time the Gorlon took one of its long lumbering steps, the vine wrapped around its foot jerked forward and dragged Molly with it.

Windslow began yelling. At first he yelled "Help!" As he began to calm down, he called her name. When Molly didn't move, Windslow forgot about his own fear and yelled at the Gorlon to stop. The black monster paid no attention to him.

Windslow still had the Book of Second Chances. He held it up. "Give Molly a second chance," Windslow screamed. "Let her go. You're hurting her."

Nothing changed. The Gorlon kept walking and Molly's little body jerked forward with each step.

"Stupid book!" Windslow screamed and slammed it shut. He shoved the book into his magic bag. "Maybe..." He slipped the bag's strap off his shoulder and twirled it around his head like a sling. He stretched as best he could and let the bag fly, aiming at the vine tangled around Molly and the Gorlon's leg. The bag hit the vine and bounced to one side. Molly dragged forward. Windslow almost panicked again when he saw the faint trail of blood Molly's body left each time the Gorlon pulled her.

"My slingshot," he said and struggled to reach his back pocket. He felt the handle and pulled out his small weapon. He found two acorns and nearly ripped his pocket feeling the corners for more. "Great," he said and sniffed. "I've screwed up everything today." Part of him wanted to start crying, the other part clung to the small hope that he could somehow free Molly.

ꕥ

When the swirling stopped, Hillary blinked her eyes. Either the closet was gone or it had changed drastically. She thought that maybe she had fallen asleep and this was a real dream she was having while she dream-slipped back home. She sat on green grass instead of the closet floor. Only a foot in front of her tennis shoes the grass stopped where it bordered the edge of a white sandy beach. Bathed in sunlight, the sand stretched merely a yard, then crept under the surface of a turquoise pond. Only a stone throw across, the far edge of the pond hid under a row of weeping willow trees, whose branches curved gracefully down to the water. Behind her a small hill rose, covered in white daisies with bright orange centers. The sun felt good and Hillary closed her eyes to enjoy the sweet perfume from the flowers. Something tickled her arm and she looked down to see a purple butterfly resting for a moment before it fluttered it wings and joined others flitting from flower to flower.

"This is really nice," Hillary said softly and leaned back. "I mean it's really peaceful and a whole lot better than that closet. I need a dream like this, but I should wake up and see if Windslow has dream-slipped back yet. I really do need to find some way to help him and Molly."

"Sometimes answers help, sometimes not," a childlike voice answered.

Hillary looked around but couldn't tell where the voice had come from. "Who's there?" she asked. "Where are you?"

"I am the oracle," the voice answered.

Movement in the willow branches caught Hillary's attention.

"I am here," the oracle's voice said. The willow branches moved again. "And here behind you."

Hillary turned around and watched the daisies sway slightly, even though there was no wind.

"And here," the voice repeated.

Hillary looked again and saw small ripples in the pond.

"The oracle the wizards told us about? Wait! That was just a statement, not a question," Hillary said and got to her feet. "I mean— You see I—" Hillary didn't finish her sentence. She stopped talking and thought. "Oracle," she asked. "I don't know the rules. I don't know how you work. I need a way to find out without asking a question. And that wasn't a question either."

"Sit, daughter of the mountain breeze. I have been expecting you. Sometimes you learn by doing. What is it you would do, if I were to answer any of your questions? Do you only want answers or do you want help?"

"You just said that sometimes answers help and sometimes they don't," Hillary said as she sat down. "I've been learning that you have to help yourself, help your friends and even help people you don't know. There are a bunch of people that need my help right now. I don't think anyone's going to magically help them, so I guess it's up to me. I'll take answers."

"I grant you a second chance because you have learned. You have not earned just one second chance, but many."

"Ha! I'm tired of hearing about second chances. That stupid book promises them and it doesn't work. Now an oracle grants me some. I thought you were going to give me answers."

The daisies moved as the oracle recited the first passage from the Book of Second Chances.

The story in this chance begins,

Found in pages locked within.

Open them with words of care.

What you seek is waiting there.

"You and your brother bring a second chance to Gabendoor. There are many dangers. You will both seek what you are looking for, but neither of you understands what it is you truly hope for."

"Are you telling me that's what the first passage means? If you call that an answer, then you're not much of an oracle. What you explained doesn't make any more sense to me than the words from the book."

"Sometimes you must reach the end of a story to truly understand it. When this story ends then you will both understand. That is the meaning of the words you and your brother have created in the book."

"We didn't create them. We just open the book. Sometimes the next page is blank. Sometimes new words show up. We don't put them there."

"It is what you do that creates the words. The book sees your hearts and minds. The book is your guide."

"This is crazy," Hillary said and stood back up. "How can the book guide us if nothing shows up until after we've done something?"

"That is a question you must answer. Your brother has used the secret of the book, but still must learn the answers. Now it is your turn."

"I don't understand."

"He gave his teacher a second chance. She set aside her fear of rejection to find her true love. He helped the wizards win back their confidence. It was your brother's magic that gave the wizards their second chance. The words in the book confirm it.

Chapter two this lesson learn,

Do not ask for what you yearn.

Magic does not come from here.

It comes from those who lose their fear

"When you wake at home in your world, there will be new words in the book. They will read:

No chances come to those who dwell

When fear has locked them in its spell.

Each second chance from courage grown,

Learn to make them on your own.

The daughter of mountain breeze

Will learn from what her brother sees.

Now with answers will she know

How to make her brother grow.

"Now you will sleep. It's time to go back home," the oracle said, her voice trailing off.

Hillary thought about the words. Suddenly her face brightened and a smile spread across her lips. "You mean that's all there is to it?" Hillary asked. "It's so simple... *yawn.* We should have figured it... out... *yawn...* a long time ago."

Hillary began to dance through the daisies, happy at discovering the secret to the book. She couldn't stop yawning and knew she'd dream-slip soon. Anxious to go back home, she curled up in a grassy spot by the flowers and fell asleep.

ꟷꟷ

Windslow loaded the first acorn. When he stretched the rubber cords back, he yawned. "Not now!" he yelled and eased the tension on his slingshot. "I can't fall asleep. I have to save Molly first." He yawned again, then quickly stretched the cords, took careful aim and released. The acorn hit its target, but bounced off the vine.

"Crud!" Windslow grabbed one of the blue magic strands and tried to stretch it to give himself more freedom to move. The magic tingled in his fingers then gave him a shock, like he got in the wintertime when he walked across the carpet in his stocking feet and touched something metal. A foot long thread of blue snapped off in his hand. The two broken ends on the Gorlon snaked toward each other. They rejoined when the ends touched.

Windslow tried not to yawn as he wound the short blue strand around his last acorn. His eyes felt heavy and he fought against the urge to sleep. He put the glowing acorn in his slingshot and sent it sailing toward the vine. It struck the spot he had aimed for but didn't sever the plant. "No," he wanted to yell, but the word came out soft as his eyes fluttered and he fell asleep.

ꙮ

The Gorlon didn't show any sign that it noticed when Windslow vanished from its shoulder. It never paused in its steady trek back to Crystal Mountain. Molly dragged behind it; the blood trail grew thicker each time it pulled her another pace forward. The acorn glowed green and soon, a silky strand of smoke curled up from the woody vine. The curl grew, as if someone were puffing on an ember. With a snap, the vine broke. Molly lay still. A small puddle of blood stained the leaves under her head. The Gorlon kept walking.

19: Truth and Lies

"Why it turn night so fast?" Tillie Truly asked as she climbed out of the water and onto the short rock shelf.

"You splash too much. Got water on sun and put it out when you dive," Nelly Never Sallyforth answered. Both she and her sister knew the answer was a lie, and that all Nelly could do was lie. It was as impossible for her to tell the truth as it was for Tillie Truly to not be truthful.

"When sun dry out, it be light again," Nelly Never continued. "We not behind waterfall."

Tillie Truly turned around and looked at the light that glowed through the cascading water. "This big cave place," she said. "We better go swim again."

"Yep, that good way to stay safe," Nelly said. "I like-a that idea better than mine. Big rock might eat us if we go that-a way." She pointed to a thin strip of light at the edge of the waterfall.

"Good thing I got smarty sister," Tillie said and headed for the narrow opening.

Once outside, the girls made their way around pond's edge until they were across from the cliff. "Hellooooh..." Tillie called with her hands cupped around her mouth. "Hey big fatty wizard guys. Hellooooh!"

"I think they all up there resting. Betcha they having big picnic lunch and waiting for us. Not much for them to worry about," Nelly Never said.

"Yep, you right," Tillie said. "They gone by now. Take-a big long time to walk way around. We better find Molly. She can play wizard with us again when we go save Window."

"That be so boring," Nelly Never answered. She sat down and pulled off her boot. "Just like-a last time."

"I get-a be Hickerwolf this time," Tillie said. She held out her hand and waited for her sister.

Nelly held up her boot, gave it a shake and then pounded the heel on the ground. Three small yellow seeds tumbled out. "I throw this one away. It belong-a Molly." Nelly picked up one seed and dropped it back into her boot. "I not be Fernbook again," she said and handed one of the seeds to her sister.

"We better find Molly first. Then eat seeds and have fun," Tillie said. She stuck her seed in a pocket on her skirt and began walking.

ᘛᘚ

The sisters had walked for nearly half an hour when they found Windslow's book bag and the Book of Second Chances still inside. They both whooped and danced over their discovery. After paging through the book, they put it back inside the bag and began running. They hadn't run far when they found their sister.

"Molly!" Tillie screamed and ran.

Nelly knelt in front of Molly. Carefully she lifted Molly's head and cradled it in her lap. Tillie used the hem of her skirt to wipe away the blood.

"Call birds. Call fast!" Tillie said. Her tears dropped on Molly's face.

Nelly put two fingers in her mouth and blew a long shrill whistle. "I not too worried," she said. "This not scare me."

"We take her to granny Gilderbun," Tillie said.

"Granny, grandpa know what to do. They fix her. Won't they?" she asked and looked up at Nelly.

ꙮ

"The Gorlon has Windslow, Hillary is lost somewhere in your closet, the Sallyforth triplets have disappeared and we're stuck in the middle of nowhere," Haggerwolf said, the anger in his voice rising. "Does that about cover it?" he yelled.

"I only said we should assess the situation," Larkstone answered as he bent a branch back away from the path and held it until the other two wizards passed. He let the branch snap back and hurried to catch up to his friends. They had waited for Hillary to reappear. Larkstone had even used his magic wand to try and make his zipper closet come back, but nothing worked. They had decided the only thing left to do was start walking.

"Hillary was right," Fernbark said as he climbed over a fallen log. "There has to be some way we can use our magic to get back to Crystal Mountain. We just haven't been creative enough."

"Face it, my friends," Haggerwolf said as Fernbark helped him over the log. "We're washed up. We have been for a long time. The only reason we're even alive is because we were too old and our magic too weak to help in the last battle. We would have died in Dreadmoor if Windslow hadn't saved us. We're just three old men."

"I've been thinking about that," Larkstone said. "Windslow says he doesn't know how to work the book. I'm sure he's telling the truth. The only thing that he did was make us think we had a chance. We took it and it worked. We saved ourselves and him in Dreadmoor. Hey, what happened to my vest?"

"I'm wearing it," Fernbark said. He stopped walking and turned around. "And Haggerwolf's wearing my boots. What's going on?"

"The book spell," Haggerwolf said. "Someone new has opened the Book of Second Chances. A bit of our warning spell must still be active."

"If we could just strengthen it." Larkstone said and pulled out his wand. "The journey wind—"

"We need to do this fast," Haggerwolf said, interrupting his friend. "Before the spell is gone completely."

Haggerwolf waved his wand. "The journey's wind will rise and grow."

"Wizards ride when the travel wind blows," Fernbark said, adding his part to the spell.

Larkstone opened and closed his mouth twice before his first words came out. "Get there fast when I... When I..."

"Come on!" Haggerwolf shouted.

"Get there fast when I blow my nose!"

ꙮ

Hillary sat up. She looked around and then pinched herself to make sure she was really back in her bedroom at home, and not just having another strange dream. Still in her jeans and flannel shirt she wore when dream-slipping, she jumped from bed and ran to Windslow's room. Being careful not to wake her parents, she opened Windslow's bedroom door and slipped inside. She breathed a sigh when she saw her step-brother lying on his side, his back facing her.

"Windslow," she said in a half-whisper. "Are you all right?" She put one hand on his shoulder. Windslow jerked away from her.

"Go away."

"Windslow, what's wrong. Are you hurt?"

"Go away. Leave me alone."

Hillary pulled her hand back and sat down on the

edge of his bed. "I was worried about you. And, Molly. Is she..."

Windslow sniffed, wiped his hand across his face and pulled his blanket over his head.

"She's not... Oh, Windslow..."

"I don't know," he said, his voice muffled by the blankets. "I tried to help her. Really I did."

Hillary sat quietly, her own eyes filled with tears. She put her hand back on Windslow's shoulder. This time he didn't pull away and she could feel him shudder each time he took in a breath between his silent sobs. "Then you don't know for sure?"

"No. She didn't move and was bleeding. I should have done something. I should have climbed the rope ladder in the first place and she wouldn't have gotten hurt. It's all my fault, just like the last time."

"What are you talking about?"

"When I fell off the roof and hurt my back. I was the one that put your doll up there in the first place. I wanted to look like a hero. Some hero. Now go away."

Hillary bit her lip and thought. "Windslow, what did you see on Biffendear's roof? What did the Gorlon look like?"

Windslow shook. Hillary could clearly hear his sobbing now. She waited.

"Like I'm going to look someday. Its legs were all shriveled up."

"It was just an illusion. You're not going... Windslow it's all right. You're—"

"A coward and a failure," he said, cutting her off. "A worthless cripple. Now leave me alone."

Hillary squeezed her eyes shut, trying not to let her fears about Molly and her brother overwhelm her. She wanted to curl up and cry too, but the words of the oracle helped her turn her thoughts away. Before standing, she looked for the magic book bag. She wasn't surprised when she didn't find it. Either it was lost or the Gorlon had it. Either way, she thought, it didn't matter. In a way it was probably good.

Quietly she slipped back to her own room to think. Bill and Trish would have lots of questions about what was wrong with Windslow. He'd probably just tell them he didn't feel good. She guessed he'd just stay in bed all day. That was probably best. She would say she stayed up too late last night, was tired and needed to do some extra homework. If she was right about the book, then today she needed to think and plan. She would need to keep busy. It would help keep her from becoming depressed over her concern for Molly. Hillary opened her small jewelry case and took out the earring that was the mate to the one she had given Molly when they first met. She took some gauze pads, tape, antiseptic ointment and aspirin from the first aid kit in the bathroom. She tucked her medical supplies and the earring into a clean sock and laid them on her pillow so she wouldn't forget them later.

She decided to wait until her parents were up before she took a shower and changed. While she waited, she sat at her desk, took out a tablet and pen and began writing ideas.

ꕥ

Tillie Truly and Nelly Never sat high up in a tree behind granny Gilderbun's cottage in Eldervale. Each girl found a broad fork in the branches of the maple tree that formed a natural chair. When they arrived in Eldervale, granny Gilderbun immediately took charge. She had Dimbleshoot carry Molly into the back bedroom and assigned other grannies to take care of Tillie and Nelly. The grannies heated water in big pots, made both girls take baths, and washed their clothes. After a big meal, both girls ran for the tree when one of the women came out with scissors and a big hair brush.

Eventually the grannies and grandpas gave up trying to coax the girls down. Now Tillie and Nelly simply waited.

It was nearing sundown when two bluebirds flitted to the tree. The birds perched and flapped their wings while they chirped wildly.

"That bad news," Nelly Never said and began scrambling toward the ground.

"Hurray!" Tillie shouted. "Molly better."

Both sisters landed on the ground nearly at the same time and stumbled over each other as they raced for the cottage. Gilderbun stepped aside at the door and simply smiled as Tillie and Nelly rushed past her to the back bedroom.

"Careful, girls," Dimbleshoot said. "She's going to be fine, but no hugs for awhile."

"Hi," Molly said. "Look-a my nose." Pillows piled up against the wall formed a backrest for Molly. She sat in bed and held a small hand mirror up in front of her face. She moved the mirror away from her face just long enough to smile at her sisters. "I not twin anymore," she said. "We not all look-a like. I got broken nose."

"You always pretty ugly girl," Nelly said and sat on the edge of the bed. "You just more ugly now. You never the best."

"What big Gorlon do to you?" Tillie asked and sat next to Nelly.

"I jump on him and blue stuff go zippity-zap. Make me fall asleep. I bonk my nose when dumb Gorlon dump me on-a ground. Lots of scratch and purple bump places," Molly said and pulled the blanket off her legs to show off her bruises.

"Me make you look pretty again," Tillie said. She picked up a piece of charcoal from the nightstand and used it to carefully draw pictures of little birds on the tape across her sister's nose. Molly watched in the hand mirror and all three girls began giggling.

"Here," Nelly said. She handed a piece of tape to Tillie. Both Tillie and Nelly drew on their own pieces of tape. When they finished, each girl put one across her own nose.

"Now we all-a like again," Tillie said. She grabbed the mirror to admire her artwork.

"Where Hillre and Window? What happen to fatty wizards?" Molly asked.

"We know lots-a stuff about all-a that," Nelly said.

"Don't know," Tillie said and shrugged her shoulders. "Gorlon must-a give Window to Fistlock by now. All-a others gone someplace. We got book though." Tillie slipped the book bag off her shoulder, reached inside and pulled out the Book of Second Chances. "We gonna save Window and give Fistlock biggie headache."

"Yep. He be real happy to see us," Nelly said. She held up her yellow seed in one hand and the one she had for Molly in her other hand. "We not gonna give him any surprises."

20: Answers

The journey wind swirled and gyrated. Three belches later it disappeared, dumping the three wizards at the spot where Tillie and Nelly had opened the book.

"Well, at least we're off that plateau," Haggerwolf grumbled as he and the other wizards changed back into their own clothes, mixed up by traveling in the journey wind.

"The Gorlon must have the book," Larkstone said as he buckled his belt.

Fernbark knelt down and looked at the ground. "The Sallyforth girls," he said. "They're alive. Two of them were here. See their boot prints?"

"Any sign of Molly?" Haggerwolf asked. "It's her that I'm worried about."

"I'm afraid so. There's some blood. It follows the Gorlon's trail. We better hurry."

They ran down the path of flattened plants and broken branches left by the Gorlon. They stopped when they found the bloody pile of leaves.

"Look," Fernbark said. "Molly was lying here. Her sisters found her. Let me see what the plants know." He walked to the nearest ferns and ran his fingers along their fragile leaves. Humming softly he closed his eyes. "Large birds of some sort carried all three of them away. At least they're out of danger. The plants don't think Molly is dead, just roughed up a bit."

"I'm glad they're safe," Haggerwolf said and adjusted his suspenders. "Those girls are nothing but trouble, but I wouldn't want to see harm come to any of them. At least they're out of our way now. They have a habit of fouling up everything they get involved with."

"Like the last time," Fernbark said, "when we were trying to find the Book of False Promises. If they hadn't messed up the clues, we might have found it. Then we wouldn't need the Book of Second Chances. Well, we better start moving. It's still a long walk to Crystal Mountain."

"I thought it was kind of fun," Larkstone said. "At least more fun than when they lost the Book of Whimsy. That time they—" Larkstone looked up and saw his friends were already far up the trail. He ran to catch up.

ഇര

"Hold it steady!" Fistlock shouted down from the top of the wooden ladder. Below him Bitterbrun struggled to hold the base in place on the slippery stone floor, just outside the Gorlon's cave.

The ladder shook as Fistlock neared the top rungs. It shook more from the wobbling of Fistlock's knees than it did because of anything Bitterbrun was or wasn't doing. "I see an impression," Fistlock called down. "The Gorlon got whoever had the book. I bet it's the boy. He must have dream-slipped home. We'll have him when he comes back. Let's see what happened. Bring me the tongs."

"But your highness," Bitterbrun protested. "Who's going to hold—"

"Now!"

Bitterbrun kept one hand on the ladder as he squatted down to grab a long pair of wooden tongs lying at his feet. Tongs in hand, he worked his way up the shaky ladder. "Here, your quiverness," he said and reached up to Fistlock.

Fistlock grabbed the tongs. Holding them in one hand he stretched the far end toward the Gorlon's orange eye. A quick grab and twist popped the shiny piece of glass from the Gorlon's face. The monster didn't move, flinch or give any other sign of discomfort. Fistlock grabbed the eye from the tongs, tucked it in his pocket and stretched for the other one.

Bitterbrun leaned out to watch Fistlock. When he leaned, the ladder began to slide to the left. Bitterbrun lost his balance and jumped. His movement shoved the ladder back to the right. Both Bitterbrun and Fistlock screamed.

Bitterbrun had the shorter fall and landed on his back. He looked up and saw Fistlock teetering just before the ladder fell. Fistlock jumped, landing on the Gorlon's chest. The blue magic sparked, Fistlock twitched and screamed. The Gorlon's sticky skin kept Fistlock from falling, but not from sliding. As Fistlock slowly slid down his black monster, cords of blue magic crackled and sparked. With each crackle, Fistlock stiffened and screamed. After nine screams he landed in a heap beside Bitterbrun.

Fistlock rolled to the side and jumped to his feet. Quickly he backed away. "You idiot. I'm finished with you. Stomp him!" Fistlock ordered, calling out to the Gorlon.

Bitterbrun scooted backward, as the Gorlon raised a foot. With a loud stomp, its foot crashed down, barely missing Bitterbrun. The Gorlon turned, took a step and stomped again. "The other way, the other way!" Fistlock screamed. The Gorlon tuned again and stomped, this time dangerously close to Fistlock.

"It can't see," Bitterbrun yelled. "You took out its eyes."

The Gorlon took a step forward. Fistlock took two steps back and stopped, blocked by the wall behind him. "Here!" Fistlock yelled and tossed his wand to Bitterbrun. "Deflate him. Quick!"

Bitterbrun snatched the wand from mid-air. He aimed

it at the Gorlon while Fistlock called out the words. "Return to the earth of the Gorlon's birth."

A thick cord of blue magic shot from the wand, as if it were a rope of silk spun from a giant spider. The far end attached itself to blue latticework of magic covering the Gorlon's body. Bitterbrun pulled his end of cord from the wand and dragged it to the side of the cave entrance. Quickly he wrapped it around a three-foot long metal spike. The Gorlon took another stomp closer to Fistlock. Bitterbrun's sweaty hands slipped from the sludge hammer when he first picked it up. He grabbed again and glanced at Fistlock. The Gorlon raised its foot over Fistlock's head. The clang of metal on metal rang out when Bitterbrun struck the first blow. The iron spike sunk six inches into the dirt. The Gorlon froze. "Clang!" Bitterbrun swung the sledgehammer again, as hard as he could. The spike sunk another foot into the ground.

Fistlock eased himself sideways along the wall, the whole time keeping his eyes locked on the Gorlon. The monster slowly lowered his thick leg. As if it were a black candle, melting on a hot stove, the Gorlon began to shrink. The blue lattice of magic sparked and thinned as it raced along the cord to the spike and into the earth. Bitterbrun's hair stood out at crazy angles from the static charge and the buttons on his vest gave off small sparks.

The oily puddle that had been the Gorlon's legs grew larger and seeped into the ground around the cave entrance. When only its arms, shoulders and head remained in the center of the pool, Fistlock hiked up his robe and stepped through the puddle, trying to stay on his tiptoes. When he reached what was left of the Gorlon, he pulled a knife from inside his robe. With a sawing motion, Fistlock carved out a chunk of the Gorlon's shoulder. Before Fistlock reached dry ground, nothing was left of the Gorlon but a large stained patch of oily sand and dirt.

"I got it," Fistlock said and held up the chunk of Gorlon shoulder. "This is all I need to make sure the boy dream-slips back. He'll return to wherever this is. Here, put it in the dungeon." Fistlock tossed the chunk to Bitterbrun. "Do it quick and I'll postpone your death."

"Thank you, your cleverness," Bitterbrun said as he caught the slippery lump of Gorlon. He turned toward the path leading around to the main entrance.

"Not that way," Fistlock yelled. "This way," he said and pointed toward the Gorlon's cave.

"But my, benevolent master, the new Gorlon is almost fully grown. It could—"

"That way! Now!" Fistlock yelled.

Bitterbrun nodded and took off running.

Fistlock grinned as he walked up the path to main doors of Crystal Mountain. He began singing a little tune that he made up as he walked. "The book is mine. The book is mine. I have all the chances and all the time. I—" He jumped up and tried to click his heels together as he sang. The jump was too low and the kick too slow. Fistlock cursed when he fell and ripped his robe. After dusting himself off, he continued walking. This time he just hummed.

Something glinted in the sunlight where Fistlock had stumbled. A short whistle sounded and seconds later a dove flew down from a nearby tree and snatched up the small tin of needle points without landing.

ꙮ

"Not here again," Hillary complained when she woke up on the bed inside Larkstone's zipper closet. "All right, let's see if all that thinking was worth it." She pulled a folded piece of paper from the back pocket of her jeans. "Hm..." she said as she ran her finger down her list of ideas. "Okay, here goes.

Hey you stupid closet," she yelled, improvising a bit from the words she had on her notes. "Larkstone needs something. He needs ME!"

ꙮ

For the last mile, none of the wizards had said anything, except when Fernbark began to whistle. Now they walked silently again, Haggerwolf in the lead with his hands shoved deep in the pockets of his robe. Larkstone came next and kicked a small stone along in front of him as he walked. Fernbark walked in back and carried a small branch he used as a walking stick. All three wizards banged into each other when Haggerwolf stopped abruptly. The zipper gave no warning when it appeared in front of him. All three stared as the shiny pull zipped downward.

"Where are we? Not still on that cliff, I hope," Hillary said as she climbed out.

"You're safe. How did you find us? What about Windslow. Are—"

Questions flew at her. Hillary wasn't sure who asked what. "Quiet!" she yelled and put her hands on her hips. "Answer my question. Where are we?"

"About a day's walk from Crystal Mountain, dear," Fernbark answered. "We're so glad to see—"

"Where are Molly and her sisters?" Hillary blurted out, interrupting him.

"Someplace safe," Haggerwolf answered. "We don't know for certain. We found their tracks and signs of birds. At least the three are together and out of harm's way. Is your brother all right?"

"Kind of," Hillary said. She spun around when she heard the zipper close and pop as it disappeared. She turned back to the wizards. "He's not feeling too good about himself right now. He's not hurt, but blames himself for letting all of us down, especially Molly. He'll be fine, but he needs some time. The good news is I know the book's secret."

All three wizard faces lit up, but before they could say anything, Hillary held up her hand. "I'm not going to tell you how it works. It's safer right now if the secret stays with me. But now that I can work it, I'm giving us a chance to save my brother and Gabendoor. But to do that, I need answers." Hillary paused and looked around, waiting to see if the swirling would start again. The wizards looked with her. She half expected to end up back at the oracle's grove.

"What are we looking for?" Larkstone asked.

"Oh. Sorry," Hillary said. "Nothing. Let's start walking. For this chance to work, to activate it so to speak, I need to know more about Fistlock. Where did he come from? Tell me about Crystal Mountain and the last war."

While they walked, the three wizards answered Hillary's questions. At first, they explained, wizards discovered their talent for magic and studied on their own. When Fistlock was a young man and learned he had the talent, he organized all the other young wizards and formed a school of wizardry knowledge.

"As the school and its knowledge grew," Haggerwolf said, "Fistlock and the others forced the three of us to retire. I have to admit, the youngsters were learning to do things we never dreamed of. They said we were old and used up. They had no use for us."

Larkstone went on to tell about Fistlock's grand idea. Gabendoor suffered a series of droughts and strange weather patterns. Fistlock said everyone had been polluting the ground. He thought up the idea of Crystal Mountain and its reservoir as a way to suck the sickness from the earth. Many of the young wizards died creating the place, but it worked. The inky blackness began filling the reservoir, rains came and the weather turned back to normal.

"So Fistlock was one of the good guys?" Hillary asked. "What happened to make him so mean?"

"Greed and vanity," Fernbark said. "We need to take that left fork here. There's a brook up ahead where we can stop and rest."

At the brook Haggerwolf told how Fistlock demanded to be named Grand Ruler of Gabendoor. The other wizards objected. That's when Fistlock created the first Gorlon. For some reason, as the world got better, magic started slipping away. It got weaker for everyone but Fistlock. Soon the war started and Fistlock had the book and the Gorlons. He could make three Gorlons a week.

"The book and the Gorlons made him invincible," Haggerwolf said. He paused and looked up at the sun. "If we walk a bit faster, we can reach a campsite not far from Crystal Mountain. It's a good place to stop for the night so you can dream-slip."

"How does all this fit into your granting another chance from the book?" Fernbark asked as they started walking again.

"I'm not sure yet," Hillary said. "There are several chances up my sleeve. I've been wondering about that black pool inside the mountain. I don't think it's a holding pond for pollution. I think it has something to do with magic. We'll take all the chances we need to solve that one. If we do, I think that will be the end of the Gorlons. The big chance for you three will come when you face Fistlock."

"Us?" all three voices said at one time.

ꙮ

Windslow knew where he was the moment he opened his eyes. He recognized the dungeon and cells from Hillary's description. He woke lying near the center of the cell. After a quick look around he moved to the back corner, pulled his knees up against his chest and wrapped his arms around them.

With a heavy sigh, he twisted his head and rested his cheek against the top of his knees.

He looked up when he heard footsteps, but only for a moment. He didn't care who was coming. He didn't care what happened. Whatever happened now he felt like he deserved.

"Well, well, well. So you're my book thief."

Windslow raised his head but didn't answer. Just as Molly had described, the man looked too skinny for his height. A long purple robe flowed beneath a slightly shorter and black outer cloak with silver trim. The man's violet pupils stared at him.

"Where is it!"

"I don't know," Windslow said. "I threw it in the woods when your Gorlon killed Molly. I hope no one ever finds it. I bet they don't. I'm the guy who can't do anything right, so you're just wasting your time with me."

"Bitterbrun!" Fistlock yelled. His assistant hurried through the door across the room and ran to his master's side.

"Yes, your loudness."

"Send some men to search the path the Gorlon took. Tell them to bring back the Book of Second Chances or they'll all end up like this wretched boy."

"In a cell?" Bitterbrun asked.

"No. Dead," Fistlock said without turning around.

"Yes, your evilness," Bitterbrun said. He turned and scurried back out the door.

"What's this?" Fistlock said as he moved his magic wand up and down between the cell bars. "A bit of magic? Stand up."

Windslow put his head back down and ignored him.

"I said, stand up!" Fistlock twitched his wand. An unseen force wrapped around Windslow. It forced him to his feet and made him take awkward steps forward.

"Hm... a bit of magic in your back. Ah, it seems you injured it. Is that why you're afraid of falling off roofs?"

"How do you know about that?"

"With these," Fistlock said and held up a pair of round orange colored glass balls. "They're the Gorlon's eyes. They record everything they see. I just need to look into them to see what the Gorlon saw. How would you like to take a walk up on the top of Crystal Mountain? It's very slippery and quite a long drop to the ground, I'm afraid."

"Do whatever you want," Windslow said.

"Not that I need your permission, yet you do have the idea, lad. Before we head to the roof, I think I'll do something about that magic patch you have."

Fistlock twitched his wand. Windslow heard a faint crackling sound and his back turned numb. He had to grab the cell bars to keep from falling. Slowly his hands slid down the bars until he sat on the floor.

"That's just something for you to think about while I wait for my men to find that book," Fistlock said. "When they do, you're going to show me how it works or I'll personally toss you off the roof. Oh and by the way, I understand you made a visit to Eldervale. You might want to know that I'm sending my troops there to burn their village. My men need a bit of practice. I've ordered them to rid Gabendoor of those useless old men and women for good. See you soon," Fistlock said and chuckled as he spun around and walked to the door.

Windslow used his hands to drag himself back to the corner. He closed his eyes and began to cry.

21: Butterscotch

Windslow didn't bother looking when he heard soft footsteps and muted voices. He assumed it was Fistlock coming back to get him. He didn't look up when he heard the slight squeak as a cell door began to open. He did look when he heard a soft voice.

"Go way, hinge-hagler. Here, take butter-rock. Go play someplace else."

"Molly?" he asked softly and turned his head.

The room stood empty, but the cell door next to him opened slowly and silently. Windslow sat up and watched the door close.

"Hi, Window," a voice whispered from nowhere.

"You pretty cute guy," another invisible voice said.

"He still look pretty ugly to me," a third voice added.

"Molly? Tillie? Nelly?" Windslow asked, a bit louder this time.

"Yep, we here," all three voices said together.

"We alla come to save you," Molly's voice said.

"Where are you? I can't see any of you."

"Right here," Tillie said.

Windslow blinked. First there was nothing but an empty cell full of dark shadows. He blinked again and the three Sallyforth sisters stood smiling and waving at him. He blinked and the cell stood empty.

"I'm going crazy," Windslow said as he stared at the shadows. "Just like prisoners in the movies."

"Hi," someone said.

Windslow rubbed his eyes. Three pairs of hands floated unattached in the air. They waved at him.

"We got shadow-glump," Molly said. "Him like-a butter-rock candy. Him help us. Watch."

Windslow looked as the three sisters appeared, disappeared, then reappeared. He dragged himself to the bars separating the two cells and looked closer. He thought Molly had something in her hand by the way she held her fingertips. When she pulled her arm around herself and her sisters, they all disappeared into a shadow in the near corner of their cell. When she moved her arm away, all three sisters were back.

"How'd you do that?"

"Told you. We got new friend. Shadow-glump, say hi to Window."

Windslow heard a faint "hello" in a deep voice. The dark shadow in the corner moved briefly.

"Window our friend too," Molly said, looking at the shadow beside her. "Window's grandpa send butter-rock magic from earth. Here, you like another piece?"

"Molly, I'm so glad to see you; all of you. But I still don't understand," he said and watched Molly unwrap a piece of candy. She held it out and it disappeared into the shadow.

"Shadow-glump one of Fistlock shadow beasties. He live in corners and dark places. He don't like Fistlock no more. He help us. See? He hide us in shadow." Molly and her sisters disappeared and reappeared again. "We get you out-a here. Come this-a way and tell us about Gorlon."

"I can't stand," Windslow said and looked away. "Fistlock took away the magic that let me walk. I was just a coward and a failure. Now I'm a crippled coward and failure.

You three better get out of here before he comes back. If you hang around me you'll get hurt again." Windslow turned his head away and closed his eyes.

"You scared of Fistlock?" Tillie asked.

"He not scared of Fistlock. He not scared of falling either," Nelly Never said.

"We scared. We scared alla time," Tillie said. "We not very big, and fatty wizards pick on us alla time. Alla places don't like us, except granny-grandpa place."

"Now you like us. We all scared. You like our brother," Molly said.

"You don't understand," Windslow said. "It's not all right to be scared. Look what happened to me. Look what I did to you. I messed everything up because I'm scared of falling again. Well, it doesn't matter. I'll never walk again. I'm a scared kid in a wheelchair who can't do anything by himself."

"You head messed up," Molly said. "Maybe big Gorlon bang you. He break my nose. See? Now we all got pretty tape."

Windslow looked at the three grinning, gerbil eyed faces. Each nose had a piece of tape across its bridge. He couldn't help but smile.

"That pretty scary time," Molly said. "Now we look alla like again. We twins."

Windslow shook his head. His smile grew. "You're triplets. Never mind. I'm still messed up."

"Maybe Window not like us anymore," Tillie said. "We mess up alla time. That why wizards don't like us."

"No. I like you. I like all of you," Windslow said. "I just feel bad about being..."

"It okay to be scared," Molly said. "Do stuff when happy. Do stuff when sad. Do stuff when scared. Alla same. Just do stuff. Only difference is feeling in here." She touched her heart. "Window got good heart. Got good head too."

"And pretty face," Tillie added.

"Shush," Molly scolded. "I fix you up. I got book now. We give you second chance to walk."

"Molly, the stupid book doesn't work. It never has. You can't fix my back with it."

"How about fatty wizard magic? I got that too. They give it to me. See?" Molly said and held out her closed fist.

"Where? Open your hand," Windslow said. He used his arms to scoot closer to the bars.

"Can't. Don't want to let it run away. Turn round. I show you. I fix back like wizard tell me. Then you see."

Windslow's heart thumped hard in his chest and his palms began to sweat as he twisted himself around.

"Pull up shirt," Molly said. Her sisters giggled when Windslow did as Molly instructed.

Molly pressed her closed fist against Windslow's back. He felt something cool and heard a crinkling crackling sound as Molly opened her fingers and pressed her palm against him. "Wizards say you not feel anything. If magic make sound then spell work. You try it now."

Windslow pulled his shirt down and twisted back to face Molly. He grabbed the cell bars and pulled. He was shaky but slowly got to his feet.

"Let go and take step," Molly said.

Windslow's face beamed brightly as he stood on his own. He took first one step backward and then another. With less wobbling, he walked backwards all the way to the other side of his cell. He stopped, broadened his grin and walked back to Molly.

"Oops, I need more magic," Molly said and reached a hand back to Tillie. Tillie took something amber colored from her skirt pocket and placed it in Molly's hand. "See," Molly said. "This same kind-a magic I fix your back with. Watch."

She stretched out her closed fist, then opened her hand, palm up. She held a piece of the butterscotch candy Windslow had asked his stepsister to give to Dimbleshoot. Molly unwrapped the candy. As she did, Windslow heard the same crinkling sound he heard when Molly fixed his back.

"The cellophane wrapper made that sound. You tricked me," he said.

"I not trick you. You trick you. You head all messed up. Butter-rock candy make you think better. Eat one," Molly said and held out her hand again.

At first Windslow didn't know what to say or do. He looked at Tillie and Nelly. Both girls smiled and stuck out their tongues. Each tongue held a piece of butterscotch candy. The tongues disappeared behind big smiles.

Windslow could only do one thing. He began to smile too. He took the candy from Molly and put it in his mouth. All three sisters grinned when he stuck his tongue out like they had.

They started to laugh but stopped when they heard the far away sound of a door slam.

"You three better get out of here," Windslow said. "You need to send a message to Gilderbun. Tell her that Fistlock is sending troops to destroy Eldervale. He plans to get rid of them all."

"We give you Second Chance Book and get you out. You stop baddie Fistlock," Molly said. She held out his magic book bag.

"There isn't time, and that book doesn't—" Windslow stopped and looked down at the piece of amber colored cellophane he had been playing with in his hand. "Take the book to Eldervale. Give it to them. Tell them it will help with any plans they come up with; even if their plan is just to hide."

"We get scritch to grab key and get you out. Then you give book to grandpas," Tillie said.

"For now, I think it's better if I stay here. I can keep an eye on Fistlock and maybe learn something."

"That not very brave," Nelly Never said. "Bet you not scared."

"I'm very scared," Windslow said. "But I think you three just taught me that I can be scared and brave at the same time."

"See?" Molly said. "Butter-rock fix your head and make you walk again. This pretty good magic stuff."

"Molly, I think the magic came from you." Windslow paused and thought about what he had just said. The words from the Book captured his thoughts just long enough for him to think about one passage.

There is no magic where you thought.

It came from things its bearer brought

These pages put you to the test

You've learned to plan and do your best.

"You three get out of here now. Deliver my message and then you can come back, but only if you can use the shadow-glump to keep anyone from seeing you. I've got some planning to do."

ꕥ

"I don't care if it's dangerous," Hillary said and kept walking. "Did you three think you could get rid of Fistlock and not be in any danger? Even with second chances there's still danger. A second chance doesn't guarantee anything. It's just a chance. You take it or you don't. I made this one myself and I'm taking it."

"All right," Haggerwolf said, "But we're going with you. Maybe we can divert the Gorlon."

"Fair enough," Hillary said. "Are you sure that's the best way in?" she asked and stopped behind a broad tree trunk. The tree stood at the forest edge, just outside the Gorlon's cave entrance into Crystal Mountain.

"The only two ways in are the main gate, and the Gorlon's cave." Fernbark said.

"What about the place Molly and I slid down from the first time I escaped?"

Larkstone peeked around the tree and pointed. "See the darker spots, higher up? There are several places like you and the Sallyforth girl used, but they're just exits at best. There's no way up to them. The glass is too slippery."

"Then we'll go through the Gorlon's cave. Even if there was another choice, I bet it's the shortest route to where I want to go. I want to be in and out fast; before I dream-slip home. Let's go."

Hillary bent over and ran as fast as she could to the cave entrance. Just inside the cavernous opening she stopped and waited for the three wizards to catch up to her.

Carved into the stone, the cave entrance stayed flat for only a few feet before the passage sloped upward and turned from black stone to crystal glass. Two buses stacked on top of each other would have no trouble fitting inside. At first, Hillary could see though the glass to the black stone behind it. As they walked up the ramp, thicker glass kept them from seeing anything but their own reflections. Sunlight angled inside the cave, bouncing off the glass in sparkling rainbow patterns that filled the whole cavern with light. The floor had a slight curve to it, and down the center a thick black residue made walking slippery. Hillary and the wizards stayed close to the wall where the footing was less dangerous.

One hundred feet in, the passage turned to the left. Hillary signaled the wizards to stop as she peered around the bend. She looked, pulled her head back, and pressed her back against the wall. "It's the Gorlon."

Haggerwolf took a quick look. "It's nearly complete. I'd say less than a day at the most and the new Gorlon will be ready. We have one thing to our advantage. Fistlock hasn't put its eyes in yet."

"Oh, gross," Hillary said.

"They're just glass balls," Larkstone reassured her. "The Gorlon doesn't feel anything. That's part of what makes it invincible. It's not very fast, but it's methodical. You can't kill it. It just wears out and melts, but not before it has done everything Fistlock tells it to do."

"And not before Fistlock has time to make another one," Haggerwolf added.

"This won't be too hard if it can't see us," Hillary said and took another look. "We'll just walk past it." She slipped around the corner.

Nearly two stories high, the puffy black form sat sideways with its back against one wall and its feet sticking out, nearly touching the opposite wall.

Hillary held a finger to her lips to signal silence. On tiptoe, she moved toward the narrow space between the Gorlon's feet and the passage wall.

The Gorlon sniffed.

Hillary froze and watched.

The Gorlon sniffed again and shifted its hulk to sit up straight. It drew one leg back and Hillary heard its chain slide across the glass.

Haggerwolf grabbed Hillary's shirt sleeve and began pulling her back. She fought against him. While they struggled, Larkstone whispered something to Fernbark. He nodded and tried to get Haggerwolf's attention. Haggerwolf ignored him as he continued to pull on Hillary's shirt.

Larkstone moved first. He grabbed Haggerwolf around the knees. Fernbark shoved, toppling the elder wizard.

Hillary screamed. The Gorlon lumbered to its feet.

Fernbark and Larkstone wrestled with Haggerwolf. In seconds Larkstone yanked off one of Haggerwolf's boots and held it out.

The Gorlon sniffed loud and turned toward them. Hillary pinched her nose and turned her head.

Fernbark let go of Haggerwolf, while at the same time Larkstone tossed the boot to the other side of the passage. "The other one too," Fernbark whispered, a bit louder than he should have.

Haggerwolf's face turned red, but he understood. Yanking off his other boot he tossed it beside the first one.

The Gorlon sniffed and took a step forward. Blindly it searched with its thick fingers while it smelled the air. It sniffed first toward the boots, and then toward Haggerwolf. Fernbark gave his barefoot wizard friend a shove and pointed.

Haggerwolf ran across the passage, grabbed his boots and held them up. The Gorlon followed the ripe scent with his eyeless face. Fernbark ran across to his friend, pulled his own boots off and held them up just like Haggerwolf. The two wizards backed down the passage.

Larkstone pressed his back against the wall and motioned Hillary to do the same. They stood motionless as the Gorlon moved with heavy steps, dragging its chain as it followed the smell from two pairs of boots and four bare feet. As soon as the Gorlon passed Hillary and Larkstone, they turned and ran up the passage.

22: Squishy Butter

Hillary and Larkstone ran the rest of the way through the winding glass tunnel. Several passages branched off to one side, but Hillary knew she only had to follow the chain restraining the Gorlon to find the black pond. When they reached it, both she and Larkstone took quick looks to make sure no one was there.

"Keep watch," Hillary said as she ducked under the brass railing surrounding the pond. "I want a sample of this to take back to my science lab."

"You're a scientist?" Larkstone asked.

"No. I go to school in my world. One of my teachers, Mr. Nick, is a chemist. I want to see what he thinks of this stuff. Do you have a bottle or jar; something I can put a sample in?"

"Not with me, but I could check my closet."

"There's no time for that," Hillary said. She thought for a moment and reached into her shirt pocket for the small lipstick case she carried. "This will work."

Hillary pulled the shiny brass cap off her lipstick tube and stuck the cap in her pocket. She twisted the base to push the bright red stick out as far as it would go, and broke it off. "Can I use your shirttail?" she asked.

Larkstone didn't question her. He ducked under the rail, stood next to her and pulled out his shirt. Hillary grabbed the cloth and wrapped it around a pen she took from her pocket. She shoved the pen and cloth inside the lipstick base and twisted several times. "I want to get the inside as clean as I can," She explained. "All right, hold onto my ankles."

Hillary got down on her hands and knees and eased herself across the slippery glass floor. At the pool's edge, she stretched out. Larkstone grabbed her foot in one hand and held a brass post with his other hand.

Hillary reached down with the empty lipstick tube. As her hand got close to the black liquid, blue sparks danced up and stung her hand. "Crud-o," she said and jerked her hand back. Hillary dug into her back pocket and pulled out the sock full of bandages she had brought in case Molly needed them. She opened a Band-Aid, and used it to fasten the lipstick tube to her plastic pen. This time the blue magic sparked along the lipstick tube, but not the pen. She dipped the tube into the liquid.

"Pull me back." Before she stood up, Hillary put the cap back on her lipstick tube and wrapped another Band-Aid around it to seal in her sample. "That's it," she said and yawned. "Let's go. I'm getting tired. I'll be dream-slipping soon."

They were about to leave when the brass-clad door to the chamber rattled. "This way," Hillary said. She grabbed Larkstone's hand and pulled him toward the side passage that she and Molly had taken when they escaped from the dungeon. They stopped just around the corner and waited.

"Here, take the eyes, Bitterbrun," Hillary heard Fistlock say. "Put them in the Gorlon so we don't have to worry about anyone coming in or out this way. Then search outside the cave. I think I dropped my little tin of needles somewhere. I need them to use on that boy when he dream-slips back to his cell tomorrow."

"Yes, your sharpness."

Hillary and Larkstone listened. They heard the door slam and footsteps fade as someone walked away.

Larkstone took a quick peek around the corner. "It will take Bitterbrun some time to put those eyes in. We can't go out that way now. If we wait, you're sure to dream-slip."

"I think I can find the other way out," Hillary said. "Look for marks on the glass like this one."

"What is it?"

"Squishy-butter. I mean peanut butter. Molly had it all over her fingers. She left a trail for us to follow. Let's get out of here."

ꟸ

"Hey, wake up. Come on. Daylight in the camp." Windslow said and gave his sister another poke.

"Wha... What? Windslow!" Hillary said and sat up in bed. "Are you all right? Fistlock—Yesterday you— And, Molly, she's—"

"Molly's fine, I'm fine, the world is fine, and you aren't so bad yourself."

"How long have you been up? Or, how long have I been asleep?"

"It's only a half hour before we're supposed to get up. I woke up early. There wasn't much to do in that cell. I'm in the same one you were in, I think. Molly's fine. She broke her nose and has some scratches. She and her sisters snuck in to help me with a jail break."

"Did you get out? Where are you?"

"I stayed in—by choice."

"What about how... how you were feeling before. You know. About..."

"You have a dope for a stepbrother. Molly set me straight. You know, I actually feel a lot better now that I told you how your doll got up on the roof and how I fell. I let you feel guilty about it when I was feeling guilty too. It really was my own fault. Well, guess what? I'm in a wheelchair. I probably will be the rest of my life. But that's not going to stop me from doing *anything.*"

Hillary leaned forward and gave Windslow tight hug. While she hugged him, she sniffed.

"Hey, why are you crying?"

"Because, dumb brother, I'm happy. I've been thinking too. I was guilty and mad because I felt like your personal servant. I was always feeling sorry for myself. I told myself I deserved it because of my guilt. But it was just a big excuse about me not having confidence in myself or taking chances."

"You? I almost laughed out loud the other day when you were ordering the wizards around at Biffendear's cottage. You're the one who everyone relies on. But now you've got me to help you, and Gabendoor has the Summerfield Teens to help it."

"Ha!" Hillary said and sat back. "I like the name, Children of the Summer Wind, a lot better."

The Book of Second Chances appeared on Windslow's lap with a loud poof! "Geeze!" Windslow yelped, and jerked back. Hillary sucked in a sharp breath, but kept from screaming.

"What just happened?" Windslow asked. "I gave this thing to Molly. It's never done this before."

As both of them watched, the book opened itself and pages began to turn. When the pages stopped, both Hillary and Windslow read the new words.

Chances always come with fear.

To overcome one perseveres.

Turn chance to opportunity.

Do not prejudge what you can be.

Courage brings a second chance,

A time for growth and to advance.

This lesson was about your guilt,
And the confidence you built.

With chances and with what you know,
Your world awaits to watch you grow.
Your futures wind through many paths,
You're free to walk them now at last.

"This is so spooky, Windslow. "The new lines are about what we were just saying."

"I know," Hillary said. "I was at the oracle. I figured the book out. I was so excited to tell you but then... Well the Molly thing happened. Speaking of Molly, you said she has the book?"

Windslow and Hillary went on to tell each other about what had happened since the last time they had talked. Hillary told Windslow about the sample she took from the pool, the oracle and being lost in Larkstone's closet. Windslow didn't have as much to tell. He skipped over most of his experience with the Gorlon and told Hillary about Fistlock's threat to Eldervale. When Trish called them for breakfast, both parents gave them strange looks. Windslow and Hillary were laughing as Hillary pushed Windslow to the kitchen in his wheelchair. Trish laughed when Bill got to the table. Hillary and Windslow had already eaten all their pancakes, half of hers and all of Bill's.

On the ride to school, their parents turned around in stunned silence when Windslow blurted out, "You know, maybe I'll be an airline pilot when I grow up."

"I'm going to be a microbiologist," Hillary said as she played with her Band-Aid wrapped lipstick tube.

ഗ്രൽ

Snort, whistle, wheeze. Snort whistle, wheeze. The snoring continued in a regular pattern as the three wizards slept soundly, confident their dome of magic would warn them of any danger. They slept in a row, on blankets spread on the soft forest ground in a small clearing in the trees. A fourth blanket marked where Hillary had fallen asleep and dream-slipped back home.

Fistlock touched a finger to his lips to signal silence. Bitterbrun nodded understanding and stepped close to his master so Fistlock could whisper in his ear. Bitterbrun nodded again and ran back to where one hundred of Fistlock's soldiers waited with pikes and swords.

While the soldiers moved quietly to circle the magic dome, Fistlock held up the bottom of his black robe and knelt on the ground. Carefully he ran a finger along the faint blue edge of the magic where it flowed over leaves and sticks. With shaking fingers, he lifted one of the sticks a half inch and propped the end up with a pebble. The twig held a tiny fold of the magic dome up from the ground. Fistlock touched his wand to the fold and muttered a spell.

With a whoosh, the magic dome sucked into his wand like a cobweb sucked into a vacuum cleaner.

The snoring stopped and the three wizards scrambled to their feet, their magic wands drawn.

"Welcome to Crystal Mountain," Fistlock said. He folded his arms and idly tapped his wand against his shoulder.

"Back off and we won't kill you," Haggerwolf said. Blue magic crackled at the end of his wand.

"How about them?" Fistlock said. "Bitterbrun, ask the men if they're worried." Fistlock said something under his breath and light filled the clearing, revealing Bitterbrun and the circle of soldiers. Each pike and sword pointed menacingly at the three wizards.

Haggerwolf lowered his wand. "We'll go peacefully," he said and stepped in front of the empty blanket where Hillary had fallen asleep.

"That seems like a better decision," Fistlock said and unfolded his arms. "Maybe you three aren't the fools you used to be. Your magic hasn't gotten any better. Captain," he said, turning to one of the soldiers. "Lock them up with the boy. Oh, and have some of your men wait by that blanket. The girl should appear there just after sun up. Lock her up too. Bitterbrun," he asked his assistant. "Did you find my needle points?"

"No, your magicness," Bitterbrun answered.

"Too bad," Fistlock said as he stepped toward Haggerwolf. "When they turn up, I think I'll use them to turn you three into shadow-glumps."

ജ൦ൽ

"Shush..." Molly whispered to her sisters and peeked around the door frame. "Wrong room," she said a bit louder. "This Fistlock bedroom, not room with book stuff."

"I got good idea," Nelly Never said. "How bout we fix up his room nice and clean?"

"Who's there?" asked a deep, insubstantial voice that sounded more like wind than speech. A shadow cast by the light of the small flames in the fireplace moved just under the bed.

"That a trundle-wraith," Molly said softly to her sisters. "He live under Fistlock bed. It me, Molly Folly Sallyforth," Molly called in a low voice. "Remember me? I help my uncle Panderflip sometime do Fistlock work. Come say hi to sisters. We not gonna hurt you."

"I'm supposed to scare you," the voice said. "Please don't tell the master."

"We be goodie friend to you," Nelly Never said.

The edge of the shadow thickened and moved, drawing itself up like a puddle of black licorice.

"Don't hide in shadow self," Molly said. "It okay to look-a way you always be."

The shadow softened and blurred. In a blink, it turned to a large fluffy dust ball with bits of lint and stray threads. It rolled out from under the bed and stopped at Molly's feet. "Why isn't anyone scared of us anymore?" the trundle-wraith asked.

"Ever-body know alla you guys. You not scary mystery thing anymore. You just thing for baddie Fistlock to be mean to. Him not nice guy like us. We got good magic."

"We share," Tillie said.

"Here. Eat whole magic," Nelly said and held out an unwrapped piece of butterscotch candy. A small piece broke off and disappeared into the dust-ball. Nelly stuffed the rest of the candy back in her pocket.

"Um... that's good magic," the trundle-wraith said and fluffed itself up a bit bigger. "Could I come with you and live under one of your beds?"

"Maybe," Tillie said. "But you not supposed to scare anyone anymore. That magic make you good guy."

"Hm... you're right," the trundle-wraith said. "I do feel better. I feel happy, friendly."

"It okay you come with us then," Molly said and backed out into the hallway. "We got-a find book room before Fistlock catch us."

"He be back soon," Tillie said. "Him and Bitterbutt not stay outside too long I think."

Molly nodded and led her sisters farther down the long wood paneled hallway. The girls moved single file and hugged the wall, trying to blend into the natural shadows. The trundle-wraith tumbled along silently behind them. They scooted around statues of men dressed in full armor, pedestals holding fat vases and tall pots planted with prickly cactus plants.

"This-a place," Molly said and pulled on the door handle. She stopped when the hinges squeaked.

"Stop making so much noise," the trundle-wraith said.

"It not me, it squeaky door hinge," Molly said.

"I meant, Horace," the trundle-wraith answered. "It's me, Horace. It's Bernie." The trundle-wraith puffed itself over to the door. "Horace is a hinge-haggler," he said to the sisters. "They make hinges squeak."

"Why are you helping them?" Horace asked.

"Cause we got magic to make you good guy and get away from meanie Fistlock," Tillie said.

Nelly took out her piece of chipped butterscotch candy. "Here," she said. "You get whole big piece." She pressed the candy into the hinge and pulled on the door handle, cracking the candy into pieces that fell on the floor. Nelly scooped up all the chunks that dropped and held one small chip back up near the hinge. The small fragment of amber butterscotch disappeared from her fingertips.

"Now Fistlock can't control you anymore," Bernie said. "You can come with us and live with the Sallyforth Sisters."

Nelly rolled her eyes and put the butterscotch chips in her pocket.

Molly led them into Fistlock's library.

A large fireplace holding only bright red and yellow embers, sat squarely in the center of the far wall. All around it, bookshelves held books of all sizes. A large table with thick carved legs and a big leather chair sat quietly in the center of the room. Atop a thin candle in the middle of the table a tiny flame danced back and forth and went out.

"It's all right, Beatrix," Horace called from his hiding place inside the door hinge. "These are our new friends. You can relight the candle."

"Are you sure?" asked a tiny high-pitched voice that spoke too fast. "Fistlock will be mad at us."

"The girls have magic that will free us from Fistlock," Bernie said. "Puff me up onto the table."

A tiny wind blew. The dust-ball spun in a slow spiral as the soft wind lifted it up to the tabletop.

"That a flame fluffer," Molly said to her sisters. "They blow out candles alla time. They like-a make it dark and scary."

Nelly put a chip of butterscotch candy on the table near the dust ball. It disappeared. "You not big oinky pig," Nelly said and carefully lifted the trundle-wraith off the table. She placed another chip of candy on the table for the flame fluffer.

"Okay, we better get-a work now," Molly said. "We take too much time."

All three girls began pulling books off the shelves. Tillie opened one on the table and ripped out three pages.

"Not so many," Molly told her. "Just one page from each. We not want Fistlock to miss any. Take lot-a pages until they this high," Molly said. She put the Book of Second Chances on the desk and patted the book's cover.

When the pile of torn sheets rose as high at the Book of Second Chances, Molly grabbed them and stuffed them and the book into Windslow's magic book bag. Molly slung the bag around her shoulder and headed for the door with her sisters behind her.

"What about us?" Beatrix asked from the candle flame.

"It okay to come, but stay shadow," Molly called over her shoulder. Bernie, Beatrix and Horace took their shadow forms and flowed down to the floor behind Nelly. As the group snuck into the hallway, more shadows flowed from cracks in the floor, corners near the ceiling, spaces behind the hall plants, and other dusty spots. They all lined up behind the girls.

Halfway down the main staircase, Tillie stopped. "This work," she said and took a penknife from her pocket. The blade made a scraping sound as she cut.

"Get two," Molly told her sister.

"Somebody not notice that," Nelly Never said. She took a piece of charcoal from her pocket. The shadows groaned when the charcoal screeched like wet chalk on a chalkboard.

"Good work," Tillie said. "Now it look even better than before." She snapped her penknife shut and hurried down the steps after her sisters.

"Almost forgot," Molly said. She took Fistlock's small tin of needle points from her pocket. "Need-a put this in baddies work room. Where scritch?" she asked.

A black form from the end of the shadow line whisked up, snatched the tin from Molly's hand and disappeared. In an eye-blink, a high squeaky shadow voice said, "I put it on his workbench. He'll find it."

"Thanks, scritch," Molly said. "We—"

"It's Fistlock and Bitterbrun," the deep voice of the shadow-wraith said. "Now what?"

"This-a way," Molly said and moved back into the shadow formed where the bottom of the staircase met the wall.

One small shadow flapped through the air like a bodiless bat. It settled into an almost invisible crack that ran along the seam where two pieces of paneling came together on the wall across from the staircase. A large section of paneling swung outward, screeching loudly as it opened. Fistlock and Bitterbrun stepped into the room.

Fistlock gave the door a kick with his boot. It slammed shut and the hinge haggler fluttered away. Without looking back, Fistlock headed for the staircase. "Lock it," he called to Bitterbrun.

His portly assistant pressed two fingers against swirling patterns in the paneling that looked like knot holes. The door clicked and Bitterbrun ran for the stairs. Halfway up, he paused and looked at the row of portraits hung on the wall along the staircase. The first painting showed Fistlock's great, great grandfather; the next, his great grandfather. Where Fistlock and his grandfather's paintings should have been, empty frames with frayed canvas edges let the wall show through. Stick figures, drawn in charcoal, showed both men with big round heads, spiky stick hair and big smiles. Bitterbrun blinked, tugged at his shirt collar and hurried up the stairs.

23: Magic

Before class started, Hillary wove her way down the hallway through the crush of students to the science lab to talk to Mr. Nick. She showed him the sample she had collected from the Gorlon's pond inside Crystal Mountain. He agreed to help her analyze it as an extra credit project, but said it looked like simple crude oil. Quick tests could confirm his assumption. If so, then he couldn't give her very many points for the project.

Later that day when science class started, she was a bit surprised. Mr. Nick gave the class a reading assignment and spent the whole time working on something in the back corner of the room. When class ended, he gave Hillary a pass to have her excused from last period study hall.

That afternoon, Hillary gave the pass to her study hall teacher and hurried to the lab. When she entered the room, Mr. Nick stood with his back toward her, his white lab coat stretched tight over his back as he hunched over one of the lab tables. Numbers and formulas covered the chalkboard near him. Straightening up, he scratched at his dark hair and moved to the board. He used his coat sleeve to erase part of a formula scribbled in blue chalk. With green chalk, he drew in new numbers and chemical symbols.

"Mr. Nick," Hillary said.

He spun around and bumped into one of the tall metal stools that circled each of the student lab tables. The stool clanged to the floor. Mr. Nick didn't bother to pick it up. He nudged it aside with one foot and hurried toward her. "This is incredible. Just look," he said, speaking fast and pointing back at the chalkboard. "See how it's working out? This could be—"

"Mr. Nick?" Hillary asked and took a step backward.

"Oh, I'm sorry. Slow down. Take a breath. Not you, Hillary. Me," he said and stood still. Dropping both hands to his sides, he drew in a long breath, held it, and exhaled. "All right, first the experiment. No, the calculations. Maybe the—Another breath," he said and took one.

"Um, could you sit at your desk, maybe? I'll sit at the lab station in front of it?"

"Yes! Of course. Got to slow down," he muttered again, turned and headed for his desk.

Hillary moved a stool to the lab station nearest Mr. Nick's cluttered desk. The lab station had a black top with a small stainless steel sink in the middle, and dual chrome-plated gas jets to one side. Hillary pushed aside some of the empty glass beakers to make room for the notebook she took from her backpack.

"Where to begin. Where to begin," Mr. Nick muttered and scratched at his forehead, leaving a green chalk smudge just over his eyebrow.

"I'm guessing it's not crude oil," Hillary said, and took out a pencil to take notes with.

"Oh, no. Not hardly," Mr. Nick said. He put his hands on his desktop, took another breath and looked at her. "I don't know what it is. Where did it come from?"

"Well..." Hillary said, drawing out the word to give herself a bit more time to think of something to say. "A couple years ago we went on a vacation to Arizona and I found this rock. A big rock," she said and held up her hands, forming a big circle with her fingers and thumbs. "It was a funny looking rock. It didn't look like any of the others around it, so I took it home. This weekend my stepbrother and I cracked it open. There was a little cavity inside with the black stuff in it. I was just wondering what it was."

"Drats!" Mr. Nick said and rested his elbows on the desktop. His eyes didn't look focused on anything as he seemed to stare off into some corner of his mind. "That's disappointing," he said and straightened back up. "But we'll save that mystery for later. I've got to show you what I've discovered," he said and stood up.

Mr. Nick showed her some of the experiments he had run and told her about others. He still didn't know what the mysterious black substance was. "First watch this," he said and put two low containers that looked like jar tops on the worktable. Each one was about three inches across and only a quarter inch high. "This one is plastic," he said as he slid them together until their edges touched. "The other one is glass."

He held up Hillary's lipstick tube and used an eyedropper to remove a tiny bit of the black goop. Hillary watched Mr. Nick squeeze the tiny drop into the glass container. She kept watching and nothing happened. "See that?" he asked.

"I don't see anything," Hillary said and looked up at him.

"Oh, of course not. I'm sorry," he said. "You're supposed to see that it doesn't do anything. But, watch this." Mr. Nick picked up the glass container and poured the tiny drop into the plastic container. When he put the glass container back down, the tiny drop of black moved. It formed a bead, rolled to the container lip, slid up and over the edges, and settled into the glass container.

"See?" Mr. Nick said. "Glass attracts it, or it's attracted to glass. I don't know which it is."

Mr. Nick didn't say anything as he used the dropper to suck another larger sample from the brass lipstick tube. He squeezed it into the tray with the first drop. Tiny, spider web thin strands of blue crackled around and over the coin sized circle of black. "Some kind of energy," he said and looked up at Hillary, his eyes wide.

"Do you know what kind?" Hillary asked. "Is it electricity maybe?"

"I thought it might be, but it's not. That's what has me stumped. I conducted a couple of simple tests. I'll show you."

Mr. Nick almost ran as he moved to another science table and back again. He held a small rectangular device in his hand. The plastic box had a dial and indicator meter on the front. A red wire dangled from one side; a black wire from the other. He put the gadget next to the goo sample. With shaking hands, Mr. Nick put the probes at the ends of the black and red wires into the crackling black sample. "Watch the arrow on the meter," he said. The meter didn't move. He took a flashlight battery from his lab coat pocket and touched one of the device probes to each end. The needle moved to the center of the indicator scale.

"At first I thought my meter was bad, so I tested a battery. Then I discovered something new by accident. Watch."

Mr. Nick put the battery on the tabletop and rolled it close to the sample container. "You won't see anything," he said. After holding the battery still for a few seconds, Mr. Nick picked it up and held the red and black probes to its ends again. The needle didn't move. "It's not electricity, but somehow it absorbs it or neutralizes it or something. I theorized that if energy goes into it, then somehow energy has to come back out. I stuck a wire into the goo and got a shock. I hooked a flashlight bulb up to a couple of wires, dipped them in the goo and nothing happened."

"But it does have some kind of power?" Hillary asked

"Yes, a very amazing power. A power like none I've ever seen or heard of before. You've stumbled across something incredible, Hillary. I've discovered something very strange, by accident. I didn't want to stir it with a glass rod because of the way it's attracted to glass. I couldn't use metal. I didn't want another shock. So I tried wood. Incredible, isn't it?"

"Um, Mr. Nick. I don't understand. What happened when you touched it with wood?"

"Well, actually two things happened. I wanted to check it for magnetism. So I grabbed a small piece of lodestone. That's—"

"Magnetic rock," Hillary said, interrupting him. "So what about the wood?"

"I had a small piece of lodestone in my hand when I grabbed a wooden stir stick and touched it to the sample. Then, WOW! Incredible."

"What, Mr. Nick? What happened!"

"That blue power formed an arc between the dish and the stick. I could feel the power flowing into the wood. When I put the loadstone down, and tried it again. Nothing happened."

"Maybe you drained off all the power?"

"Not even close. That substance holds a lot of something. Watch this." Mr. Nick looked at Hillary and grinned. He held open his lab coat and took out a thin wooden stick from an inside pocket. At the bottom end of the stick, Hillary could see the small magnet peeking out through the silver duct-tape Mr. Nick had used to fasten it in place. He touched the stick to the sample goo from Crystal Mountain. The blue power leapt from the dish to the end of his stick until Mr. Nick pulled his hand away.

"Here, try using it now. It's ready," Mr. Nick said and handed the stick to Hillary.

&

Working late in the evening, Fistlock's excitement helped him fight the urge to sleep. He wanted everything ready for the morning and hummed to himself as he went over his last preparations. Bitterbrun waited patiently at Fistlock's side, both men standing at the table in the center of Fistlock's workroom.

"A scritch found it, Your Happiness," Bitterbrun said as Fistlock took the top off his small tin of needle points.

"Hm... just enough," Fistlock said as he counted the needle points. "One for the boy, the girl, three for the wizards and one for the new Gorlon. I'll let you stick the Gorlon."

Fistlock carefully picked a needle point out from the tin and fitted it into the small hole in the top of his magic wand. "Stick the Gorlon in the morning," he said and handed the wand to Bitterbrun. "After I get the book from those children, I'll send the Gorlon out to help the troops wipe out Eldervale. The soldiers should be there by noon tomorrow."

"Yes, Your Evilness," Bitterbrun answered and tucked the wand inside his vest "Should I start another Gorlon after I release this one?"

"No, I don't think so. I won't need another one for awhile. By this time tomorrow, Eldervale will be destroyed, those troublesome wizards will be dead along with those horrible Earthlings and I'll have the Book of Second Chances. All that will be left are the Sallyforth girls. They're no threat. You can kill them later. After preparing the Gorlon, get the Spire ready."

"The Spire, Your Wickedness? You're really going to use it?"

"Call it a test, so to speak. I'm going to turn everyone in Wartville, Chubbytown and Shortyvale into shadow-glumps all at once. No use wasting a Gorlon or troops on those places. One blast ought to work. I need to build up a supply of shadow beasts to send to Earth." Fistlock snapped his needle tin shut and stuffed it into a pocket in his robe. "Go get some sleep. I don't want you bumbling anything up."

"Yes, your Graciousness," Bitterbrun answered. He turned and scurried out the door. Fistlock looked around his workroom. Satisfied everything was ready he headed for his bedroom. He hummed a little tune he made up as he walked.

Three old wizards trapped in a cell
Stuck with my needle, one didn't feel well.

Two little wizards trapped in a cell
Gave one a push to send him down the well.

One puny wizard trapped in a cell
Gone with a poof, from my clever spell.

No little wizards trapped in a cell.
I am the greatest when I do so swell.

ꙮ

"Mr. Nick is going crazy over that sample I gave him," Hillary told Windslow as they sat in his bedroom that night. "I told him we found it inside a rock in Arizona. He had me point out a place on a map."

"Where did you point to?" Windslow asked.

"I just picked a place outside Tucson. He said he might take a leave of absence and go there searching for rocks. I don't know what I'm going to do. I can't let him do that because of a lie."

"Tell him you made a mistake. Tell him my grandfather gave me that rock. Tell Mr. Nick that grandpa told me it was a meteorite he found when he was little."

"Good idea. I don't want him leaving," Hillary said and began filling her pockets with things she thought they might need when they dream-slipped. "He's one of the coolest teachers at school."

"Next to Ms Christensen, or Mrs. Christensen, I should say," Windslow said. "She got married this weekend."

"Didn't she change her name?" Hillary asked.

"Na. She's keeping it. Oh, I almost forgot. She and her husband decided to adopt some kids. She said they thought it would be nice to give some orphans a second chance. I think that's pretty cool too." Windslow adjusted his pajama top. Underneath his pajamas, he wore a sweatshirt and jeans.

"You know, that book is really helping lots of people," Hillary said. "Maybe some of it really does work."

"Hillary, you know the book is bogus. Well, at least for being magic. Well maybe not that. It does do magic stuff, like the way words appear."

"And like the way it popped into your hands from nowhere."

"Do you think Fistlock knows its secret?" Windslow adjusted his pillow and the Book of Second Chances hidden under it.

"Lights out in ten minutes," Trish called from down the hall.

"Okay, Mom," Hillary called over her shoulder and turned back to Windslow. "I hope Fistlock doesn't know. Otherwise, what would he need you for? You'll have to keep him guessing for another day, at least. We need to get everything in place for our plans. If you see Molly, tell her the wizards and I will meet her at Eldervale. Then we'll come back and help you take care of Fistlock."

"Show me the wand again," Windslow said and held out his hand.

Hillary stood and rolled up the right cuff of her jeans. From inside her calf-length white shock, she pulled out the stick with the magnet taped to the end and gave it to her stepbrother.

Windslow grinned at her and pointed the stick at his desk lamp. "Lamp off," he said. A small click sounded and the lamp went out. "Lamp on," he said and the bulb spread its yellow glow around the room. "It's better than that clapper thing on TV," Windslow said and pointed it at the pile of clothes near his closet. "Hang up," he said and the clothes leapt to hangers, the hangers hooked themselves over the pole in his closet and the door shut. "Cool," Windslow said and handed the stick back to his sister.

"Idiot, those are your dirty clothes," Hillary said, but her smile betrayed her true feelings. "Enough playing. I don't know if the thing wears out or not, and Mr. Nick played with it all afternoon. Right up until the explosion."

"I didn't even hear it," Windslow said.

"Well, it was more like a firecracker. He did burn his fingers. When the magnet touched the black goo stuff, the magic strands really started crackling. The whole dish turned red hot and started to melt. When the melted glass and the goo mixed together, they exploded. Mrs. Taralynn really got mad at him. It was kind of fun to see the principal hollering at a teacher for once."

"I'm getting sleepy and I don't want Trish or Dad checking on us because the lights are still on," Windslow said. "Be careful on your way to Eldervale."

"And you watch out for Fistlock," Hillary said. "We'll show him firsthand how second chances work."

24: Captives

Windslow rubbed his eyes and sat up. A single torch, stuck in a wall bracket on the far side of the dungeon, cast a yellow glow that thinned as it stretched barely to the well and large square table in the center of the room. Shadows scurried across the grey stone blocks that formed the walls. Neatly mortared, pumpkin-sized stones formed a three-foot high circle of the well. The slightly shorter table sat next to it. Through the hole in the ceiling above the well, Windslow could see the bottom of the wide tarnished bell. The table, well and bell shaft above it looked almost as Hillary had described them. There was only one small change. A metal grating made of finger-thick bars blocked the bell shaft as a possible escape route.

"Are you all right, boy?" a voice asked from the darkness in the cell next to Windslow.

"Haggerwolf?" Windslow asked. He stood and moved to the black metal bars separating the two cells.

"We're here too," Fernbark said. "All three of us."

"What about Hillary?" Windslow asked. "If she—" Windslow cut his sentence short when he heard the sound of boots coming down the hall that led to the dungeon. The door opened. Hillary stumbled forward into the room.

"Don't push, you creep!" she hollered and caught her balance. Behind her, three of Fistlock's soldiers stepped into the light. Two held her arms while the third approached Windslow's cell. Without speaking, the guard unlocked the cell and motioned Windslow back. The other two guards brought

Hillary forward and gave her another shove. Windslow grabbed his sister to keep her from falling.

"If you jerks touch me one more time I'll... I'll...!" Hillary yelled as the guards slammed the bars shut with a loud clang and twisted the key in the lock.

Windslow held her back as the guards turned and left. "What happened?" he asked. "If they hurt you—"

Hillary pushed herself away from her stepbrother. "Those morons were waiting for me when I dream-slipped. I kicked a couple of them, but they have stupid leather armor. They wouldn't say anything. They just searched me and dragged me in here. At least I know the way out now. At the other end of the—"

"Hillary!" Windslow said, almost shouting. "Did they hurt you?"

"No. I told you," she said and folded her arms. "I'm just mad. This screws up all of our plans. What are we going to do now? Maybe the wizards can do something. They weren't there when I woke up."

"Um...They're kind of here too," Windslow said and scrunched up his face.

"We didn't have a chance," Fernbark said from the next cell.

Hillary looked at the three forms pressed against the bars.

"That's just terrific," she said and slumped down to the floor. "Now what are we going to do?"

"Hillary?" Windslow said softly. He touched his sister on the shoulder and pointed.

Across the dungeon, an unlit torch on the other side of the door lifted itself from the wall bracket. It floated in the air as it moved slightly up and down, moving closer to its lit companion. When the torches met, more light spread to the edge of the cells as the floating torch danced back to its wall bracket.

"Hi, Hillre." a voice called from nowhere.

"We alla gether," said another voice.

"Even crabby wizard here too," said a third voice.

"Quit hiding," Windslow said. "Can you get us out of here?"

"Peek-ee boo," Molly said and pulled the shadow-glump away from herself and her sisters. "Scritch get us key. We get alla you guys out now."

"Molly, I'm so glad to see you," Hillary said. She pressed herself up against the cell door and stretched her arms out through the bars as Molly ran over to her. As best she could, Hillary gave her tiny three friends a hug. She let go and took the key. "We're not going to escape," she said and shoved the key into her pocket. "If we do that, Fistlock will send his men after us and we'll just end up right back here. We need a new plan."

"We got plan," Tillie said.

Haggerwolf cleared his throat and spoke just loud enough to be heard. "A plan for disaster, if those three thought it up."

ꕥ

Bitterbrun reached inside his vest and took out the magic wand Fistlock had prepared the night before. He checked to make sure the needle point was in place at the wand's tip. Shaking just a bit, he knelt next to the long chain that rose from the pool and stretched out of sight down the passage to the Gorlon's cave. The black goo from the pond wove a finger-thick cord in and out though the chain links and connected the pond to the monster. Bitterbrun held the wand up high and jabbed it downward. The Gorlon didn't roar like

Bitterbrun had expected, but the chain did jerk and Bitterbrun jumped to the side. Glad this assignment was finished, he hurried back to Fistlock's bedroom.

ജ്ഞ

"I prepared the Gorlon," Bitterbrun said as he took Fistlock's robe from the chair back and handed it to his master. "The earth girl is locked up in the dungeon with the others. Are you going to get the book from them now? The boy has it."

Fistlock hummed to himself as he finished dressing. "I will, soon enough. First I'll turn the wizards into shadow-glumps and let them help us torture those meddlesome earth children. When we have the book's secret, 'KA-BOOM,' I'll blow up a few cities. How's that sound for a fun filled day? Let's go meet our guests. We must be polite. It wouldn't be nice to keep them waiting."

ജ്ഞ

"Not Switch-lily seeds," Haggerwolf said.

"Where did you get those?" Larkstone asked as the three Sallyforth girls each held out a small white seed in the palms of their hands. "Switch-lilies have been extinct for a hundred years or more."

"They grow alla place." Tillie said. "They alla round our house."

"Harrumph," Haggerwolf scoffed. "They may as well be extinct then."

"If they're all around Molly's home, then why would anyone think they're extinct?" Windslow asked.

"Because, no one knows where these three orphans live. They won't tell anyone and no one has ever been able to find out," Haggerwolf said.

"So, big deal," Hillary said and sat down on the cell floor. "Let them have their privacy."

"It's important, or was important," Larkstone said, "because their great grandfather is the one who created the Book of Second Chances in the first place."

"Are you serious?" Hillary asked. She glanced at the wizard before she turned to look at Molly.

"Yep," Molly said. "Grampy make alla kind a book. Big one, little one."

"The Book of Broken Promises, the Book of Whimsy, Lessons In Calamity, Lost Ways and many more," Fernbark said. "Their great grandfather was one of the great wizards of Gabendoor. Some of us thought that if we could find his home, then we might find some of his other books."

"Molly, why do you keep this all a secret?" Hillary asked.

"Grampy make us do big promise before he die. When that happen ever-body start to be mean to us. But that not matter. Now we got best new friends. We got Hillre and Window."

"Did you ever ask the triplets how the book works?" Windslow asked and stared intently at the wizards.

Haggerwolf looked down at his feet and played with his beard. Fernbark looked up and scratched at his ear. Larkstone shoved his hands in his pockets and softly said, "No. We never thought to."

"I can't believe it," Hillary said and pulled up the leg of her jeans. She pulled the magic stick from behind her sock and stuck it in her back pocket. "Why not?"

"Hillre not wait to find out," Nelly Never said. "You ask right away, too."

"We're so dumb," Windslow said. He retrieved the book from the corner of the cell where he left it when he dream-slipped that morning. "Molly, can you tell us how this thing works? We think we know, and I'd like to find out how close we were to figuring it out."

"It work just like this-a one," Molly said. She slipped Windslow's magic book bag off her shoulder. When she stuck a finger inside the bag, it expanded.

Windslow's eyes widened as he looked at what Molly took from the canvas pouch and placed on the floor. It was some kind of a book, or at least an attempt at making one. The cover was canvas, stretched and glued over a thin square piece of wood. Someone had tried to paint the canvas brown, but when Windslow looked close, he could see Fistlock's portrait through the color. The book's cover was slightly smaller than the pages. Ragged edges peeked out. It looked as if the sisters had simply scooped up a pile of pages and bound them together. Black hand-painted letters, tipped at slightly different angles read. DO CHANCE AGAIN.

"How does the book work, Molly? Not your new one," he said. "The one your great grandfather made."

"It work like all book. It teach."

"Here," Hillary said and opened the real Book of Second Chances. "Show us how. Tell us what all this means."

"Oh, good," Tillie said. "We like-a read and tell story."

"I'll read what's here and you tell us what it means," Hillary said and began reading.

The story in this chance begins,

Found in pages locked within.

Open them with words of care.

What you seek is waiting there.

"It just mean you new guy with book. It gonna teach you stuff."

Something lost in time long past,
Chancing love she thought would last.
You helped her think of what to do.
A link once cut she now renews.

"That about Window's teacher. He smart guy and tell her to take chance. He help her think of one to take."

A second chance you granted them.
Teachers reach for hope again.
The first of four you did not waste,
Although you wished the chance in haste.

"You get one, two and one, two chance to learn from book. But Window not think much about words. He just jabber, jabber," she said and shook her finger at him.

Chapter two this lesson learn,
Do not ask for what you yearn.
Magic does not come from here.
It comes from those who lose their fear.

"Don't say you want lot-a stuff. That not do no magic. Got to do stuff. Magic not from book. It from inside guy who learn from book."

"It pretty simple stuff," Tillie said. "Grampy say he don't want book be too hard-a read."

Windslow closed his eyes and shook his head. Haggerwolf rolled his eyes. Hillary kept reading.

Chances hide when first you look.

Seek your answers from this book.

The words placed here for you to see,

Came from what you made them be.

"Book teach." Molly said. "I tell alla you that. It show you what you do right or when you do goof up."

There is no magic where you thought.
It came from things its bearer brought.
These pages put you to the test.
You've learned to plan and do your best.

"That when Window help meanie wizards. He give his magic to wizard. He help wizards believe they important guys so they not give up so fast."

The Gorlon comes, it brings a chance,
For one who takes a special stance.
If puzzled out one wish will come,
A prize for something that you've done.

"You big scardy-cat sometime," Molly said and looked at Windslow. "Book want you to try stuff even if you scared. Okay to be scared. Book watch to see if you learn. Book say you be big winner if you learn."

Chances do not guarantee.

Results are what you make them be.

You took no chance to win or fail.

A chance is lost if not availed.

"Hillre learn this one good. Chance not mean you get wish. Chance mean you work hard. Want chance, you just take one. Work very, very hard second time. Give you better chance than first time."

"Like learning to have confidence in myself," Hillary said.

Molly nodded.

You made your choice when two fears came

A copied chance works out the same.

Something different, something new.

Is what second chance gives to you.

"That mean you do same thing alla time, Window. Let big scary stuff stop you. If old way don't work, got to try new way."

No chances come to those who dwell

When fear has locked them in its spell.

Each second chance from courage grown,

Learn to make them on your own.

"Now you know it okay to be scared. Just do stuff anyway. Do stuff even if hard and scary sometime."

The daughter of mountain breeze

Will learn from what her brother sees.

Now with answers will she know,

How to make her brother grow?

"That when you learn to take charge, Hillre. You learn not to feel sorry for Window. You let him do stuff himself. Book want you to help him. Book want him to help you."

Chances always come with fears
To overcome one perseveres
Turn chance to opportunity
Do not prejudge what you can be.

"This really good part," Molly said and looked at Windslow. "You try lot-a stuff and save me from Gorlon. You get confidence back too, just like Hillre."

Courage brings a second chance
A time for growth and to advance
This lesson was about your guilt
And the confidence you built.

"That mean you learn to feel good about you. Like

granny and grandpas in Eldervale. They know they old. It not matter. We gonna teach them to beat baddie Fistlock army."

"We'll talk about that in just a minute," Hillary said and read the last section in the book.

> With chances and with what you know
> Your world awaits to watch you grow.
> Your futures wind through many paths
> You're free to walk them now at last.

"That mean you learn alla lesson in the book. You make own second chances. Magic come from lota hard work and from when you don't let stupid stuff stop you."

"I was right!" Hillary said. "That's what the oracle helped me figure out. Now we need to use what we learned to stop Fistlock."

A black shadow swept past Nelly Never's ear. "You got lot-a time for that," she told the others. "Scritch just say that Fistlock not be here in about five minutes."

"Okay," Hillary said. "First, I have something for you." Hillary unrolled the turned up cuff of her jeans. Four small squares fell on the floor. "It's called bubblegum," she said and handed one to each of the Sallyforth girls. "I know you three like candy. I mean biggie earth magic."

"And I have more butter-rock for you." Windslow pulled out a bag of the amber colored butterscotch candy from inside his shirt.

"Good luck everyone," Hillary said. "While you tell us your plan I'll show you how to blow bubbles." She unwrapped her piece of gum and popped it into her mouth.

"Candy and children," Haggerwolf mumbled.

"But they're the children of the summer wind," Larkstone said. "We need to learn from the Book too. We're not just three old wizards. This is our second chance and we'd be fools not to make the best of it."

25: Switch-lilies

Windslow took a step back when Fistlock strode into the dungeon. Hillary didn't flinch. She stood her ground, just a foot back from the cell door. Fistlock's long purple robe flowed out behind him. His violet eyes stared at her stepbrother, or at least at who he thought was her stepbrother.

Bitterbrun stayed behind his master as before. His marshmallow face looked flushed and his squinty eyes looked tired. He wore the same yellow shirt as before, with a few added food stains. It stretched across his overstuffed belly and over the top of his orange pants.

When Fistlock passed the table, he glanced at Hillary. She felt an invisible force push against her. She stumbled awkwardly backward until the cell wall stopped her. It was difficult to breathe with Fistlock's magic barrier pressing against her. More determined than ever, she stayed silent and scowled defiantly at Fistlock. She doubted he noticed. His attention was focused back on Windslow.

Fistlock stopped two feet in front of the cell. He studied Windslow for a few seconds, and backed up to the table. After parting his robes, Fistlock boosted himself up and sat with his hands folded on his lap and his legs dangling. He cocked his head slightly and reached to his side where the magic wands from the three wizards lay in a pile of items his men had taken from Windslow and Hillary. After picking up the first wand, he snapped the thin wooden stick in half and threw it on the floor. Windslow jumped slightly at the sound. Fistlock snapped the second wand in half. Windslow took a step forward and placed his hands on the cell door bars. Fistlock started to break the third wand. He grinned and pointed it at the cell.

Hillary watched the Book of Second Chances float upward off the floor. When it was waist-high it stopped, turned sideways, and floated forward, slipping through the narrow space between the cell bars. At the table, the book turned again, opened and settled gently into Fistlock's lap. Fistlock broke the third wand and threw it on the floor with the others. Hillary saw the small piece of loadstone fall loose from its hollow space in the wand's end. The black rock bounced and tumbled until it stopped only inches from the cell.

"Hm..." Fistlock said as he read one page and turned to the next.

Hillary felt the barrier fade. Relieved, she took a long breath but held still. Moving her head slowly and as little as possible, she looked sideways. The three wizards sat at the back of their cell, their knees drawn up against their chests and their arms folded. Haggerwolf winked at her. Hillary hoped that Fistlock wouldn't notice or question the tiny bit of orange coloring at the tip of the wizard's long beard.

She slowly turned her head back. Fistlock and the table blocked some of her view, but she thought she saw a large shadow slip out the dungeon door.

"You've been busy, but haven't done anything useful with the book. You're a fool," Fistlock said and looked up at Windslow. "Maybe not too big a fool. You do know how to work it. Now tell me its secret!" he said loudly and slammed the book shut.

"He can't tell you," Hillary said. "The wizards put a spell on him."

"They did? Oh, no," Fistlock said, his voice in a high and mocking tone. He put both hands to his face. "I'm so worried. What am I to do?" He glanced at Bitterbrun who leaned against the side of the table.

Bitterbrun grinned.

"Might I have my wand back?" Fistlock asked his assistant.

Bitterbrun stood straight before bowing deeply at the waist. Reaching into his vest he pulled out Fistlock's wand and handed it to his master.

Fistlock held the smooth wooden stick in one hand while he reached into his cloak with the other hand. From an inside pocket he took out his small tin of needle points and placed it on the table.

"If you try to use magic on him," Hillary said, taking a step forward, "his tongue will blow up. Then he won't be able to tell you anything."

"There's no such spell," Fistlock said. He leaned over and opened the lid on his needle tin.

"Don't do this. I'm warning you," Hillary said and took two more steps forward until she stood just behind Windslow.

Fistlock pointed his wand straight up and recited a spell.

For many years, I have looked.

Tell to me, secrets of the book.

"Your rhyming stinks," Hillary said and put her hands on Windslow's shoulders.

"Close enough," Fistlock said, not bothering to look at her.

He controlled his voice, but Hillary could see anger building in his eyes. Fistlock lowered his wand and pointed it at Windslow.

"No, Windslow, no!" Hillary yelled, trying to make her voice like she was scared. Inside she actually was. Not as much about Fistlock's spell as she was about Molly's plan working. She looked over at the wizards. Fernbark still had his arms folded but Hillary saw his arms move slightly and caught a quick glimpse of the stick Mr. Nick had made. Fernbark gave a small nod.

Windslow's mouth began to move. His jaw worked back and forth, up and down, but his lips stayed closed.

"Now!" Fistlock said sharply and slid off the table. He thrust his arm out straight and pointed his wand directly at Windslow's mouth.

Windslow's jaw stopped for just a second. Slowly his lips parted as his pink tongue pushed outward.

Fistlock's eyes widened. Bitterbrun took two steps backward.

Windslow's cheeks puffed out as his tongue began to swell. It started out dark pink and quickly formed a nearly perfect round ball at the tip of his lips. Windslow's tongue grew bigger each time his cheeks showed another puff.

Bitterbrun moved behind the table. Fistlock unconsciously moved backward until the well stopped him.

As Windslow's tongue grew, its color changed from dark pink to a pale transparent shade.

"No!" Hillary yelled. "Reverse your spell, Fistlock. Do it before it's too late!"

Fistlock stared at her for a second and fumbled with his cloak pocket, not realizing he still held the wand in his hand. When he looked down, Windslow's tongue burst with a loud *POP*! Fistlock looked back up, froze and stared. The skin from the exploded tongue covered Windslow's face from chin to eyebrows. Windslow raised one hand and picked at the thin film of pink skin. After plucking most of it free, he put it back in his mouth and began chewing.

Fistlock watched as another bubble grew from Windslow's lips. When the bubble grew larger than the first, Fistlock bent his knees, slouched down and closed his eyes. When he opened them, he pointed his wand at Windslow and nearly yelled as he spoke.

"Reverse my spell.

Let no tongues swell."

"Too late!" Hillary shouted as she pulled Windslow to the back of the cell. She stood in front of Windslow, with her back toward Fistlock to block the evil wizard's view. As Windslow slid to the floor, he opened his mouth and used his tongue to try and pull bubble gum from his face. When his tongue stuck out, Hillary heard a soft whoosh. The image of Windslow shimmered and Tillie sat in front of her, the small Switch-Lily seed sitting in the middle of Tillie's tongue. Tillie grinned and pulled her tongue back in. Another soft whoosh sounded and Tillie changed back to Windslow. "Don't do that!" Hillary whispered before she turned around.

ꟾ

"All clear," Molly's voice said. In the empty hallway that led from the dungeon, a shadow along the wall moved. Suddenly she Windslow and Haggerwolf appeared from behind the cover of the shadow-glump.

Molly moved forward, down the hall. At the next door she stopped. Windslow waited just behind her. "Check other side," Molly said and held out a small chip of butterscotch candy. A shadow crossed her palm. Both the shadow and the candy chip disappeared. A second later the shadow brushed across her ear. "Scritch say can't go this-a way. Baddie men in their sleep room on other door side." Molly took a small key from a chain around her neck. "We go like Hillre and I do last time. This a way. Bend down. Gota use shoulders."

Windslow squatted down and steadied himself by holding his hands against the wall. Molly climbed up on his shoulders. He carefully stood up as Molly slid her hands along the wood paneling.

"Too high," Molly said.

Windslow bent his knees. He heard a click just before Molly's foot shoved against his shoulder. When her weight was gone, he looked up. She grinned down at him from one of the access panels Hillary had told him about. He boosted Haggerwolf up high enough for Molly to grab the wizard's hand. After Haggerwolf's boots slid out of sight, Windslow reached up, grabbed the edge and pulled.

Molly backed up to let Windslow pull himself inside the four-foot square wooden passage. He barely had his feet inside when she squeezed past him, pulled the panel door shut and locked it.

"Which way?" Windslow whispered as Molly slid back past him.

"Like last way. Don't know," Molly said and began crawling forward.

"That figures," Haggerwolf said and pressed himself back against the wall to let Molly pass.

They hadn't crawled far before Molly stopped and pointed at scratches on the wooden floor. "Gorge-gobbler marks," she said. "This-a way me an Hillre go. We not lost now."

After a few minutes of crawling, they reached the passage opening into the hallway near the Crystal Chamber.

Windslow slid down first and then helped Molly. She ran to the copper clad door and placed her fingers in the small secret indentations.

"Cool," Windslow said as the door opened and gave him his first look inside Crystal Mountain.

"Good," Molly said and ran ahead. "Gorlon still here. I go see if tricky-stuff work."

ꕥ

Fistlock straightened, adjusted his cloak and glanced back at Bitterbrun. His assistant peeked from behind the table, stood up and shrugged. Fistlock tried to boost himself back up to sit on the table, but slipped. A bit slower, he eased himself onto the wooden planks, wiggled a bit and placed his hand on his tin of needle points. "Very clever," he said.

Hillary walked back to the cell door but kept herself between Fistlock and the masquerading Tillie, just in case. "I warned you," she said and grabbed the bars.

Fistlock nodded as he picked up his tin and opened the lid. "Well, it occurs to me that you know the book's secret too," he said as he picked a needle point from the tin. He fitted the small sliver of metal into the hole in the tip of his wand. When he waived a hand, the torches behind him burned brighter, sending more light into the wizard's cell. Fistlock pointed his wand as he mumbled something Hillary couldn't hear.

Haggerwolf unfolded his arms and stood. With exaggerated jerking steps, he marched toward the front of the cell and stopped.

"If you don't tell me the book's secret, I'll turn your little wizard friend into a shadow-glump."

"You probably will anyway," Hillary said and folded her arms. "Why should I tell you?"

"If you do, I'll just toss you and your brother down the well. If you don't, I'll turn you into shadow-glumps and then throw you down the well. One way you die. The other way you and your brother live on to haunt your own world forever as my shadow creatures. Trust me, death is the better choice." Fistlock slid off the table and walked to the wizard's cell. "Hold him, Bitterbrun," Fistlock said to his assistant.

Bitterbrun scurried from behind the table. He grabbed Haggerwolf's arm and held it steady against one of the bars.

"Well?" Fistlock asked and held his needle pointed wand just inches away from the wizard.

ꕥ

"Look. It work," Molly said.

Windslow looked where Molly pointed. She knelt and picked up a small needle point, barely visible where it rested on the glass floor against the Gorlon's chain.

"Why didn't it go in?" Windslow asked.

"We scritch box from Fistlock. Tillie wash alla stuff off needle. Nelly rub pointy part on rock. See?" she said and pressed the needle point against her palm. "Not pointy now. Not sharp. We fix alla them. Now we gota find key. We set Gorlon free."

"What does the key look like?" Windslow asked. "Do you know where Fistlock keeps it?"

"Don't know. Big secret place inside glass thing," she said and pointed to one of the many thick glass pillars inside the pond room.

Windslow and Haggerwolf began searching each pillar, looking for anything unusual. Windslow stopped when he found one with chocolate smudges on the glass. "Someone pressed right here,"

Haggerwolf placed his fingers on the chocolate fingerprints. When he did, a click sounded and the glass turned to stone. A rectangular door panel swung open.

Windslow pulled out a long metal rod with a T handle across the top and a flat miniature profile of Fistlock's head at the other end.

"Yep, that key," Molly said and helped Windslow and Haggerwolf drag the key to the large padlock near the black pool.

Together, they lifted the key into the lock and twisted. When the lock clicked, it disappeared, along with the chain and black cord that had run from the pool to the Gorlon.

"That good sign," Molly said.

"Didn't you think it would open?" Windslow asked.

"Yep. Sure about key. Not sure about Gorlon. Is good he not make big howling sound. Maybe he sleeping. We go wake him up."

"If I had a better idea, I'd be against this plan," Haggerwolf said and stared down at his boots. "But I have faith in you two," he added. Looking back up, he stepped to Molly and gave her a hug. "You be careful, dear. I'll be waiting here with the others when you get back. Good luck."

Molly smiled and gave the wizard's beard a tug before turning around. She glanced at Windslow and headed down the Gorlon tunnel.

"Wait for me, Molly," Windslow called. Either she didn't hear him or she ignored him. He took a deep breath, blew it out and ran to catch up to her.

ꟃ

"You win," Hillary said. "I'll tell you what you want to know."

"Smart girl," Fistlock said and handed his wand to Bitterbrun. "Be ready to stick the wizard," Fistlock said and moved back near the well. He sat on the table, adjusted his robe and placed the Book of Second Chances on his lap. "Well?" he asked and looked at Hillary.

"First snap the latch closed," Hillary said and glanced at Fernbark. She saw his arm move as he gave a small nod.

Fistlock pushed the brass ends of the leather strap together until he heard a snap.

"Now press the brass acorn to unlock the strap and open the book. The pages should be blank."

Fistlock's hands shook as he followed Hillary's instructions. "They're blank," he said and looked up at her for a second. Looking back down at the book, he tried to turn a page. "The pages don't turn," he said and looked back up. Fistlock turned his gaze to Haggerwolf. "Speak to me," he said. "Bitterbrun, point my wand at his head."

A soft blue glow formed around Haggerwolf's head and just as quickly it disappeared.

"Just a bit of magic to make sure you're telling the truth," Fistlock told Hillary. "I'll have the wizard confirm your answers. If they don't match, things won't be pleasant for either of you."

"Is she telling me the truth about the book's latch?" Fistlock asked as he stared intently at Haggerwolf.

"She tell you big truth alla time," Haggerwolf said.

"Ah... Your Magicness, the wizard doesn't sound right," Bitterbrun said.

Fistlock flipped one hand at his assistant. "Side effect of the magic. Just stay ready to stick him and let me handle things," he said and turned back to Hillary. "Now what?"

"Just start thinking about what you want to do with the book," Hillary said. "Close your eyes. Imagine you are looking at the pages, and focus on what you want to do with your first chance. Bitterbrun, maybe you should shut your eyes too, but only if your boss wants your help with his chances."

"Do what she says," Fistlock said and squeezed his eyes tightly shut.

Bitterbrun shook his head and rolled his eyes before shutting them as instructed.

Hillary gave a quick nod to Fernbark. He jumped to his feet and moved to the bars separating the two cells. He handed the stick with the taped end to Hillary and quickly sat back down. Haggerwolf stuck out his tongue. Hillary shook her finger at Nelly. The small girl grinned, winked and pulled her tongue and the Switch-lily seed on it, back into her mouth. Hillary scowled at Nelly as her image switched back to Haggerwolf.

Hillary pointed the stick at the small black pieces of magnetic rock that had fallen from the broken magic wands. The three small stones jumped from the floor and settled softly into her open palm. She stuffed both the stones and stick into her back pocket.

"All right," She said to Fistlock. "Open your eyes and look at the pages."

"Do I open mine too?" Bitterbrun asked.

"Maybe not yet," Hillary said.

"Does it matter, wizard?" Fistlock asked Haggerwolf.

"It make biggie difference. Better do what Hillre say."

"You've got your answer," Fistlock told his assistant. "It's working," he said softly as he turned the first page and read the lines aloud.

The story in this chance begins,

Found in pages locked within.

Open them with words of care.

What you seek is waiting there.

ꙮ

Molly skidded to a stop when she came to a bend in the tunnel. She held her hand back toward Windslow, motioning him to wait. "Oops, he not asleep," she said when she rounded the corner and saw the Gorlon standing in front of her, its head nearly touching the cave ceiling.

Its orange eyes glowed when it spotted her.

26: Battle of Eldervale

Gilderbun stood ready. The ribbon she wore in her silver hair was from the same material as her pink dress. Today she had exchanged her white apron for an older one made of blue gingham. It matched her husband's vest and was as close to a uniform look as she could manage. She was proud of the way Dimbleshoot looked standing next to her. He stood taller and straighter than usual, his cane in one hand and a shovel in the other. His dark blue pants and white shirt gave him more of an "official" look than her.

"Fistlock's troops will be here soon," Gilderbun said.

"What? Speak up!" Granny Fiddlewish yelled from the middle of the crowd. She held the spout end of a funnel to her ear and turned the wide end toward Gilderbun. "We can't hear you back here."

"They will be here soon!" Gilderbun said, pausing slightly between each word and shouting as loud as she could. "We can't hope for any help. There's no one to stop Fistlock's men but us. But beat them or not, let's show them we're not the helpless old fools they think we are!"

"YES!" many of the grannies and grandpas called out. Shovels, rakes, brooms and mops waved in the air.

"We'll show them," a voice yelled.

"Wake up, Hatterbush," another voice called.

Gilderbun saw granny Brushendust give her husband a poke in the ribs with her broom end. He snorted and opened his eyes.

"Everyone get in place," Dimbleshoot called and pointed toward the barricade they had crafted at the west end of the town square.

It wasn't much of a barricade, made from wagons, carts, bed frames, kitchen tables, bales of hay, and lots of wooden chairs all piled together. Gilderbun knew her husband didn't care what it looked like. He and the others were proud of their effort.

The grannies and grandpas moved at various speeds, taking their assigned places along the only thing that separated them from Fistlock's approaching troops. Some of the Eldervale residents walked fast. Others moved slower, using canes or crutches. The slowest ones needed help from friends, to push them in their wheeled-chairs. Most of the men wore cooking pots on their heads. Some had several layers of leather aprons wrapped and tied around their chests. Here and there were bits of rusty armor dug out of storage chests. Only one or two women wore pots. Others had baskets on their heads. Most of them wore their best bonnets, and fanciest dresses. There had been much talk and discussion about looking good one last time.

"Here they come," Dimbleshoot yelled. "Bring up the ammunition. Get the slings in place."

A group of men moved forward, pushing handcarts toward the waiting grannies and grandpas at the barricade. Another group of men set big Y shaped posts into narrow holes dug in the ground. From the Y branches hung long strips of elastic, some still trimmed with silky white lace that had been part of the undergarments the elastic came from. A broad flat basket dangled from each set of elastic straps. Dimbleshoot moved behind one of the three slings that had black suspenders added to reinforce the elastic. He had personally designed these slings for long range.

Two hundred yards on the other side of the barricade, Fistlock's troops marched forward. They approached from the open field rather than the forests that sheltered the other sides of Eldervale. Ten rows of soldiers in shiny metal armor stood almost shoulder to shoulder in the knee-high grass. They formed a wall twenty men deep. A man on horseback drew his sword and held it high over his head. The soldiers stopped marching. The air filled with the sound of scraping metal as the soldiers drew their swords and held them up like their mounted captain.

"Load!" Dimbleshoot shouted to the men who stood ready at the other slings.

Women with their heads protected by baskets ran to the pushcarts. Each woman grabbed a handful of pies, an armful of jelly jars or over baked cookies as hard as rocks and rushed to one of the slings. Dimbleshoot held the basket of his sling steady while Gilderbun loaded it with a large ham.

The captain pointed his sword toward Eldervale and yelled, "Charge!"

ꕥ

"Now, what?" Fistlock asked as he looked at Hillary.

"You have to shut the book, hold it on top of your head and spin around twelve times as fast as you can. When you stop, you must be facing south or nothing will happen."

"Is she lying to me, wizard?" Fistlock asked Haggerwolf.

"Nope. She not too smart for girl. She not think up stupid stuff for you to do. She not want-a make biggie Fistlock look like fool. You be smart fellow to do fancy stuff she says."

Fistlock nodded and slid off the desk. He held the closed book on his head and started to twist, but suddenly stopped. "Which way is south?" he asked Bitterbrun.

"Um... that way," his assistant said and pointed toward the dungeon doorway.

Fistlock spun. His robes flared out near his knees, making him look like a tall spinning cloth bell. Around and around he spun.

Hillary counted. When she reached twelve, Fistlock stopped spinning. He staggered to one side, but managed to stay on his feet. "Now, as fast as you can, take six deep breaths," Hillary shouted.

Fistlock, his back toward the cells, bent forward and began sucking in and blowing out air. When Hillary counted five, Fistlock teetered for a moment and passed out.

"Grab Bitterbrun!" Hillary shouted.

Nelly spit out her seed and grabbed Bitterbrun's wrist. Larkstone and Fernbark jumped up and ran across the cell to help her hold the wriggling assistant. They pulled him toward the bars, but not before he jabbed Fistlock's wand into Nelly's wrist. In seconds, Fernbark had his arm wrapped around Bitterbrun's neck, pinning him to the bars.

Hillary opened her cell door and hurried to unlock Nelly and the wizards.

"Give me your wand-stick! Hurry!" Larkstone shouted. "Bitterbrun stuck Nelly. She'll turn into a shadow-glump if I don't figure out some way to reverse the needle's effect."

Nelly put both hands to her neck as if she were choking herself. She twisted and turned in jerky movements, and made coughing sounds as she sank to the floor. "Oh, I almost dead," she said. Her legs jerked and kicked. "Needle make me die before meanie wizard start-a like me."

"We like you," Larkstone said and knelt beside the frail girl. "We always have, haven't we, Fernbark?"

Fernbark finished tying up Bitterbrun, using the fat man's belt, suspenders and strips torn from Bitterbrun's pants. "Yes," he said and knelt beside his friend.

"The stick, Hillary," Larkstone asked again.

Hillary rolled her eyes and checked to make sure the wand-stick was in her pocket. "Come on," she said. "Fistlock could wake up any second."

"But we can't just leave poor Nelly to die," Fernbark said and stroked Nelly's head while Larkstone checked her arm.

"There's no puncture wound," Larkstone said and twisted Nelly's arm to look at the other side.

"Ouch," Nelly said and opened her eyes. "I not like-a friend wizard no more when he hurt me."

Hillary started for the door, then stopped and turned around. She pulled her magic stick from her pocket. "Larkstone's closet," she said and the magic zipper closet appeared in front of the startled wizard. "Nelly is all right. She and her sisters did something to the needle points so they aren't sharp or magic anymore. She's just playing with you. Larkstone, find some shackles in your closet and we'll put them on Fistlock."

Nelly smiled and got up. Larkstone harrumphed, and unzipped his closet.

Fernbark gave Nelly a big hug while Larkstone placed metal cuffs, linked by a chain, around Fistlock's ankles. Hillary snapped the second set of shackles around Fistlock's wrists.

"Now that we don't need to worry about him anymore, let's take a look at that pond. I've got some ideas about it from Mr. Nick's experiments. I want to check a couple of things before we go help Windslow and Molly."

The others lined up behind her and Hillary moved through the dungeon door. Halfway down the hallway she stopped. "There's a secret passage here that leads out to a courtyard. If I can just find the right..." Hillary didn't finish her sentence as she moved her fingers along the wood paneled wall. "There," she said when a small click sounded. She pushed and a narrow door opened. Without waiting for the others, she stepped through the door and out into a bleak courtyard.

Hillary looked around. The courtyard was small, about four times the size of her garage back home and empty except for a dead tree in the center. She dashed across to the far wall where a lever stuck from the stones that formed the outer wall. When she pulled it, a door opened.

"We'll go out this way, run down the path, and go back in through the Gorlon's cave," she told the others. "Let's hurry!"

ꙮ

Fistlock blinked his eyes and rolled over onto his back. In disbelief he looked at his shackled hands and screamed. The few remaining shadows slipped quietly across the doors and walls and disappeared, sliding under the closed dungeon door.

"Bitterbrun!" Fistlock yelled.

"Yes, your Immobilness," Bitterbrun called from the cell door.

"Get over here. Get me out of these."

"I can't, your Angerness. They tied me up. I can't move."

Fistlock rolled to his stomach and pushed himself up onto his hands and knees. "Where's my wand!" he shouted.

"Behind me, Your Loudness."

Like a big purple inchworm, Fistlock moved across the floor. When he reached his wand, he bent his head down until his nose touched the polished wooden stick. "Open duffs," he said, his words sounding like he had a stuffed nose. The cuffs clicked and fell free.

Fistlock grabbed his wand and stood. He checked for the book and smiled when he found it on the floor where he had dropped it. He picked it up and carefully dusted off the cover.

"Your Forgetfulness," Bitterbrun said. "What about me?"

Fistlock turned around and placed the book on the table. After he checked to see if any new words had appeared, he pointed his wand toward Bitterbrun without looking. As he muttered something, the belt and strips of cloth that bound Bitterbrun burst into small flames and burned away.

His pudgy assistant stifled a small scream as he swatted at the charred bits of cloth that still clung to him.

"They're fools," Fistlock said and closed the book. He tucked it under one arm. "They gave me the book and told me how it works. They can run as far as they want. It just means they'll be tired when they die. Did you prepare the Spire like I told you to?"

"Yes," Bitterbrun said. "All you need to do is lower the end, aim it and it's ready."

"Good," Fistlock said. "Let's go blow up Eldervale and anything else that annoys me."

"Yes, your Friendliness," Bitterbrun answered and followed behind his master.

ꙮ

Pulling back on the basket, Dimbleshoot stretched the elastic straps of his sling as far as he could. He let go. The elastic jerked, flinging the ham high over the barricade. The ham-grenade sailed downward and with a loud thump smashed into the captain, knocking him off his horse. Flying pies spattered blueberries, cherries and apples into visors of the charging soldiers. Some men fell, others stopped to wipe goo from their faces, and one or two licked their fingers.

Jars full of jelly or jam, hit their targets and shattered into pieces. Luckier shots clunked hard enough against helmets to make dents or knock over a soldier. Cookies rained down, adding to the mess. Soldiers slipped and fell, but most marched steadily ahead.

Now only fifty yards away, the first row of soldiers broke formation and ran. They yelled battle cries and swung their swords over their heads as they rushed the barricade.

"Hand weapons!" Dimbleshoot yelled and bent over to grab his shovel. "Gilderbun, help me up!" he yelled to his wife.

Gilderbun shuffled to her husband as quickly as she could. He stood bent over at the waist, his hands just inches from his shovel. Squatting down, she grabbed the shovel and tipped the handle up so Dimbleshoot could use it to straighten up. Behind them, they could both hear chopping sounds of swords hacking at the barricade. They heard screams mixed with battle cries and curses. Steel from metal rakes clanged against swords and dull metal thuds sounded each time a sword smashed a pot.

When they turned around, Dimbleshoot hobbled to the barricade to help defend it. Soldiers were already ripping down the top layer of chairs and tree limbs.

"Women to the houses!" Gilderbun screamed. She took one last look back at Dimbleshoot before joining the retreating women. He stood at the barricade near a broken wagon. He swung his shovel like a club and a soldier tumbled from the top of the barrier. She hoped the red she saw on her husband's arm was strawberry jam.

"Retreat!" Dimbleshoot yelled.

The men who were able to walk fast or run, stayed at the barricade to give their less nimble comrades a head start. Dimbleshoot waited and watched from the front door of a house at the far side of the town square. By the time the last defender reached the line of houses that would be their last means of defense, the soldiers had cleared a large gap in the barricade.

The soldiers didn't rush the houses as Dimbleshoot expected. Instead, they moved through the opening and waited for their captain. His armor stained by pumpkin pie, rotten plums and a plate of spaghetti, the captain stood in front of his men and stared at the houses. "Bring the torches!" he yelled and used his fingers to pick a large clump of white noodles off his shoulder. He took several steps forward and shook his fist at the wooden homes. "I'll burn you out!" he screamed. "If you want to fight with food, then let me show you how to cook grandparent pie!"

Several men ran forward, each holding a long wooden torch with black pitch at the top. In a few moments, all the torches burned with dark yellow and orange flames that gave off plumes of black smoke curling upward into the afternoon sky. The captain stood in front of the other soldiers who held torches. With them marching behind him, he moved forward.

After his first few steps, the captain stopped. A shadow moved past him and his torch flame flickered. He looked up, as if expecting to see where the breeze came from. He took another step and the flame flickered again, and then bent over from a hard puff of wind. The captain looked at the treetops at the far side of the town. The branches didn't move. He stepped again and a harder puff blew out his flame. Cursing, the captain turned around to relight his torch from one of the others.

More shadows raced past. All the torch flames flickered and bent. Some flames twisted down along the torch handles and nearly burnt the hands that held them. Before the captain could relight his torch, all of the torches puffed out.

"What's happening?" Gilderbun asked her husband who stood at one of the boarded up windows. He had his face pressed against a space between two of the wooden planks nailed across the opening.

"I can't see very well," he answered. Everyone packed into the small house began to push forward. "I think it's flame-fluffers," he said. "Something puffed out their torches, and there's no wind."

"It can't be shadow beasties," someone near the back of the room scoffed. "Why would they help us? They're Fistlock's creatures. It must be—"

"Shush!" Gilderbun said. "Everyone be quiet!"

Voices hushed. Gilderbun and the others listened. A delicate painted teacup made a tiny rattling sound from the shelf where it sat. "Someone give me that cup. And a saucer too," Gilderbun said. She shooed people away from the table and put the cup and saucer in the center of the checkered tablecloth. "Some water. Quick!"

They all crowded around the table and watched the cup. Tiny rings formed in the water. They circled outward from the center to the cup's edge, as if water were dripping into it in a steady rhythm.

"Something's shaking the ground," Dimbleshoot said. "It's making the cup shake. I can feel it. Put your hands against something solid."

The crowd pushed and shoved, everyone trying to get close to a wall. Those in the center of the room stooped down and felt the floor.

Outside, the captain threw his useless torch across the town square and started to draw his sword. The hilt only moved an inch before it gave off a screeching sound like a rusty hinge. Something pushed his visor down. When he tried to push it back up, it made the same hinge-squeak sound.

He reached back for his sword. It was gone. In frustration, he pulled off his helmet and threw it on the ground. All around him, his soldiers struggled with their visors or watched swords and other weapons disappear as faint shadows swirled around them.

The ground shook harder. Now even the soldiers noticed it.

Dimbleshoot and the others inside the house all jumped when they heard a loud thud on the roof. Dimbleshoot chanced a quick look out the front door. He looked up, but all he saw was an eagle flying away just over the rooftops. When he looked down, his heart nearly stopped.

"Hi, ever-body," Molly said, her large eyes sparkling. "Why alla you inside? Big fight gona start. It big second chance for you."

"Molly, dear," Gilderbun said as she pushed past her husband. "Get inside, child. It's not safe out there."

"I know that," Molly said. "Fistlock baddie guys in biggie trouble now. Look what Window have for you." Molly reached inside the magic book bag and pulled out the book she and her sisters had made. "We make special copy, just for alla you. Got this too. Secret earth magic," she said and held up a large bag of butterscotch candy. "Shadow-glumps, scritch, flame-fluffer, alla shadow guys your friends now, too. They help. They already out there. It lota fun for them."

"Dear, girl," Dimbleshoot said. "Do you really think we have a chance?"

"Sure," Molly said. "Shadows already scritch alla swords and stuff. Now you got book. Now you got fair chance. And Window coming with Gorlon. Look," she said and pointed.

Far out past the barricade the Gorlon walked with long pounding strides. Barely visible on the creature's shoulder sat Windslow.

"Let's get them!" Dimbleshoot shouted and stepped outside. He and other men began beating on house doors to tell the others. "Attack!" someone yelled and the grannies and grandpas grabbed their shovels and brooms.

ꕥ

"Through there!" Windslow shouted to the Gorlon. "Go to that wall of junk and kick it out of the way."

The Gorlon silently followed Windslow's commands. When it reached the barricade it stopped and kicked.

"Not like that!" Windslow yelled as carts, chairs and tables flew toward the town square. "Kick them to the side. Make a big opening so the soldiers have a way to get out. Yes. Like that," Windslow said as the Gorlon turned and kicked again.

Windslow raised one arm over his head and closed his fist. Across the square, he saw Molly and the people of Eldervale running from their homes. When they reached the confused soldiers, brooms, mops, shovels and heavy frying pans began bashing against armor. Soldiers fell and tried to crawl away on their hands and knees.

"Inside," Windslow commanded. The Gorlon turned again and lumbered toward the soldiers. "Now I... I want you to..." Windslow felt strange. He looked at his hands. They seemed to shimmer and he could see through them. The blue magic of the Gorlon crackled around him and the creature stopped.

The grannies and grandpas stopped fighting. The soldiers turned around.

Molly stood near Gilderbun. The wrinkled old grandmother held the Eldervale Book of Second Chances up high, but began to lower it. "What's happening?" she asked Molly.

Molly shrugged. Windslow disappeared. The Gorlon stopped moving and Fistlock's men began getting to their feet.

ꟷ

"Windslow. Windslow," a soft voice called to him. He floated through the stars. To one side a bright white star called to him. It called his name. To his other side, a brilliant blue star pulsed. Somehow he knew it was Gabendoor. He heard his name again and the stars faded.

"Windslow, wake up."

Windslow opened his eyes. A face leaned over his and he tried to swing his hand. He couldn't. His blankets pinned him down.

"Windslow, it's me, Trish. You're having a nightmare, Honey."

Windslow blinked his eyes to chase away the sleep as he realized where he was; back home in bed.

"What happened? What's wrong," he asked. "Is Hillary all right?"

"Shush," his stepmother said softly. "She's sleeping. We don't need to wake her up too. You were dreaming. It must have been some dream. You were tossing and turning and yelled about going through something. I got up for a drink of water and heard you all the way from the kitchen. Here," she said. "I brought you a drink too."

Windslow took the glass she offered and took a sip.

"Do you want to talk for a bit? I could stay in your room tonight if something is bothering you."

"No. I have to get back to sleep. I mean... I mean... I was... Ah... stuck late after school. That's what I was dreaming. And then a spaceship landed and..."

"Well, that doesn't sound too bad."

"Um... No," Windslow said and took another sip of water. "I'm fine now. I'm really tired. I think I'll go back to sleep."

"Sounds like a good idea," Trish said and tucked the covers around him. "I have something for you. Something that was mine when I was little. It helped me sleep. It's a lucky horseshoe." Trish held out a small thin flat piece of metal shaped in a U.

"It's not a real horseshoe," Windslow said and held out his hand. "It's a toy magnet."

"I know," Trish said and smiled. "When I was little, my mother told me it was from a tiny magic horse that you could ride in your dreams. It takes you through a magical sleep door where there are only happy dreams. She said I used to gab in my sleep a lot. I believed in the story for a long time. I even named the horse 'Gabin.' Actually, I think the horseshoe does work. I didn't have many bad dreams after I began sleeping with it under my pillow. I called it riding through Gabin's door. I think it needs a new owner; a new dreamer."

Windslow felt his face flush. He blushed even more when Trish leaned down and kissed his cheek. She reminded him of how much he had loved his own mother and the times she would comfort him.

"Good night," she said as she stood paused at the door.

"Good night... mom," Windslow said.

Trish bit her lip and her eyes glistened. She stepped back to the bed, bent down and hugged him. Windslow's eyes began to water when he saw a small tear ease across his stepmother's cheek. Without saying anything, she stood, moved into the hallway and closed his door.

"Oh, oh. Gabendoor, the Gorlon and Eldervale," Windslow said softly to himself. He closed his eyes, not sure if he could sleep or where he'd dream-slip to if he did.

27: The Spire

When Windslow reappeared on the Gorlon's shoulder, the cheers and shouts he heard startled him. When he looked around, a smile spread across his lips. People of every age filled the crowded town square. In the center of the crowd sat Fistlock's soldiers, their hands tied behind their backs. Grannies and younger women tended to the soldiers' wounds, wrapping bandages around banged heads.

Gilderbun yelled something Windslow couldn't hear, and the mass of people began moving to clear a path for Molly. She walked quickly, nodding to the people she passed. Many of them stopped her and shook her hand or patted her on the shoulder.

Windslow glanced at the Gorlon. Raspberry jelly smeared its new mouth. None of the jelly had made it inside. The Gorlon's mouth didn't have an opening. Windslow suspected the mouth was Molly's work. Unwrapped pieces of butterscotch candy were stuck into the black goo like slices of carrot stuck in the face of a snowman. The pattern gave the Gorlon a goofy happy-face smile. While Windslow watched, the Gorlon used two big fingers to scoop more jelly from a large milk pail. It smeared its fingers across its face, adding more raspberries to the mess already dripping down its chin.

"Now I Captain," Molly said, calling up to Windslow. "They see ear thing Hillre give me. They think it mean I big soldier boss for Window army." Molly turned her head so Windslow could see the tiny earring his sister had given Molly when the girls first met.

"Molly, what happened?" Windslow asked as he

climbed down from the Gorlon.

"I send birdies to tell other places to come help granny grandpas. Alla them know we got two Book a Chances now and that you ride Gorlon. They come and help. It pretty fun big battle. We win."

"General Windslow," Dimbleshoot said from behind Molly. "On behalf of Eldervale, I want to thank you for the chance you gave us. Without your—"

"Oh, oh," Molly said, interrupting Dimbleshoot as a bluebird flitted to her shoulder, chirped rapidly and flew away. "Birdie just tell me there biggie trouble at Fistlock place. We all in danger."

ᘐᘑ

Fistlock and Bitterbrun checked the equipment in a large room three levels above the goo pond. Rising from a hole in the center of the glass floor, a large smooth wooden timber the thickness of a telephone pole, rose upward and continued out a matching hole in the domed ceiling.

"Did you check the spire top?" Fistlock asked his assistant.

"Yes, Your Detailness. The tip sticks up as high as the workers could build it. It's the largest magic wand that ever existed."

Fistlock ran his hands along the wooden spokes of a mechanism near the wall. Mounted on a thick pedestal and stretching five feet across, it looked like the steering wheel from a ship. The wheel connected to arm-thick ropes that ran through a maze of huge wooden pulleys.

Fistlock grabbed one of the spokes and pulled, turning the wheel a quarter turn. The ropes tightened and creaked. The large pole slid downward, barely six inches.

"Good," Fistlock said. "I need to control how much power I draw in. No sense wasting the magic. Besides, I don't want to obliterate everything. I will need some survivors or I won't have a supply of people to turn into shadow-beasts. Let's give the spire a try," he said and moved to the other side of the room.

On top of a pedestal fastened to the floor, another smaller wooden spoked wheel sat with its own set of ropes and pulleys. Fistlock inspected the mechanism and gave the wheel a small tug. "Tell me when I'm aiming at Eldervale," Fistlock said.

Bitterbrun watched a flat wooden ring that circled the spire timber. The ring looked like a three-foot wide dinner plate with a hole in its center, except for one small detail. A triangular point stuck out at one edge. The point rested between two marks carved into the wooden floor. One mark had the word 'Wartville' carved above it. The other mark had 'Eldervale.'

Fistlock gave the wheel another pull and the triangle rotated, moving closer to the line below 'Eldervale."

Bitterbrun bent over and rested his hands on his knees. He watched the marker. "Just a bit more, Your Aimlessness," he said.

Fistlock pulled again.

"Stop! It's aligned," Bitterbrun said and straightened up.

"This is going to be so much fun," Fistlock said and rubbed his hands together as he hurried across the room to the larger wheel. "What does the power reading say?"

Bitterbrun checked near the ceiling for the set of grooves the workers had carved around the spire trunk. He couldn't see them. Workers had designed the grooves to show how close the bottom of the spire was to the goo in the pond room far below.

"It's much too high, Your Tallness," Bitterbrun answered. "I can't read the first marker until you lower the spire closer to the pond."

Fistlock nodded and began turning the wheel.

ꟸ

Hillary stood with her stomach pressed against the brass rail that surrounded the black pond inside the crystal chamber. She looked up when she heard the creaking noises and saw the bottom of a large timber expose itself through a wide hole in the glass ceiling above the pond. "What's that?" she asked.

"Big stick in hole," Tillie said.

"The rumors are true," Haggerwolf said. "He actually made it."

"Made what?" Hillary asked. She watched as the pole moved downward another foot.

"A gigantic magic wand. He calls it the spire. It's something Fistlock dreamed up when he was a young wizard. Everyone scoffed at the idea. There isn't a source of magic large enough to power such a thing. There still isn't."

"Haggerwolf, just what do you think that pond full of goo is?" Hillary asked.

"We told you before. Fistlock invented this place to suck all the pollution out of the ground. This pond is all the bad stuff the mountain collects."

"I have a surprise for you," Hillary said and pulled the wand-stick from her back pocket. She held it out toward the pond and a small thread of blue energy lifted from the goo and attached itself to the end of Hillary's stick. The thread thinned and disappeared as she pulled the stick back. "This pond is raw magic. Fistlock has sucked it out of your world and has been collecting it here."

"Then the spire could work?" Larkstone said, looking at the other two wizards. "If that's true, then we're all in great danger. No force exists that could stop a wand with that power."

"That's what you said about the Gorlon," Hillary said and turned back to the rail again. She looked up and watched the pole move down two more feet. "Let's try something. See the end of the pole? The end is hollowed out. It's full of lodestone; magnetic rock. That's why my stick wand works. Watch this."

Hillary reached into her pocket. She took out one of the small pieces of stone that she had collected when Fistlock broke the wizard's wands in the dungeon. She tossed one chunk into the black goo.

When it landed, blue sparks leapt from the surface and the latticework of crackling blue strands of energy grew thicker. They crackled louder where Hillary had thrown the rock. Small bubbles pressed against the surface of the black goo and popped. Several strands of energy lifted up from the pond and briefly attached to the end of Fistlock's spire still high up in the domed ceiling.

"An excellent demonstration," Fernbark said, "But I think it's a bit dangerous."

"The reason I wanted to come in here was to test a couple of ideas. I have to take the risk," Hillary said and tossed a second piece of stone into the pond.

The latticework crackled and snapped. Large patterns of blue lifted up from the pond, tore apart and collapsed. Strands rose up and danced along the brass rail surrounding the pond, buzzing and humming until they broke away. The pond's surface began moving in thick rolling unorganized waves that sent up splashes of black when they collided.

They heard more creaking and groaning from above and watched the spire lower until it was no more than fifteen feet over the pond.

"I think this pretty safe place to be," Nelly Never said and backed up.

"You wrong about that," Tillie said and moved against the wall with her sister.

"I'm guessing you have an idea about what you're doing," Larkstone said. He moved to Hillary, took her arm and tried to pull her back. "But whatever it is, you don't want to put yourself in danger. If you hurt yourself here in Gabendoor, you'll carry your injuries back to earth when you dream-slip."

"I know," Hillary said and pulled her arm away from the wizard. She took the third stone from her pocket. "I just want to try one more piece."

ꕥ

"Molly, we need to get back to Crystal Mountain," Windslow said. "Can you call your eagle friends? We have to get there fast."

"Eagles not fastest way," Molly said and pulled a piece of butterscotch candy from her pocket. She put the candy on the ground and stomped on it, breaking the amber sugar candy into small pieces. "Hey, scritchey guys," She yelled. "Come get butter-rock. Take us to Gorlon cave and I give you more."

Small round shadows, the size of tennis balls, made zipping sounds and as they appeared from nowhere. The first to arrive began bouncing, making soft 'ka-pluck' sounds each time they hit the ground. Ka-pluck, ka-pluck, more scritches came and bounced with the others. Molly stepped back. A small *whoosh* sounded as the mass of scritches moved over the candy. Ka-pluck, ka-pluck and the candy was gone. One scritch leapt from the main group. It made a pockety-pock sound when it moved from the group to Molly's shoulder.

Pockety-pock, pockety-pock. More scritches attached themselves to Molly until only her head showed above the mass of shadows. Pockety-pock, pockety-pock. Windslow looked down and saw himself covered to his chest. Pockety-pock, pockety-pock and he had to close his eyes as more scritches covered him.

The sounds stopped and Windslow wondered what would happen next. He didn't have to wait long to find out. He heard a muffled whoosh and felt himself pressed back against the soft cushion of scritches. His stomach felt like it had been left behind. He barely had time think about the feeling when another whoosh sounded and he stopped. This time it felt like his stomach kept going. It was worse than the wildest ride he had ever taken at the amusement park. Pockety-pock, pockety-pock and the scritches were gone. Windslow took a deep breath and wrapped his arms around his stomach. Molly stood next to him.

"That not so much fun," she said.

"I know. I'm just glad I didn't have anything to eat. I'd be throwing up now if I had."

"Here. Eat butter-rock," Molly said. She put a piece of candy in her mouth and handed one to Windslow.

Even though he didn't like butterscotch, he unwrapped the candy and put it in his mouth. He took a couple more breaths. Feeling better he looked around. Just ahead was the entrance to the Gorlon's cave. This time he didn't wait for Molly to take the lead. He headed inside.

ꕤ

As Windslow moved farther down the glass tunnel, he saw flashes of blue light reflect off the walls. Soon he heard long buzzing sounds and crackling. The air filled with a smell like the time he melted a foam cup in the microwave oven back home. When he stepped into the pond room, he heard his stepsister yell.

"Stop, Windslow! Don't come any closer. You'll get burned if one of the strands touches you!"

Across the pond, Hillary, the three wizards, and Molly's sisters, huddled behind one of the pillars. Blue strands danced in the air. They struck out at the brass railings and hummed until they crackled away. More strands lanced out like miniature lightning bolts and crackled up and down the glass pillars. Haggerwolf held his hands together. Windslow could see the edges of a white bandage peeking out from underneath the wizard's fingers.

"What's happening?" Windslow yelled back.

"I threw three magnetic stones into the pond. Look up there," she called and pointed. "Fistlock is lowering that pole toward the pond. It's a gigantic magic wand. When it's charged, who knows what he's going to do with it. Is Eldervale safe?"

"Molly's plan worked. Well, there were some minor changes. Mom woke me up. She thought I was having a nightmare. When I dream-slipped back, the battle was over."

"I General now!" Molly yelled and touched her earring.

"Where's Fistlock?" Windslow asked.

"There's a control room a couple levels up!" Fernbark yelled, cupping his hands around his mouth as he shouted.

Hillary ducked as a blue strand attached to the glass column she and the others hid behind. After the energy strand crackled, sizzled and disappeared, she peeked her head back out. "We've got to stop him, but we're trapped in here. Got any ideas?"

Windslow thought for a moment about what Hillary had said about Mr. Nick's experiments. "I've got an idea. I'll be right back."

ജര

"How close is the marker?" Fistlock asked after giving the wheel another quarter turn.

"It depends on what setting you want, Your Twistedness," Bitterbrun answered.

The first marker groove carved around the pole was only two feet from the floor. Above the groove was the word, 'PLAYFUL." Two feet higher was another groove and the word, 'SERIOUS.' Above that, another groove read, 'DEADLY.' The top groove read, 'ALL GONE.'

"Let's forget *Playful*," Fistlock said. "I'm tired of fooling around. Let me know when it's at *Serious*. That should take care of Eldervale and everything for a mile around it. Now I just need to think of what spell to use."

"How about that one you used on the army of Wizards last time," Bitterbrun said as he watched the marker groove move closer to the floor. "You know. The one that goes, pitch and hot oil, human blood boils?"

"An excellent idea," Fistlock said and gave the wheel another turn.

ꙮ

Hillary knew it was only minutes, but it seemed like hours before Windslow and Molly reappeared at the entrance to the Gorlon tunnel.

"We're back!" her stepbrother yelled from across the room.

Hillary watched as Windslow and Molly both held dead branches up like cloth-less umbrellas above their heads. Windslow took a cautious step forward.

The blue magic strands shot out but didn't touch him. They crackled around the bare twigs and thinner branches over Molly and him. Together, they walked around the pond.

"I got the idea from what you told me about Mr. Nick," Windslow said when he reached his stepsister. " Without any magnets, the sticks just attract the magic, they don't absorb it. Now how do we get up to Fistlock's control room?"

"We don't," Haggerwolf said. "I saw the layout when Fistlock and the younger wizards built this place. It's sealed off. There's only one way in or out and it locks from the inside."

"Think, Haggerwolf," Hillary said. "Remember how many times you said something couldn't be done. Then you met us and you starting doing things you said were impossible. This is your chance to do it again. There has to be a way."

"There are windows," Haggerwolf said as he scratched his beard. "They are spaced around the room so Fistlock can look out and cast his spells. Maybe one of Molly's birds could fly me up there."

"Birdies not go there," Molly said. "Small birdie can't carry wizard. Big ones not fit in window."

"Maybe Window can do window," Tillie said.

"What?" The three wizards asked at the same time.

"Tillie, you mean Windslow can do window?" Hillary asked.

"That not what she say," Nelly said.

Hillary glanced at her stepbrother and then back at Tillie. "But how would he get up there?"

"I'd climb," Windslow said. "Molly, take me to that opening where you and Hillary slid down the first time you escaped."

28: Another Chance

Windslow stood on the narrow glass shelf and looked up the side of Crystal Mountain. About three stories above him, he could see a window. "Do you think that one opens in the spire room?" he asked.

"It has to," Haggerwolf said and grabbed the end of his beard to keep the wind from blowing it up in his face. "It's the only opening I can see."

"You can't do it," Hillary said. "It's too dangerous."

"I can, Hillary. I really think I can. I at least have to try. Before I fell, I was the best tree climber, the best roof climber, the best anything climber around. You know, now that I think about it, I'm not afraid of climbing. I've been afraid of failing. When I fell off the roof, I was showing off. I wasn't careful. I was stupid. It was my own dumb fault and no one else's."

"That still doesn't change anything. You could hurt yourself, or worse!"

"I know what it's like to hurt myself. Remember? Do you think I want to be in a wheelchair here too?"

"Worse, Windslow! It could be worse. Do you know what that means?"

"Yes," Windslow said. He took a deep breath and blew it out. "Look close. The glass isn't perfectly smooth. The angle will help and I think there are enough little ridges and rough spots for me to grip. I have to try. That's what second chances are all about."

"But it's glass, Windslow. It's not like rock climbing or roof climbing." Hillary turned to Larkstone. "Do you have any suction cups in your magic closet?"

"I might," Larkstone said. "What are they?"

"They're sticky rubber things that— Never mind," Hillary said.

"Need sticky stuff? That easy part," Molly said. "Hey, scritch, get me Hillre magic stick."

Hillary grabbed for her pocket but was too slow. Molly already held the magic stick-wand.

"Make butter-rock pile," Molly told her sisters.

Tillie and Nelly each pulled a handful of butterscotch candy from their pockets. They unwrapped each piece and piled them on the glass floor.

"Now bubbley gum," Molly said and put her piece on top of the candy.

"I not like this stuff anyway," Nelly said and took a couple quick chews before adding her piece to the pile.

"Melt alla stuff to sticky goop," Molly said and pointed the wand-stick at the pile.

The magic followed her instructions and the pile melted into a thick amber puddle with three pink spots. The puddle swirled until the pink blended in.

"Use shoes like this," she said and put one of her boots into the puddle. When Molly pulled it out she pressed her foot against the glass just inside the doorway, gave a little jump and held her hand against the ceiling. She stayed in place for several seconds before her boot began to peel away from the wall, leaving threads of candy stuck to the wall.

"Molly, you're brilliant," Fernbark said and gave her a hug.

"This mean you not like alla us anymore?" Nelly asked.

"Well yes... I mean no," Haggerwolf stammered. "I mean we like you. Is that clear enough?"

"They understand," Hillary said. "We all understand, but we don't have time for this. We need to stop Fistlock. Windslow, are you sure about this? We don't even know what you can do if you get up there."

"I have to try it, unless you think of something else in the next few seconds," Windslow said. He stepped into the amber puddle of candy. "The rest of you should slide down and get out of here."

"I can't," Hillary said. "I still have one more magnet left from my stick-wand. But my brother is right," she said to the others. "The rest of you have to go."

"I go," Nelly said. She turned and walked back inside Crystal Mountain.

"Me neither," both Molly and Tillie said together.

"Same for us," Larkstone said. "We're all in this together."

"All right," Hillary said. She stepped to her brother and gave him a kiss on the cheek. "Be careful."

"Wait!" Windslow said and pulled the small horseshoe shaped magnet from his pocket. "We can make another magic wand. Maybe it will help me with what I need to do. Molly, break a stick from those branches. Hillary, do you have any band aids left?"

Molly handed him a six-inch long piece of stick while Hillary took out a Band-Aid. After they taped the magnet to the bottom of the stick, Windslow shoved it into his back pocket.

"Let's see how I am at playing wizard," he said and stepped to the corner of the ledge.

Hillary watched her stepbrother. He hesitated, took another breath and put one sticky shoe against the glass to test his weight. Molly's trick seemed to be working. Windslow reached, found a handhold, and climbed up two feet. He hugged the glass and closed his eyes. Hillary didn't like it when she saw his legs shaking. She wanted to close her eyes, but didn't and watched him scan the glass above him, reach, step, and climb again.

"Haggerwolf, you stay here and watch my brother," Hillary said and picked up one of the branches. "I'm going inside."

ꕥ

"A few more inches and it should start charging," Fistlock said as he gave the wheel three more twists. "Is the mark lined up?"

"Yes, Your Readiness," Bitterbrun answered.

"Good. It's time to consult my book."

Fistlock opened the Book of Second Chances. He was pleased to see he could turn another page. Eager to see the new words, he flipped the page and read.

Something lost in time long past,

Deeds of good that did not last.

Your chances seek an evil way.

A course you follow on this day.

"Ha! It's working, Bitterbrun. It's working!"

"Yes, Your Excitedness," his assistant answered.

"Maybe there's more. Which way is south?"

"That way," Bitterbrun answered and pointed.

Fistlock put the book on his head and began spinning. When he stopped, he glanced at his assistant. "In case I faint again, seal the place up," he said and began drawing in deep breaths.

Bitterbrun watched Fistlock's face go pale. His tall master teetered and fell over. Bitterbrun thought twice as he moved to the lever that would seal off all the entrances to Crystal Mountain. The open door seemed to tug at him, but his fear of Fistlock helped him make a decision. Bitterbrun pulled the lever.

ꕥ

Hillary and Molly each held one of the branches over their companions. The group was barely inside the passageway when they heard Haggerwolf's yell. Hillary spun around and saw the glass bars that blocked the opening to the outside.

"Fistlock has sealed the exits," Haggerwolf said. "Your brother's fine. He's halfway there already. I'll slide down and see if I can find some help."

"All right," Hillary said. "We'll try to meet by the Gorlon's cave. Yell up to Windslow and tell him too."

"Good luck," Haggerwolf said.

Hillary waited until Haggerwolf sat and slid out of sight. "This isn't going like I hoped it would," she muttered and walked past her waiting friends. "Let's go see what other surprises are waiting for us."

ꕥ

Inside the pond room, they found only one surprise. Glass bars blocked any chance of exit through the Gorlon's tunnel.

"You four check the brass door," she said to Nelly, Tillie and the two wizards. "If you can open it, your job is to keep it open. Molly, you stay with me to hold the branch. I might need both hands free."

"What are you up to?" Larkstone asked as he checked the brass door.

"If I throw enough magnets into the pond, the whole room might melt and eventually blow up."

"What?" Larkstone shouted and spun around. "You can't be serious. At least let the Sallyforth girls out of here before you do it."

"I don't intend to blow any of us up," Hillary said and looked down at the magic wand stick she held in her hand. "First of all, I don't know if I have enough magnets. Second, the place won't blow up fast. We should have time to get out if you can get that door open."

"It's locked from the other side," Fernbark said as he pressed his fingers against the indentations that should have made the door open. "Let me borrow your wand."

Molly held the branch over their heads as she and Hillary moved back to the wizards. "Here take it," she said and handed the wand to Fernbark.

"Locked door, closed no more," Fernbark chanted and pointed the wand at the door. "Drats! It didn't work," he said after pressing his fingers against the indentations again.

"Be smart wizard," Tillie said. "Think about door without magic."

"Hm..." Larkstone said and stroked his chin. "If I didn't have magic I'd break it down or I'd... I'd... I'd pull the hinge pins! Let's see. A good spell for that would be—"

Nelly grabbed the wand from Fernbark, pointed it at the door and yelled, "Fixed!" Both hinges made loud creaking sounds and dropped to the floor. The door teetered toward Fernbark and nearly hit him before he caught it.

"Check down the hallway," Hillary said.

"I know way," Molly said. She handed Hillary the branch and ran through the doorway, pushing past her sisters and the wizards who followed after her.

While Hillary waited for her friends to return, the sounds inside the pond room grew in her awareness. When things had been busy and her friends had been with her, the sounds from the pond had faded into the background. Now the crackling and static from the blue webbing and strands of power grew louder. As Hillary listened, new sounds added in, coming from the voice of magic itself.

Long melodic tones began soft, grew quickly, and softened again. High-pitched chirps and sharp whistles mixed in. Calls came from every direction, mimicking the recorded sounds of whales that Hillary had listened to at school.

Another sound caught her attention—ropes groaned and squealed as they strained against pulleys. Hillary looked up and saw the bottom of the spire lower another foot. When it stopped, the lattice of blue power strands lifted to the wooden pole and connected it to the pond. The magic stopped calling. It screeched as if it were crying out until the crackling and snapping sounds of static overpowered it. The wooden spire trembled.

ꕥ

The wind puffed at Windslow's shirt before a blast rushed past him. He tightened his grip on a small walnut sized imperfection in the glass and pressed himself against Crystal Mountain.

"Yeah, I'm scared!" He yelled to the wind. "But this is my second chance and you're not stopping me. Maybe I'll never walk again back in my own world, but nothing is going to be the way it used to be. I'm Windslow Summerfield! My sister is Hillary Windgate-Summerfield. We know the secrets of the Book of Second Chances!"

The wind buffeted him again and he pressed his cheek against the glass. He could feel his heart hammering inside his chest. Windslow gritted his teeth, turned his head and yelled.

"I'm the son of the summer storm and she's the daughter of mountain breeze. We're here to free Gabendoor!"

The wind stilled. His heart calmed. Windslow let go with one hand, wiped it on his jeans and stretched for another handhold. Looking up, he could see the open window only a few feet above him.

Another hundred feet up at the top of Crystal Mountain, he saw blue clouds forming. Mist swirled and thickened. Crackling blue lightning raced back and forth, lighting up the darker sections of the cloud. His palms began to sweat again and his arms and legs still shook when he climbed another foot. He didn't stop until his fingers reached the window ledge. One more pull and he looked inside.

ഌ☙

Fistlock lay on the floor with his eyes closed. The open Book of Second Chances balanced across his chest. It rose and fell with each breath the unconscious wizard took. Bitterbrun, his back toward Windslow, bent over his master.

Windslow eased himself over the ledge and silently slid to the floor. He crept toward the larger wheel mechanism as Bitterbrun took out a small vial and pulled its stopper. From his hiding place Windslow watched Bitterbrun move the vile back and forth under Fistlock's nose. Fistlock snorted. His eyes fluttered. Windslow ducked his head and pressed his body deeper back into the space between the wooden wheel and the wall.

Fistlock sat up, pushed Bitterbrun away, and looked around the room as he sniffed the air. "There's a new magic in here," he said softly as he got to his feet.

ഌ☙

"Alla ways blocked," Molly said as she led the others through the door and back into the pond room. "Only way is crawl places to bell tower in dungeon."

"Molly's right," Fernbark said and handed the wand-stick back to Hillary. "We'll have to crawl back through the passages and find our way to the bell shaft. We can climb down the way you and Molly climbed up when you escaped the dungeon the first time."

"That's good enough," Hillary said. "From there we can go out through the courtyard. All we need to do is let Windslow know where to meet us."

"Assuming he finds a way down from the spire room," Larkstone said.

"Crud-ola," Hillary swore. "I shouldn't have let him climb up there. I don't like the idea of what he's trying to do."

"It wasn't your decision to make," Fernbark said and put his hand on Hillary's arm. "You've known that all along. He wanted to do this for his own reasons, and not just to stop Fistlock. Windslow's a smart lad. He'll be fine."

"I just wish we had some way to coordinate things. I don't know if I should wait, act, or try to think of something new."

"The spire is in place," Larkstone said as he watched the blue strands connecting the pole to the pond snake back and forth. "Fistlock is charging his spire now. There's not much time left for us to do anything."

"I not like-a see Granny Grandpa place blow up," Tillie said. "I think it time Hillre do earth magic."

"You're right," Hillary said. "Get back inside the doorway. I'm not sure what's going to happen when I do this." She held up her magic stick while her friends moved back inside the doorway. When they were in place, she threw the stick and magnet attached to its end, into the pond.

29: Wizard Battle

Windslow knew he had to act. He just wasn't sure what to do. After opening his Swiss Army knife, he sawed the blade across one of the thick ropes that ran from the mechanism to a pulley fastened to the floor.

He had barely cut a fourth of the way through the rope when a force tightened around his throat and lifted him to his feet.

"You're a troublesome boy," Fistlock said, his wand pointed at Windslow. "But not much longer. I assume you snuck in through the window. It doesn't matter. That's the way you're leaving. I don't suppose you know how to fly, do you?" Fistlock asked and smiled.

Still hanging in the air and held by Fistlock's magic, Windslow struggled to reach into his back pocket. When he was barely a foot from the window, his fingers touched his magic wand. "Duct-tape sunglasses!" he shouted.

Windslow dropped to the floor and scrambled back to his feet as Fistlock yanked at the silver tape across his face. "Double-strength trash bag," Windslow yelled and pointed his wand at Bitterbrun.

In a "poof" a black plastic trash bag formed around Fistlock's pudgy assistant. Parts of the bag bulged and stretched as Bitterbrun tipped over, kicking and struggling inside.

Windslow ran back to the rope and began sawing at it with his knife again. Barely halfway through, he looked up to check on Fistlock.

One eye free of the tape, Fistlock pointed his wand. "Poison darts!" he screamed.

"Big dartboard!" Windslow called back. Thirty small darts sounded, *thack, thackety, thackety, thack, thack, thack* as they sunk harmlessly into the round cork target he held out like a shield.

"Fireball!"

"Waterfall!" Windslow screamed and sawed.

"Stone of death!"

"Catcher's mitt!" Windslow called back and stood just in time to catch the black stone that hurled across the room toward him.

"Not bad," Fistlock said, and began moving along the wall toward his bagged and wiggling assistant. "But did you know you don't actually need to say the words for a spell? All you have to do is think them." He leveled his wand at Windslow.

Windslow tensed, ready to react to whatever magic Fistlock created. For a moment, Windslow thought Fistlock might be bluffing. Then he heard a small *clunk*, and looked down. The magnet that had been taped to his stick now lay next to his tennis shoe. "Wand fixed," Windslow said and grimaced when nothing happened.

"Oh, dear. Is your wand broken?" Fistlock asked. He kept his wand pointed at Windslow as he slowly bent down and untied the strings holding the trash bag shut. "It's time for you to die."

ꕥ

Hillary threw the wand and ducked, not knowing what to expect.

The pond settled for a second, as if tasting the small magnet before swallowing it. The pond heaved, and bubbled like black mud boiling in a pot. The blue strands leapt higher than before and hummed as many of them attached to the brass railing. Both the railing and the brass poles glowed red. In seconds the longer sections sagged like soft candles before plopping to the floor. Hillary felt the heat on her face as the brass melted into puddles that thinned as the molten metal flowed into the pond.

"Is it working?" Larkstone called from the door.

"I'm not sure," Hillary yelled back. "Have everyone get into the access tunnel. I'll be there in a second. That last magnet still might not be enough. The brass melted but it doesn't look like the glass is getting hot. There's nothing else I can do."

"I know where there's another magnet!" Larkstone called over the sound of the buzzing and crackling blue power strands. "Up there in the bottom end of the spire!"

Larkstone ran to Hillary's side as the others headed for the access tunnel. "I don't need a magic wand for this. Closet," he said.

Larkstone's zipper closet appeared. He reached inside and took out a bow and a handful of arrows. "I wasn't too bad a shot when I was young," he said as he strung the bow. "If I can slice some of those ropes..."

Larkstone took aim and shot his first arrow. Blue strands lanced out and struck the arrow. The feathered shaft disappeared in a slender puff of smoke. "Drats!" he hollered and tried another shot. Four more tries had the same results. "Time to go," he said and took Hillary's arm. "You did your best. We all did. We better get out of here while we can. It's all up to your brother now."

ꙮ

Windslow dove for the floor and pressed his stick against the magnet. "Backward football helmet!" he screamed.

The magic did his bidding. Fistlock stumbled forward, his head covered by a football helmet with its faceguard sticking out behind him. "Busted wand! Glue him up! Chained to the wall!" Windslow yelled.

Fistlock's wand crumbled. When he grabbed at the helmet, his hands stuck fast, glued to its sides. A chain snaked out from the wall and attached itself to the helmet's facemask.

Bitterbrun pulled a long slender knife from his boot and pointed it at Windslow.

Windslow's heart raced. Somehow, the knife scared him more than Fistlock's magic had. "Now's your chance to get away from him," Windslow said and stood his ground. He pointed his useless stick at Fistlock's assistant. "Get out of here or I'll turn you into a toad."

Bitterbrun hesitated. He looked at Fistlock and back at Windslow.

Windslow took a quick step forward and thrust out his stick. Bitterbrun yelped, dropped his knife and ran for the door.

"Whew!" Windslow said and turned back to look at Fistlock, whose curses were muffled by the football helmet.

The wizard jerked at his hands and yanked hard at the chain.

"Now what should I do with—Ouch! Crud-o," Windslow said and jumped.

Blue strands of power snaked along the side of the spire. The end of a strand broke free and buzzed as it attached itself to the stick in Windslow's hand. "Ouch!" Windslow yelled again and dropped the stick.

More strands wove their way up the spire. The room began to shake and the pole banged back and forth, hitting the edges of the openings for it in the floor and ceiling. "I better find the others," Windslow said and headed for the door.

"Trish's lucky magnet," he said and stopped in the doorway. He turned and ran back to where it lay on the floor, close to the spire. In his haste, Windslow kicked the magnet as he bent down to grab it. The horseshoe shaped piece of metal gave a small thud as it scooted across the floor and banged against the spire. Before Winslow could grab it, the magnet slipped through the space between the spire and the edge of the hole.

ຂ໐ଔ

"Wait! Something's happening," Hillary said and pulled her arm away from Larkstone. "Hear that? It's the voice of the magic."

They both listened. The blue strands suddenly disappeared. The pond settled and the calling began. The long low warbles sounded again, with fewer chirps than before. Hillary could feel the sound as it vibrated through the floor. She looked up and saw Trish's magnet resting on a rope that wrapped around the end of the spire.

"Do you see that, Larkstone?" she asked and pointed. "Do you have any arrows left?"

"No," Larkstone said and unstrung his bow. "I don't need one." He held up the wooden bow and bent his arm back, ready to throw as he checked his aim. When he threw, the bow sailed straight toward the spire and balanced magnet. A small splash sounded when the horseshoe magnet dropped into the pool.

The room stilled, except for the sound of Hillary's heart beating. All at once, a shrill high-pitched whine pushed away the silence. Blue strands leapt from the pool. This time they didn't dance in random patterns. They ran straight upward and split into fine webbing that spread across the glass domed ceiling. Grey smoke drifted upward and collected in a thick layer that hid the blue webbing. Tiny lightning bolts struck out. One bolt struck a glass pillar on the other side of the pond, shattering it into large pieces. Another strand crackled loudly. The pillar it hit didn't shatter. The glass turned yellow, then red. As Hillary watched, the pillar melted and the glass flowed to the pool, mixing in with the black goo.

"We did it!" Hillary yelled. She grabbed Larkstone's arm and jumped up and down. "Windslow did it. You did it. We all did it! That last magnet was just enough. It won't be long and this whole place will..."

She looked at Larkstone and bit her lip.

"Will what?" he asked.

"Explode!"

ᘓᘐ

"Crud-o," Windslow cursed. "Now which way?" He ran along the hallway until he found another staircase and headed down. Three levels later he stopped. He caught a glimpse of Bitterbrun as the fat man ducked out of sight around a corner up ahead. Windslow ran after him.

When Winslow rounded the corner, he heard a door slam. Up ahead he found the door. After trying the handle, he cursed, kicked at it and slammed against it with his shoulder. "Now what?" he said and ran back down the hallway, checking other doors.

The castle shook, almost knocking Windslow off his feet. A suit of armor fell over. The sound made Windslow jump. The floor shook again and vases rattled off of pedestals and pictures dropped from the walls. Where one of the pictures had hung, Windslow saw an access panel.

ᘓᘐ

"Which way, Molly?" Hillary asked. They huddled together inside the four foot square access passage at a spot where two of the long crawlways crossed.

"This-a way," Molly said and pointed to the wooden floor. "Squishy-butter marks from last time."

Hillary saw the smears and turned down the new corridor. When they climbed into one of the connecting equipment rooms, Hillary recognized it and headed for the access door on the other side. Before she reached it, the panel door swung open and Windslow tumbled from the shaft, landing on his hands and knees on the floor.

"Window!" Tillie shouted and scooted over to help him up.

"I'm so glad you're safe," Hillary cried. She ran to her stepbrother and hugged him, nearly crushing Tillie.

"I not part of sandwich," Tillie said and squeezed out from between them.

"What happened? What did you do to Fistlock?" she asked.

"He's sort of stuck in the spire room. I followed Bitterbrun out, but he gave me the slip and locked me in a hallway. I found an access panel and I've been lost in this maze of passages. I hope you can find a way out of here for us."

"We don't have time to rest. The place is going to blow up. Remember what happened to Mr. Nick? The glass in the poolroom was starting to melt. The magic has changed. I don't know how long we have, but I'm pretty sure this place is going to explode any minute."

"I know way from here," Molly said. "See? You lucky girl, Hillre. Lucky thing you trade me for ear thing long time ago." Molly smiled and tugged at the shiny earring Hillary had given her when they first met. "This-a way."

Molly climbed into the corridor Windslow had just come from. The others crowded in behind her.

They crawled as fast as they could. Several times, they stopped as the walls shook and the floor bounced. They heard wood cracking and groaning. Smoke drifted toward them from around the corner of a side passage as they made their way forward.

"We here," Molly said and used her feet to kick open an access panel.

Hillary looked. "Molly's right," she said. "It's the bell shaft over the well in the dungeon. We need to—"

The building shook. Hillary ducked her head back inside the passage when several small bricks fell past, nearly hitting her. "We need to get out of here fast. But be careful. There are ladder rungs to step on. But don't anyone slip. If you do, you'll fall into the well. We've all made it this far. I don't want any accidents. I'll go first."

Hillary turned around and eased herself into the bell tower. She climbed down several rungs and stopped to watch Molly climb out next. When her friend was above her, Hillary started downward.

The bell below them clanged each time the shaft shook. By its sound, Hillary knew they were getting closer.

"Hillary!" Windslow called from up above. "There might be a problem. When we were in the dungeon I saw bars across the bell tower opening. What are we going to do about them?"

"I don't know," she yelled back. "But it's our only way out."

The bell clanged, struck by another brick that fell past them. The sound hurt Hillary's ears but she kept climbing downward. Before the sound faded, she saw the bell and metal grating just below her. Carefully she climbed onto the bell and grabbed the chain it hung from. First, she tested the grating with part of her weight. The bars didn't move.

"Be careful!" Larkstone yelled. "If that grating breaks loose and you fall down the well, you'll die."

Hillary eased her full weight onto the bars and jumped. Nothing happened. In the distance, she heard a small explosion. She was going to jump again when the tower shook so hard she fell, banging her knees on the bars that trapped her and her companions.

"It can't end this way!" Windslow yelled from up above.

30: The Well

The bell shaft shook as another explosion sounded in the distance. Three more bricks fell and clanged as they hit the metal grate.

"We've got to think of something!" Windslow yelled.

"We got plan," Molly said from where she hung onto the ladder rungs up above him. "Alla you gota squeeze back. Make room."

"Make room for what?" Larkstone asked.

"Make room for Sallyforth sisters. We gona fix bar."

"How, Molly?" Hillary called up.

"We use magic butter-rock and good idea," the small, doe-eyed girl said as she and her sisters began climbing higher. "First we got stuff for alla you. Hey wizzie guys, I tell you where grampy Sallyforth house hidden. It up in Nelly's room behind the clock. That one of grampy's riddles. It easy one, though."

"Yep. It up in my room," Nelly said.

"It got lots more of grampy's books," Tillie said and climbed until she was with her sisters.

"How are you going to fix it, Molly!" Hillary called again.

"We knock it loose," she said and handed pieces of butterscotch candy to her sisters. "You guys alla time nice to us. Even wizards. Tell Haggerwoof he good guy too."

"Molly! Tell me how!" Hillary screamed.

"Window, you make book work. You hero now," Tillie said as she unwrapped her piece of candy and popped it in her mouth.

"Hillre, you like-a big sister for us. You give me first present I ever get," Molly said and touched her earring. "We like-a twins when we both got one."

"Molly, Tillie, Nelly! Don't do this!" Windslow shouted.

The girls ignored the pleas from all their friends.

Hillary pressed tight against the bell tower wall. It shook again and she closed her eyes. When she opened them, three amber candy wrappers floated past her. Hillary looked up when she heard Molly count.

"One, two, one!"

Hillary and Windslow both screamed. Three bodies plummeted downward. The sisters hit the grate with a dull thud followed by wood splintering and a loud clang. Three of the fasteners holding the grate tore free. The metal bars tipped downward with one edge acting like a hinge still connected to the ceiling. The three small girls disappeared into the darkness of the well.

"No!" Both Hillary and Windslow screamed. Windslow shut his eyes. Hillary began crying. "It's not supposed to be like this," she said, her voice shaking.

"Don't let their sacrifice be wasted," Fernbark said, speaking only loud enough to be heard. He wiped his eyes with his shirtsleeve. "We need to climb out of here."

Hillary sniffed and let out a breath. Without saying anything, she climbed down on the bell, carefully stepped to the top of the well, and jumped to the tabletop. She helped the two wizards and her brother.

"Maybe they..." Windslow said. He slid to the floor, moved to the well and looked over the side into the darkness.

"They always had a way of... of..."

"We need to go," Larkstone said and took Windslow's arm.

Windslow jerked his arm free. "No! There's got to be a way..." His words trailed off and he slumped to the floor.

Larkstone and Hillary both helped Windslow to his feet. Reluctantly, he walked with them.

When they reached the dungeon door, a loud crash and clang startled them. They spun around and saw the bell tipped at an angle and stuck in the well. The dungeon shook when a much louder and much closer explosion sounded. The bell groaned as the brass scraped the stones that formed the well. With a final clang, the bell dropped out of sight as a section of the well crumbled.

"I think we need to run," Hillary said and pushed through the door.

ꙮ

"Over here!" a voice called from near the trees at the far side of the clearing.

Windslow stood at the courtyard door, holding it open for the others. He spotted his friend a hundred yards away. "It's Haggerwolf," He told the others as he pointed. "Run!"

Windslow, Hillary, Fernbark and Larkstone ran as fast as they could. Behind them more explosions sounded. When Hillary looked back, she saw the top of Crystal Mountain glowing deep red.

"I have hippograffs in a clearing up ahead," Haggerwolf said. "Where are the Sallyforth sisters?"

"They fell down the well. They're gone," Fernbark told him.

"I'll go back for them. I've got a replacement wand," Haggerwolf said and reached inside his vest.

Fernbark grabbed his friend's arm. "It's too late. The well's destroyed. The bell fell in after the girls. There wasn't anything we could do then, or that you can do now."

Haggerwolf turned his back to them. Hillary watched the tough old wizard pull a handkerchief from his pocket and wipe it across his face. After he cleared his throat and stuffed the handkerchief away, he turned back around. "This way," he said without looking up. He headed for the woods.

ꙮ

Riding hippograffs, they sailed over the forest just above the treetops. Behind them, Crystal Mountain sagged like melting ice cream. Explosions sounded but the distance gave them more of a rumbling sound. Soon, the group could no longer see Fistlock's stronghold. Everyone stayed silent, the only sound was the steady buzz of hippograff wings.

They landed at Eldervale. The grandfathers and grandmothers gave them a grand welcome and introduced people who had come from other cities. Everyone wanted to shake their hands, pat them on the back or give them a bag of cookies to take home. Hillary and Windslow tried to smile and said "no thanks" to the treats.

Dimbleshoot saw Hillary and Windslow yawn. He and his wife shooed the other well-wishers away and offered their back room and small beds to the brother and sister team. Weary from the day and still thinking about the Sallyforth triplets, Windslow and Hillary both welcomed the chance to sleep and looked forward to dream-slipping home.

ꙮ

Three times that week, Hillary and Windslow slept through the night, neither dream-slipping nor having normal dreams that they could remember. Two times they did dream-slip back to Eldervale. They were pleased to see the new statue in the center of the town square. Standing on a huge block of marble, carved to look like a piece of butterscotch candy, were figures of the Sallyforth Triplets. Hillary cried the first time she looked at the statue. Windslow spent much of his time as he did this afternoon, sitting quietly on the grass beside the stone tribute to the girls.

"Things seem so quite now," Haggerwolf said.

Windslow looked up and smiled at the three wizards as they walked towards him. "I know," Windslow said and stood. "I still wish it could have ended some other way."

"Best to not think about that for now," Larkstone said. "Hillary!" he called and waved at Windslow's sister who stood near a small group of women. "Come over here. We have something for you."

When Hillary joined them, Larkstone reached inside his coat and took out a small blue pouch with a shiny brass zipper. "This is for both of you," he said and held it out.

"We couldn't make two of them," Fernbark said. "We tried. Magic is getting stronger now, but these things are hard to make. I think most of magic is busy turning the grass and tree leaves green again."

"Or maybe we're just not good at being wizards," Haggerwolf stammered as he blushed.

"You three are wonderful wizards," Hillary said. She gave each of them a kiss on the cheek. "We couldn't have done this without you three."

"Or the— or the Sallyforth girls," Haggerwolf said. He cleared his throat, scratched at his beard, and gave Larkstone a small shove. "Well, show them what we made."

"Oh," Larkstone said. "It's like my zipper closet. Not as big, of course. Well you can make it bigger. See?" Larkstone held both ends of the zipper and pulled until he had stretched it nearly two feet long. He grabbed the blue cloth, stretched it, and whispered, "Smaller." This time when he moved his fingers, the cloth and brass zipper shrunk until the pouch was no bigger than a small change purse. "Oh, it stays put, too. It can't be scritched. Watch." Larkstone held out his arm, opened his fingers and let go. The pouch floated in the air. He grabbed a corner and moved it down a foot. After grinning at Hillary and Windslow, he pushed it sideways and then up, using only one finger.

"Quit playing with it," Fernbark said. He grabbed the pouch, stretched it out a bit and pulled the zipper. "It's actually connected to Larkstone's closet. It won't hold nearly as much, but we thought it might be useful."

"It's really cool," Windslow said and took the pouch from Fernbark. Hillary smiled when her brother unzipped it and shoved his arm in, up to his elbow.

"You look goofy with only one arm," Hillary said. "Let me see it."

After Windslow handed it to her, she turned it over and saw the letters, M T N embroidered in fine golden thread. "For Molly and..."

"Yes," Haggerwolf said as he reached out and turned the pouch back over.

"Why aren't we dream-slipping here every night like we did before?" Windslow asked.

"You don't have the book anymore," Fernbark answered. "The book's magic drew you here."

"I think... I think we need to say our goodbyes while we have the chance," Haggerwolf said. He rubbed his sleeve across his nose and looked at the ground.

The rest of that afternoon, Hillary, Windslow, Larkstone, Fernbark and Haggerwolf stayed near the statue and talked about unimportant things. Hillary didn't think any of them wanted to talk about the adventure because of the Sallyforth triplets.

ꕥ

The next day at school, Mrs. Taralynn, the principal, made several announcements over the public address system. One said that Mr. Nick was leaving school at the end of the year to become a geologist. The other said that Mrs. Christensen-Forth was leaving too. She had unexpectedly been approved to take in three foster children and would no longer be teaching. Both Hillary and Windslow were disappointed after learning the news about their two favorite teachers.

"Is this really your last day?" Windslow asked after the other students had left, even though Mrs. Christensen had confirmed the announcement in class.

"Yes it is, Windslow," she said and moved from her desk to stand beside his wheelchair. "I'll be packing up my things this weekend."

"It won't be the same without you," Windslow said. He looked down and played with one of the straps on his backpack.

"You'll be just fine. You've grown a lot this year. Inside here," she said and touched his shirt, just above his heart. "I understand that you've decided to go ahead with that operation you were afraid of."

"Yeah," Windslow said and shrugged. "The other operations hurt a lot. This one will too. But at least the doctor thinks there's a little chance. Once in awhile I get some feeling in my legs. It comes and goes."

"If anyone deserves another chance, it's you, Windslow. I better go now. My new family is waiting for me in the staff parking lot."

Mrs. Christensen bent down and gave Windslow a small kiss on the cheek. When he looked up, she was already walking through the classroom door.

Windslow sat silently. It was less than a minute before Hillary came into the room.

"Ready to go home?" she asked and began pushing his wheelchair.

"Almost. Take me out the side entrance by the gym. I want to watch Mrs. Christensen go."

When they reached the sidewalk by the tennis courts, Windslow looked and saw Mrs. Christensen's blue mini-van. Her husband drove across the parking lot toward the street exit.

Mrs. Christensen saw Windslow and waved to him. "They're triplets!" she yelled out the window. "Molly, Tillie and Nelly!"

Windslow and Hillary looked at each other.

"It can't be," Hillary said. She ran across the tennis courts and headed for the corner of the parking lot. The van slowed, waiting for traffic before it could turn onto the road. When Hillary was fifty feet away, a small head turned in the side window. The sun glinted off a single earring in the little girl's ear. Just before the car turned, Hillary saw something drop out of the window.

Nearly out of breath, Hillary ran to the corner. Lying next to the curb was a single piece of butterscotch candy. She clutched it in her hand and hurried back to her brother.

"Windslow! You're not going to believe this," she said and held out her hand.

"I've got something you're not going to believe either," Windslow said. "Look."

Lying in his lap was a leather bound book. Gold letters embossed into the brown cover read: The Book of Broken Promises, by Riddle-Quip Sallyforth.

☙ The End ❧

The Secret Books of Gabendoor.

Book 2, The Book of Broken Promises

Hillary and Windslow return to Gabendoor to save it from the wizard Gristle-tooth and his time-mists.

His spirit is free and his time-mists will end all life. Magic helps Hillary and Windslow dream-slip back to Gabendoor to battle the wizard Gristle-tooth and his assistant, Aghasta, for *The Book of Broken Promises.* No one understands the secrets in the book or which promised to keep and which to break. One wrong choice and the Book will grant Gristle-tooth's promise to destroy everything.

Join the Children of the Summer Wind on their second adventure in Gabendoor along with their three wizard friends and the Sallyforth triplets. Dream-slip across time and space to the world of Gabendoor.

Continue the incredible saga that began in *The Book of Second Chances.*

Book 3, The Book of Twisted Truths

With their mother traveling to Gabendoor, Windslow and Hillary must weave white lies that could cost lives. The truth reveals her startling secrets.

A third magic book from the Secret Library summons Hillary and Windslow, the Children of the Wind, back to the world of Gabendoor to stop an invasion. Life becomes complicated when their mother, Trish, "dream-slips" into the middle of their adventure. Trish thinks she's going crazy, and reveals twisted truths from her childhood that link her to Gabendoor. It's up to the Children of the Wind to unravel that link and solve the mysteries of the magic book. Without the book, truths will stay hidden. Without the truth, Gabendoor will go to war. With war, many could die, including the Children of the Wind and their mother.

Book 4, The Book of Library Secrets

Just who are the Sallyforth triplets? In their most dangerous adventure yet, Windslow and Hillary must stop the wizard, Dreadlore, before someone dies.

Whoever solves the ancient riddle of Gabendoor will learn the location of the Secret Library and its magic

books. Whoever learns the secret of the mysterious ratStone will control the stars. The books and the magic stone both hold the power to destroy Gabendoor and to save Gabendoor. Using either one will mean death for Hillary, Windslow, or one of their companions. In their most dangerous adventure yet, the Children of the Wind race against time and the evil wizard Dreadlore. They must succeed. Back on Earth, their mother's life depends on what they do in Gabendooor.

www.gabendoor.com

Amarath, The Birth of Magic

A new epic fantasy adventure by J. Michael Blumer
Books 1-3 now available.

The Ghost of the Keepers Monk is part legend, part mystery. It holds two of three mysterious stones that control all magic. The war lord, Murthra, controls the third and most powerful stone. He's using it to help him conquer all of Amarath.

Daran, a teenager who calls himself Rat Boy to shield his real identity, unravels the ghost's secrets, and is "adopted" by intelligence in the Monk's two stones. The stones control events and pit an unwilling Daran against Murthra. The stones' first task for Daran's alternate identity is a rescue, but there's a problem. The princess he's sent to rescue, despises Rat Boy but drams of a romance with Daran, not knowing they're the same person.

When Daran tries to sort things out, the magic further complicates his life, manipulating him into a third identity and deeper into the politics of the growing war. Daran wants to resume his quiet life as Rat Boy, but the magic stones of Amarath have other plans.

Biography

J. Michael Blumer is a long time storyteller who finally found time to become a writer thanks to encouragement from his family. Long ago, his children dubbed him an "alternative life form" because of his "creative" parenting techniques, such as making them sing their arguments. He's married to a second grade school teacher which explains why his marriage has lasted so long. His wife knows just how to handle him. Mike lives in Stillwater, Minnesota with his wife Jane, and the wildlife that wanders through their backyard. Read more about the world of Gabendoor at www.gabendoor.com.